KU-218-621

100 Reasons to Celebrate

We invite you to join us in celebrating Mills & Boon's centenary. Gerald Mills and Charles Boon founded Mills & Boon Limited in 1908 and opened offices in London's Covent Garden. Since then, Mills & Boon has become a hallmark for romantic fiction, recognised around the world.

We're proud of our 100 years of publishing excellence, which wouldn't have been achieved without the loyalty and enthusiasm of our authors and readers.

Thank you!

Each month throughout the year there will be something new and exciting to mark the centenary, so watch for your favourite authors, captivating new stories, special limited edition collections…and more!

The Millionaire's Seductive Revenge
by Maxine Sullivan

ᐅ ᒉᐟᑫ ᐊ

"You should smile at me more often, Kia."

"But if I smile you might think I like you," she said with false sweetness.

As if he realised he had let his guard down, the smile froze on his lips. "We wouldn't want that to happen, now would we?"

Thankfully, the song ended. She cleared her throat and went to move away. "Thank you for the dance, Brant."

But he surprised her by holding on to her arm.

"Say it again, Kia."

She blinked. "What?"

"Say my name again."

"Brant Matthews," she said defiantly.

Looking satisfied, he dropped her arm like he'd drop her heart if she dared let him near it.

The Tycoon's Hidden Heir
by Yvonne Lindsay

ᗝᘏᚹᕉ

Mason caught her face between his hands – forcing her to meet his gaze.

Then, suddenly, her body was empty of his possession.

"No! Please, don't stop now." Helena begged as Mason pulled away from her and got up from the bed. "What's wrong?"

Under his cool scrutiny Helena felt reduced to little more than a butterfly on a pin. She desperately wished she could cover her naked body from the emptiness in his gaze.

"There's nothing wrong." His answer was delivered at subzero temperature.

"Then why? Why did you stop?"

"Because I can." He tossed her clothes on the bed. The inference in his action was clear. Get dressed and get the hell out of his room. "And because now I know how far you're prepared to go."

Available in March 2008
from Mills & Boon® Desire™

Thirty-Day Affair
by Maureen Child
&
The Prince's Mistress
by Day Leclaire

ᗡ◌⋈ᗝ

Expecting a Fortune
by Jan Colley
&
Fortune's Forbidden Woman
by Heidi Betts

ᗡ◌⋈ᗝ

The Millionaire's Seductive Revenge
by Maxine Sullivan
&
The Tycoon's Hidden Heir
by Yvonne Lindsay

The Millionaire's Seductive Revenge

MAXINE SULLIVAN

The Tycoon's Hidden Heir

YVONNE LINDSAY

MILLS & BOON
Pure reading pleasure

*First published in Great Britain 2008
by Harlequin Mills & Boon Limited,
Eton House, 18-24 Paradise Road, Richmond, Surrey TW9 1SR*

The publisher acknowledges the copyright holders of the
individual works as follows:

The Millionaire's Seductive Revenge © Maxine Sullivan 2007
The Tycoon's Hidden Heir © Dolce Vita Trust 2007

ISBN: 978 0 263 85896 9

51-0308

*Printed and bound in Spain
by Litografia Rosés S.A., Barcelona*

THE MILLIONAIRE'S SEDUCTIVE REVENGE

by
Maxine Sullivan

Dear Reader,

I'm thoroughly delighted to say that this is my first book, and, like any firstborn, it's very special to me. It's an unbelievable feeling holding my "baby" in my hands and knowing it will be read by romance readers around the world. There's nothing more thrilling to me than being able to share this very first book with others who will appreciate it.

My story is set in Darwin, in the tropical north of Australia, where I lived for many years. Writing the book allowed me to revisit a city that holds treasured memories for me and my family, so it was only natural I chose such an exotic place for my characters to fall in love. No handsome hero will be able to resist a beautiful heroine once those mesmerising sunsets start to work their magic.

With such a perfect setting for love, is it any wonder I used Darwin as the setting for a further two books? Look for the second AUSTRALIAN MILLIONAIRES book in May.

Happy reading!

Maxine

MAXINE SULLIVAN

credits her mother for her lifelong love of romance novels, so it was a natural extension to want to write her own romances that she and others could enjoy. She's very excited about seeing her work in print, and she's thrilled to be the second Australian to write for the Desire™ line.

Maxine lives in Melbourne, Australia, but over the years has travelled to New Zealand, the UK and the US. In her own backyard, her husband's job ensured they saw the diversity of the countryside, including spending many years in Darwin in the tropical north where some of her books are set. She is married to Geoff, who has proven his hero status many times over the years. They have two handsome sons and an assortment of much-loved previously abandoned animals.

Maxine would love to hear from you, and she can be contacted through her website at www.maxinesullivan.com.

For Andrea Johnston, Suzanne Barrett,
and Noelene Jenkinson, Critique Partners,
Mentors, and Friends

One

Every man in the room was staring at Kia Benton. And Brant Matthews was one of them. He'd seen many beautiful women in his life but none who affected him like the woman who'd entered the ballroom of Darwin's Shangri-La Hotel. Australia's most northerly city may possess a tropical lifestyle that was the envy of the rest of the country, but it still didn't hold a candle to this woman's beauty.

Dressed for an evening that promised glitz and glamour, Kia looked stunning tonight, with her ash-blond hair pulled back in a stylish chignon, her perfectly made-up features accentuated by the black liner circling her eyes.

The eyes of a seductress, Brant mused, his gaze

sliding down over bare shoulders to the shimmery silver dress that hugged her breasts, then slid over slim hips and long legs.

But it wasn't just her looks that coiled sexual hunger in the pit of his stomach. She had something that called to him on another level. A quality he'd never found in another woman, not even in his ex-fiancée, Julia. Hell, definitely not Julia. Julia had only been about one thing.

His mouth tightened. He had to remember that Kia was no different. Both women wanted the same thing.

Money.

He'd been suspicious of Kia from the moment he'd stepped onto the plane on his way back from Europe and caught sight of a photograph of her and his partner Phillip in the society section of a Darwin magazine. It was being read by the man next to him, and the picture had shown her arm in arm with Phillip at a cocktail party, looking very pleased with herself. The last he heard, Phillip still had his secretary from years back. This Kia was a total shock.

The caption had read, "Has one of Australia's richest bachelors finally been hooked by his new personal assistant? Miss Kia Benton obviously knows a thing or two about getting 'personal.'"

Yes, this woman knew how to get her hooks into someone all right. But what she didn't know was that he'd heard her on the telephone when he'd gone into the office the next day.

Of course I'm working on getting myself a rich man, she'd been saying when he'd passed by Phillip's office and seen her leaning against the desk, looking for all the world as if she owned the place. Then she'd laughed and said, *It's as easy to love a rich man as a poor one, right?*

This was the reason she'd made herself indispensable to his business partner so quickly. Within two months she'd had Phillip eating out of her hand. Oh, yes, she was a gold digger, this one. A beautiful, deceitful gold digger.

"Oh, don't they make a lovely couple?" one of the executive wives tossed into the conversation going on around him, pulling Brant from his thoughts and dropping him back into the Christmas festivities that were a necessary evil at this time of year.

"Yes, they're perfect together," one of the others agreed after all heads turned toward Kia and Phillip standing beneath the Merry Christmas sign in the doorway.

Then the head of the Legal Department's wife put her hand on her husband's arm. "Hon, I don't know what they're putting in the water at your office, but she's beautiful."

Simon puffed up with an odd sort of fatherly pride. "That's Kia. She's got brains as well as beauty."

Brains as well as beauty.

And she had no qualms about using those assets, Brant thought, hating the pull of her attraction but unable to do anything about it.

Dammit. If only he'd met her first. But two months ago, as senior partner, he'd gone to Paris to establish their new office and get everything up and running. Phillip hadn't wanted to go because he'd been heavily involved with his then girlfriend, Lynette. Yet when he'd returned a month later, Phillip's secretary had resigned due to ill health and Kia had been firmly ensconced as Phillip's personal assistant during work hours.

And his constant companion out of hours.

Like now.

Of course, if he'd seen her first, they would have been lovers straight away. No doubt about it. He'd known it from the moment he'd gazed into her sparkling aquamarine eyes.

Why?

Because she knew what she did to him, that's why. She knew the attraction he felt for her. This deep, pulsing need to make her his own. She merely had to glance his way and sizzling heat coursed through his veins. Even now he could feel himself burning to be inside her, feeling her close around him as he moved ever so slowly in and out, watching her eyelids flutter against her cheeks, hearing his name a murmur on the parted bow of her lips.

"She's got a brand new car, too," someone interrupted his thoughts, making him stiffen in disbelief. "A Porsche. It's fantastic."

"Lucky girl," one of the guys said. "Did Phil buy it for her?"

Simon darted a look at Brant, as if he knew this wasn't a subject they should be discussing in front of the boss. "Er…I'm not sure," the other man said awkwardly.

"It's understandable," Simon's wife added in a sympathetic tone. "He probably doesn't want her to have a similar accident to the one he had."

Pretending to ignore the conversation, Brant leaned back in his chair and took a sip of his whiskey. Late one night, Phil's car had broken down after he'd gone out on a date with Kia. When he'd stepped out to check the problem, a passing vehicle had clipped his leg, busting up his knee and breaking his ankle, leaving him with what would eventually be a permanent limp.

And Kia…God bless her, Brant mused cynically… had been quite happy ever since, going back and forth between the hospital and the office, assisting Phil with his workload. Through it all she must have been manipulating him to get the car. And a Porsche, to boot. Bloody hell. His friend and business partner deserved better than someone who was only using him for his bank account.

He was tempted to show Phil what sort of woman he was involved with. Kia would be easy enough to get into bed if he really put his mind to it. Only he couldn't. Not for *her* sake but for Phillip's. He knew how it felt for someone close to steal your woman.

And he'd be damned if he'd put the business at risk. He may've had to correct some of Phillip's poor decisions since they'd started buying up other businesses three years ago, but the last thing Brant wanted was instability within the company that was now riding the wave of phenomenal success.

Yet all of it could be jeopardized because of a woman who was out to get everything she could, he reminded himself as he watched the pair moving through the tables toward him, Kia pushing Phil's wheelchair but stopping to talk to people on the way. Oh, she was good at what she did. She knew how to work her audience.

Sickened that such beauty hid a heart of stone, Brant stood up. "Back in a minute," he muttered to no one in particular and headed for the exit behind him. His date had vanished into the nether regions of the ladies' room a while back, so he was unconcerned she would miss him until his return.

He needed to get outside and let the ocean air fill his lungs and clear away the smell of deception. Then maybe his body wouldn't ache so much for a woman who deserved nothing more than his contempt.

After finally reaching their table, Kia sat back with a glass of champagne and tried to relax. Brant seemed to have disappeared for a while, though she knew he'd be back. And he always affected her in some crazy way, no matter how hard she tried not to let him.

Tonight, for instance, it had started as soon as she entered the ballroom. She'd felt his eyes upon her, scrutinizing her, undressing her. This wasn't the only time she'd sensed his desire. Far from it. From the moment she'd met him she'd known he'd wanted her, despite himself. In his bed and out of it. Anywhere and anytime.

And as much as she had fought it, his want always bonded with a need deep inside her. That knowledge had pulsed through her veins tonight, making her breathless, wanting more, wanting him.

"Everything all right, Kia?"

She took a breath and fixed a smile on her lips for Phillip, fully aware of the attention from the other tables guests. "Everything's fine."

His gaze slid to her throat and a glint of humor appeared in his eyes. "I'm glad you like your present."

Her hand went to the sparkling diamond necklace he'd asked her to wear. He'd wanted her to keep it, but she'd refused, so they'd compromised and she'd said she'd wear it only for the night. "It's fabulous."

"A fabulous gift for a fabulous lady."

She shifted in her seat. Did he have to lay it on quite so thick? Just because he wanted to give the impression they were a couple didn't mean they should act like characters in a thirties melodrama. It made her uncomfortable.

Suddenly the hairs on the back of her neck began to rise. There Brant was, dancing with a woman at the far end of the dance floor. Her breath caught at the sight of him, desire shooting to every region in her body.

He was certainly something to look at. Handsome, wealthy, extremely sexy in a black suit that matched the color of his gleaming dark hair and fitted his lean body to perfection. He exuded an attraction she found difficult to deny.

"Who's that dancing with Brant?" a visitor to the table asked the question on Kia's mind.

"That's his date," someone replied.

Kia hid her surprise. Brant usually only dated blondes. Beautiful blondes with gorgeous figures and impeccable style, if the photographs in the newspaper were anything to go by. Certainly the women who frequented his office were blond and beautiful. And according to Evelyn, his personal assistant, so were the women who called him constantly on the phone.

This brunette was definitely not in his league. The woman wasn't beautiful, though she wasn't unattractive either. She just lacked the confidence of those other women, and that red-and-white floral dress looked totally wrong on her. It seemed to swallow her up. Just as Brant's presence seemed to be doing.

And didn't she know how *that* felt, she scoffed to herself as the other woman smiled shyly up at him and Brant returned the smile with a devastating one of his own. The woman stumbled, and who could blame her? Brant Matthews, Womanizer Extraordinaire, had struck again. Maybe she could suggest he have that printed on his business cards.

All at once she realized Phillip had spoken. "Sorry, Phillip. What did you say?"

"I said she's my new physiotherapist."

Ah, so this was Serena. They'd spoken on the telephone. But why had *Brant* chosen her as his date? It didn't make sense.

Then it hit her.

"Phillip, you didn't," she said for his ears only.

"Didn't what?"

"Fix them up together."

He frowned. "Why not? I thought it would do Serena good to be asked out by someone like Brant. He didn't mind."

Oh, that poor girl. Why were men so insensitive at times?

"That's exactly why he's wrong for her."

His brows drew closer together. "What do you mean?"

"She'll know people will be wondering what Brant sees in her and that'll make her feel even worse."

"I was only trying to help," he said a touch defensively.

Kia's heart softened. "I know you were. It's just that…" How to explain the mind of a shy, insecure woman? It wasn't easy delving into her own past and reliving her inadequacies.

"Merry Christmas, Kia."

Without warning, Brant was beside her, his lips brushing against her cheek in a gesture that meant nothing yet everything. Kia's pulse almost fell over itself as his warm hand touched her bare shoulder and she caught a whiff of his masculine scent. Her throat went dry.

Then he moved away and held the chair out for his date. "Serena, this is Kia, Phillip's personal assistant."

"We've spoken on the telephone," Kia said with a smile as the woman sat down opposite her.

"Oh, yes." The other woman gave a wavering smile in return, and empathy stirred within Kia, helping her recover from the shock of Brant's greeting.

"Serena's a lovely name," Kia said, wanting to put her at ease.

Serena smiled tentatively. "You think so?"

"It suits you," Brant said before Kia could respond.

Serena blushed, looking quite pretty. "Thank you."

He sat down and handed her a glass of champagne.

"Not too many women are as restful as you to be around, Serena."

Kia saw his eyes flick toward her. Was he saying *she* wasn't restful to be around? What a cheek. It wasn't her fault he wanted her but couldn't.

"Some men aren't restful to be around either," Kia pointed out, not willing to let him get the upper hand.

He eased back in his chair, confident but with a dark look in his deep blue eyes that sent shivers down her spine. "Are you saying that some men disturb you, Kia?"

Was he asking if *he* disturbed her?

"People only disturb you if you let them. I don't ever intend to let any man disturb me."

"Really?" His eyes slid across to Phillip at her side, then back to her again. They hardened, reminding her that from the day he'd met up with her outside the hospital room after he'd returned from his trip, this man had grown more and more hostile toward her. He hid it well, but she knew it was there. She could only assume that because Phillip had been going home after a date with her, Brant blamed her for the accident.

And that was totally unfair, but she wasn't about to challenge him over it or he might start delving into her and Phillip's relationship and discover the truth. How it had all started when Phillip had begged her to be his partner at a business dinner with people who knew his ex, Lynette. Things had snowballed after that and now they were out of control. Totally out of control.

Glancing at Brant, she saw a muscle pulsating in his lean cheek. Then, as if he'd had enough of her, he turned away to talk to one of the others.

She felt a spurt of anger at his dismissal. Was this the way he treated women when he had enough of them? Did he use them to amuse himself, then get rid of them once they'd passed their use-by dates? Of course he did. So why did she feel surprised? Did she think she was any different just because she shared in this intense physical attraction?

Schooling her features, Kia sipped at her champagne and watched the couples dancing out on the floor. She could hear Phillip talking about going home to Queensland to be with his family for Christmas. It reminded her of her own plans to fly south to Adelaide to spend Christmas with her mother and stepfather. She was looking forward to having some downtime with her family. She badly needed time away from the office—and the men who ran it.

All at once, Phillip leaned forward and said loudly across the table, "Hey, Brant. How would you like to dance with Kia for me?"

"Wh-what?" Kia said before she could stop herself. She didn't want to be in Brant's arms. Close to him. Touching him.

Brant's eyes narrowed slightly, but was she the only one to see the flash of hunger in them? "Maybe Kia doesn't want to dance," he said, giving her an out, telling her that as much as he wanted her in his arms, another part of him didn't.

She managed a short laugh. "Phillip, don't be silly. I don't need to dance."

"I saw your foot tapping to the music," he said, surprising her because she hadn't been aware she'd been doing that.

She opened her mouth to say she really didn't feel like dancing but then noticed all eyes upon her. Making a fuss would only make them wonder why she objected to dancing with Brant. And if that happened...

"Okay, Phillip. Anything for *you*," she emphasized, making sure Brant knew it wasn't for *him*.

And then, like a gentleman, Brant stood beside her, helping her out of her chair. She tried to smile, but already his closeness affected her. Every nerve in her body suddenly started to tingle as he led her out onto the dance floor and straight into his arms. Knowing she was in danger of melting against him, she stiffened and pulled back.

"We're only dancing," he mocked, knowing full well the effect he had on her.

On any woman.

On women in general.

"Mr. Matthews—"

His mouth thinned. "I've told you before. Call me Brant."

"You're my employer. I prefer to keep it formal."

"Why?"

"I was brought up to respect my elders."

His laughter was low and throaty, his lips showing

the tip of perfect white teeth. *All the better to eat you with, my dear,* she thought.

He moved his hand more comfortably against the small of her back. "Thanks for putting me in my place."

"I try." She moved to dislodge his fingers. They were an inch too low for her liking.

"I know you do." He tilted his head. "It makes me wonder why."

She looked somewhere past his shoulder. "Because you're the boss."

His hand moved imperceptibly lower, snatching her breath away, drawing her eyes back to him. "If I'm the boss, then you should do what I say," he murmured, making the simple statement sound very, very personal.

Recovering, she squared her shoulders and lifted her chin. She was beginning to feel as if she were some sort of puppet to be manipulated. "I never *was* good at doing what I was told."

"Shame." His eyes hardened. "But I bet you know how to get your own way now."

"Doesn't everyone?" she quipped, not sure where this was heading.

"Every *woman,* you mean."

Ah, so the womanizer had a low opinion of women. Color her surprised.

"Actually, I meant every *person*. Man. Woman. Child. Even animals—"

"I hear you've got a new car," he cut across her. "A Porsche."

Her mind reeled in confusion, not only at what he'd said but at the hint of accusation in his tone, though what she was being accused of she had no idea.

"Yes, I do have a new car."

His lips twisted with a touch of cynicism. "We must be paying you well."

His animosity was growing in leaps and bounds. "You get what you pay for," she pointed out coolly.

"I'm sure we do." He leaned closer so that his lips were practically pressed to her ear. "Or should I say *Phil* gets what he paid for."

She stiffly drew back. "What do you mean by that?"

The corners of his mouth curved in a smooth smile that didn't match the piercing glint in his eyes. "Merely that you're a top-notch PA. I'm sure Phil believes he's lucky to have you."

"That sounds like a backhanded compliment."

"Does it?" He pulled her slightly closer again, making her feel his heat.

Well, if he could be hot, she would be cold. Let him think she couldn't care less about his little games.

"Serena seems nice," she said, pasting on a cool smile.

He appeared casually amused by the change in subject. "I'm enjoying her company."

"Naturally," she said somewhat sourly. No one was safe from a womanizer like Brant.

The amusement left his face and he scowled. "What does that mean?"

"What do you think it means?" Two could play at this.

"Are you going to answer all my questions with a question?" he said, the scowl still in place.

"Is that what I'm doing?"

His glance sharpened. "You thought I'd ignore her, didn't you?"

The thought had briefly crossed her mind, but she knew he would never miss an opportunity to charm a woman, whether young or old, beautiful or plain.

But she had to admit she was still annoyed with Phillip. "Actually, I know Phillip meant well, but I wish he hadn't put her in this predicament. Believe me, I know what it's like being an ugly duckling."

His head went back in shock. "You? Never!"

"It's true. I was always very plain-looking."

"You're kidding, right?"

"I'm not. Ask my father. He was very good at telling me how plain I was." She smiled grimly, remembering all the hurt. How many times had she looked into the mirror and wished she was beautiful? "Naturally he was delighted when I suddenly started to blossom into something resembling a female."

Brant's eyes probed far too deeply. "Shouldn't a father's love be unconditional?"

"Not my father," she said, on some level surprised she was telling him so much. "He only likes being with women who are beautiful."

"Women?"

She pretended not to care. "My parents are divorced. Luckily my mother settled down to a life of bliss with a man who truly loves her. Dad's on his third marriage, to a model half his age."

"How do you feel about that?"

"I'm thrilled my mother found happiness."

"And your father?"

She'd suddenly had enough. Already she'd told him more than she should have about herself.

She glanced back at the table to where the others were talking. "We were talking about Serena."

His eyes said she wasn't fooling him but he'd accept the change in subject anyway. "Serena's a nice kid."

"She wouldn't appreciate being called a kid. She's not much younger than me."

"But you're so much more—"

"Cynical?"

He broke into a sexy half smile. "I was going to say mature."

Before she could stop it, she found herself smiling back at him.

"You should smile at me more often, Kia."

As Serena had, she stumbled—just a little—then recovered. "But if I smile, you might think I like you," she said with false sweetness.

As if he realized he'd let down his guard, the smile froze on his lips. "We wouldn't want that to happen, now would we?" he said, but his voice sounded flat and he'd withdrawn into himself.

Thankfully the song ended. She cleared her throat and went to move away. "Thank you for the dance, Brant."

But he surprised her by holding on to her arm. "Say it again, Kia."

She blinked. "What?"

"Say my name again."

In a way, she was grateful the womanizer was back. "Brant Matthews," she said defiantly.

Looking satisfied, he dropped her arm the way he'd drop her heart if she dared let him near it.

Not that she would, she told herself on the way back to the table, then forced her face to maintain a calm expression when Phillip gave her an odd look. Phillip didn't know it, but he'd taken on the role of a buffer between her and the man who was her principal employer.

She spent the next hour listening to a couple of speeches, then talking to the other guests at the table and to the staff who stopped by to pay their respects to the top table.

"Hello, Phillip."

Kia blinked as a wave of apprehension swept over her. She'd seen a picture of this woman hidden in Phillip's desk. Lynette Kelly. Phillip's ex-girlfriend.

Phillip smiled coldly. "Lynette. What brings you here?"

The other woman straightened her shoulders. "I'm here with Matthew Wright," she said quietly, looking beautiful in a silky black evening gown, her dark hair framing a lovely oval face with high cheekbones and a dainty nose.

"So you've finally found your Mr. Right, have you?" Phillip said rather nastily, and Kia turned to look at him in dismay. He and Lynette had been deeply in love until her career as a flight attendant had come between them.

Lynette's chin lifted with an odd dignity. "Yes, Phillip. I believe I have."

Kia was sure she was the only one who heard Phillip suck in a sharp breath. Thankfully the others at the table didn't appear to realize what was going on.

Except Brant, she noted.

"What a coincidence," Phillip said, recovering quickly as he picked up Kia's hand and eyed Lynette with cold triumph. "I've found the right one this time, too. Kia's agreed to marry me."

Two

"Ma-marry?" Lynette stuttered just as there was a lull in conversation at the table. Then all hell seemed to break loose.

"Marry? Who's getting married?"

"You and Kia are getting married?"

"Oh, I just *knew* something serious was going on between you two."

Kia was frozen in her seat. It wasn't often she was lost for words, but this time she was, shock causing any protest to wedge in her throat. Had Phillip just said what she thought he'd said? In front of everyone?

He looked at Kia, brought her hand to his lips and kissed it. "I know we were going to wait until after Christmas, darling, but I think now's as good a time as any." He smiled, but his eyes implored her not to make a scene. "Forgive me for telling everyone our little secret?"

She was going to kill him. Doing a favor for her boss was one thing, but this was going too far. But what could she do? Make him look a fool in front of everyone? In front of Lynette? The other woman had been the reason for all this pretence in the first place.

A faint thread of hysteria rose in her throat. "I—"

"Details," someone cut across her, which was probably best because she had no idea what she'd been about to say.

"Yes, give us details. We want to know everything."

"Yeah, like where's your engagement ring?"

Phillip laughed. "We don't have any details yet. I only proposed tonight." He smiled lovingly at her. "We'll pick out a ring after Christmas, won't we, darling?"

Still in shock, Kia was trying to think what to say. "Um…"

"How romantic," one of the women said on a sigh.

"Yes, isn't it," Brant said, a penetrating look in his eyes that made Kia feel as if he knew everything about them and didn't like what he saw.

Yet Phillip had been insistent when they'd started this charade that no one know about it but themselves. Not even Brant. *Especially* not Brant, Phillip had said, worried his business partner might think he was being irresponsible. Apparently Brant still hadn't forgiven Phillip for some silly error he'd made with one of their clients. It hadn't been that important, Phillip had told her, but Brant had been watching him like a hawk ever since.

And she'd gone along with the secret for her own reasons. It had afforded her some degree of protection against the desire she saw in Brant's eyes. Always he was around...watching...waiting...as if ready to pounce on her the minute Phillip was out of sight, both physically and mentally.

"You're a lucky woman, Kia," Lynette suddenly said in a quiet voice, her face pale as she took a shaky breath. An awkward silence fell. "Well, I must get back to my table." She looked at Phillip, her bleak eyes riveted on his face. "Congratulations, Phillip. Goodbye."

His very breath seemed to leave him, then he appeared to gather his resolve. "Goodbye, Lynette," he said brusquely.

She walked away with stiff dignity that made Kia inwardly flinch. God, she felt bad about her involvement in all this, having met the woman now. It had started out so innocently...so uncomplicated. No one should have gotten hurt.

But Lynette was hurting badly right now. And so was Phillip. He couldn't have known she'd be here. Couldn't have prepared himself for—

Suddenly something fell into place and Kia realized that Phillip *had* known Lynette was going to be here tonight. It was the reason he'd been distant after lunch. The reason he'd given her the diamond necklace to wear. And the reason he'd asked Brant to dance with her, making sure she was on the dance floor and on show for the other woman.

To *hurt* Lynette.

The thought tore at Kia's insides. She'd never deliberately hurt someone in her life and didn't appreciate being a part of this now. She'd tell Phillip on the way home and make him promise to set things right after this once and for all.

It was as well the DJ announced he would take a break while they served the meal, and everything became a flurry of people returning to their tables.

All at once she realized Brant was watching her with narrowed intensity. Every instinct inside her told her not to let him figure out the truth just yet. He was the senior partner—the boss—and he would take no hostages.

She felt uneasy as Brant continued to watch them while they worked their way through each course. By the time dessert was served she felt as though her relationship with her new fiancé had been scrutinized.

Suddenly Phillip pushed his wheelchair back from the table and gave a weak smile to the other guests. "You'll have to excuse me, but I think I'll call it a night. My leg is really starting to give me hell." He looked at Kia apologetically. "Darling, you stay and enjoy yourself."

She'd been concentrating so hard on Brant that his announcement took her completely by surprise. Come to think of it, Phillip hadn't eaten much and he'd been very quiet throughout the meal.

Probably from guilt, she decided, anger building at him even *thinking* about leaving her here and throwing her to the wolves. Or should that be *wolf?*

As in, Brant Matthews.

"I'll come with you," she said, reaching for her purse, determined to get away from all prying eyes.

He gave her a tired smile that was offset by the wary gleam in his eyes. "There's no need, darling. I'll be going straight to bed."

Kia wasn't about to let Phillip get away with this. They needed to talk. *Tonight.*

She pushed her chair back farther. "Still, I think I'll go home, too."

Phillip put up a hand. "Please stay, darling. I don't want to spoil your fun."

What fun? She didn't call Brant's company fun, not with him watching her, waiting. And if Phillip called her "darling" one more time, she was going to scream. She was no man's "darling," not when her father liked to call her his "darling girl."

She turned back to Phillip, ready to insist on going with him. Only the look in his eyes stopped her dead. Seeing Lynette again had upset him.

Compassion stirred within her, diminishing her anger to a degree. "Okay, Phillip. I understand. You just get plenty of rest so that we can go to the art exhibition tomorrow." Her eyes said she intended talking to him then about all this.

His eyes darted away uneasily. "I'll call you in the morning."

"I'll make sure she gets home safely," Brant said out of the blue.

Kia's heart lurched. She couldn't imagine being in

the confines of a car with Brant. Why, even the ballroom wasn't enough to stop his silent seduction.

"No, that's okay," she said quickly. "I'll take a taxi."

"Not in that, you won't," Brant said arrogantly, giving her breasts a raking glance in the clinging silver dress. "There was a woman attacked just last week after she left one of the hotels by herself."

"Yes, and they caught the guy, remember?" she pointed out, resisting the urge to tug at her bodice and cover her cleavage. "It was an old boyfriend." She turned to Phillip. "I'll be fine."

But Phillip was frowning. "No, Brant's right. You're too attractive to be out on your own late at night."

Okay, this was getting crazy.

"Phillip, don't be ridiculous. I'm a grown woman. I know how to take care of myself."

Phillip opened his mouth, but it was Brant who spoke. "I don't think it's ridiculous that your..." He paused. "...*fiancé* is concerned for your safety."

She grimaced inwardly. What could she say to that? "Fine. You can drive me home then."

God help her.

Satisfied with that, Phillip fobbed off someone's suggestion that they announce the engagement over the microphone before he left. She shuddered at the suggestion, knowing it would be public knowledge soon enough. Oh, heavens, and wasn't that idiotic journalist who'd written the comment about her getting her hooks into Phillip going to just love all this?

Thankfully Phillip's male nurse, Rick, was in the

hotel and was ready and waiting by the time Kia pushed the wheelchair through the ballroom doors. She tried to speak to Phillip, but all she got was a quick apology and a promise to talk later.

Then Rick wheeled him away. Suddenly the hardest thing to do was turn around and walk back into that room. Brant would be there with his arrogance and his hostility, and if he said so much as one word out of place, she would pour his drink over his head.

She smiled to herself. As a matter of fact, she hoped he did, she mused as she pushed open the doors and immediately felt those hard eyes eating her up from across the room. They scorched her with a look that bordered on physical intensity.

Unable to stop herself, she glanced at Brant. Through the sea of people and smoke-filled air, her knees weakened as sexual heat enveloped her, even as he pretended to be listening to something Simon said to him.

And it *was* a pretence. Every feminine instinct told her that he'd like nothing more than to sweep her into his arms and lose himself in her body. *Her body.* She had to remember that's all he wanted.

"Hey, babe. Wanna dance?"

Startled, she turned and looked into the face of Danny Tripp, the teenage son of one of the executives who worked a few days a week in the accounts department, and who turned beetroot-red whenever she came into the room. She'd never been able to get him to say more than two words at a time.

But not tonight, it seemed. Tonight tall, young,

clean-cut Danny Tripp, fortified by alcohol, had a silly grin on his face and was game for anything, especially with a group of his mates egging him on.

Great. Now she had *two* men lusting after her. Well, one was really only a boy in a man's body. And the other? Yes, Brant Matthews was all man. And more. Much more.

She glanced across the room and saw the alert look in his eyes that told her he sensed another male moving in on his territory. *His* territory. How ridiculous to think that way. Yet she couldn't shake the feeling.

Dragging her gaze away, she gave Danny a friendly smile so that he wouldn't feel embarrassed in front of his friends. "I'd love to dance with you, Danny."

"You would?" For a moment he appeared stunned. Then he grabbed her hand and dragged her out onto the dance floor.

She stumbled into his arms when he spun around to face her, and before she knew it, he'd slid his hands onto her hips, pulled her close to his lanky body and buried his face in her hair. There was none of the finesse Brant had exhibited earlier when he'd taken her in his arms. This was pure adolescent male, hungry for sex, and all the better with a woman he fancied.

Slightly alarmed—and hearing his pals' whistles over the slow music—she put her hands against his chest and forced some distance between them. "Danny, I—"

"Don't talk, babe." He went to pull her back into position.

She held firm against him. "Dan-ny…" The tone of her voice must have gotten through to him, because the hold on her hips slackened. She breathed a sigh of relief and looked up at him, pleased to see some of the alcoholic glaze disappear from his eyes.

He gave her a self-conscious grin. "Sorry, Kia. I guess you went to my head."

She relaxed with a smile, finding his boyishness easier to handle. "I think the drink had more to do with it than me."

He shrugged wryly. "Yeah, well, I'm not used to drinking rum."

Kia suspected he wasn't used to drinking at all. "I once got drunk on brandy and was sick for a full week."

"*You* got drunk? No foolin'?"

"I was young once, too, you know," she joked, even while her heart cramped with pain at the reason she'd been drinking. It had been the day her father had married his second wife. He hadn't wanted his "plain-looking" daughter at the wedding—or that's what he'd been telling her mother when Kia had accidentally picked up the telephone to make a call.

She'd been crushed by his rejection, though at fifteen she should have been used to his insensitivity. Afterward she'd feigned ignorance when her mother had gently explained about her father's remarriage. She had then gone out and gotten rotten drunk at a friend's party, learning the hard way that drinking didn't solve a thing.

"I hope you won't spread that around?" she said now, pushing aside her painful memories to smile up at Danny.

"Er…" His eyes darted to his friends at the table behind them, then back to her. "Sorry. What did you say?"

Someone yelled out, "Yea, Danny," but she pretended not to notice. They were only having fun. "I said I hope you won't tell anyone that I once got drunk. I have a reputation to uphold," she teased.

His gaze went beyond her again, seemed to hesitate. Then, taking a deep breath, he pulled her up close once more. "I won't say anything," he said as if whispering sweet nothings in her ear. "I promise, babe."

He was obviously more concerned with his own reputation than hers, so it was silly to feel a flutter of apprehension just because he wanted to show off for his friends. He was really just a kid who'd had too much to drink.

Should she wait until the music stopped, then go back to her table? Or go now? The room was full of people. Surely nothing would happen to her in the middle of the dance floor....

She jumped when he began to nuzzle her neck. Okay, no way could she let this go any further. "Danny, I—"

"Let the lady go," a deep male voice said beside them, startling them both, the warning in Brant's voice clearly evident.

Danny shoved himself away from Kia, a slightly belligerent look on his face until he caught sight of who'd spoken. His cheeks began to turn red as he looked at Brant's thunderous expression. "I'm sorry, Mr. Matthews," he said quickly. "I wasn't doing anything wrong."

"I know exactly what you were doing, Daniel." Brant jerked his head at the table behind them. "I suggest you go back to your table before I decide to tell Mr. Reid what you were trying to do with his PA."

Danny looked horrified. "I was just fooling around, Mr. Matthews—promise," he said, then scurried away, obviously terrified he would lose his job.

Kia couldn't help but feel sorry for the young man. Brant could be a formidable figure when he chose to be, though why he chose to throw his weight around now was anybody's guess.

She winced inwardly. That wasn't quite true. She knew *exactly* why he wanted Danny away from her. But before she could think further, Brant swept her into his arms and began to lead her around the dance floor. His touch was impersonal enough, so why did she feel acutely aware of him and his sexual power over her?

Angry with herself for her reaction, she shot him a look that would make a lesser man stumble. "You didn't need to frighten him like that."

"Yes, I did."

And she saw that deep down he did. It fit his dangerous persona. The predator who never gave up his prey without a fight. All very subliminal, yet it was there, hidden beneath his civilized exterior. God, was she the only one who saw it? Who felt it? She must be.

She swallowed a lump of apprehension. "You had no right to interfere."

His grip tightened. "I had every right. Philip would expect me to protect his…fiancée."

She ignored another insulting pause. "Danny's just a boy. He was having some fun, that's all."

A cynical smile immediately twisted his lips. "He's a young man who was almost having his way with you right there on the floor." He shrugged. "But, hey, if that's how you get your kicks, then maybe—"

"Shut up, Brant."

For a moment it was hard to tell who was the more surprised, but then a satisfied light came into his blue eyes. "Hurrah! She said my name."

Kia found herself exchanging a subtle look of amusement with him. Okay, so he'd won that small victory. She could allow him that, seeing he really had saved her from a possibly unpleasant situation.

"If it'll make you feel any better, I'll talk to Danny on Monday," he said. "For now, it'll do him good to stew over the weekend. He needs to learn a lesson about not making a move on the boss's woman."

Which boss? she wanted to ask, a tingle running down her spine at the thought of being Brant's woman. She grimaced. *One* of Brant's women. "Thank you."

There was a moment's pause, then, "So congratulations are in order," he said in a harsh voice that suddenly matched his eyes.

Unable to bring herself to say yes, she merely nodded.

"I'm surprised," he continued. "Most women couldn't have kept it a secret."

"I'm not most women."

"True." But it didn't sound like a compliment. His burning gaze slid down the column of her throat, to the necklace, and rested there for a moment. "Diamonds look good on you," he said almost as if he disliked her for it. "Another expensive gift from Phillip?"

"Another?"

"As well as the Porsche."

Good grief. Did he think Phillip had bought the car for her? She felt her cheeks redden. "Phillip did *not* give me the Porsche."

His eyes flickered with surprise. "But he gave you the necklace, right?" His expression darkened, grew stormy. "He's generous to a fault."

The way he said it was as if Phillip was generous and *she* was at fault. For a moment she wondered what she'd ever done to this man—apart from *not* hopping into bed with him.

As for the necklace, how could she tell him she was giving it back to Phillip? He'd have to ask why. So let him think what he liked. He did anyway.

After that, he seemed to sense her withdrawal, because he remained quiet while they danced around the floor. Kia fought hard to concentrate on being angry with him, but the music was growing insistent, bringing his body against her own, each step sensuously rubbing leg against leg.

His hand rested on her hip, every movement making his palm slide a little up, a little down.

Up. Down.

Hot. Cool.

In. Out.

Oh, God.

"Are you all right?"

His husky words snapped Kia's head back and she gazed into eyes that smoldered with awareness. Her heart lurched sideways, his magnetism so potent, so compelling that she could imagine him taking her right here and now in a raw act of possession that had everything to do with pure sex and erotic pleasure and nothing to do with reason. And he knew. Oh, yes, he knew, because that feeling was rushing through him, too. She could see it in his eyes. In every beat of his heart.

"It's—" she moistened her lips "—a bit hot in here, that's all," she said, pretending it was the crowd of people on the dance floor affecting her, and not him. "Too many people wanting to let their hair down, I guess."

His gaze dropped to her mouth, and the blue of his eyes darkened. Then he glanced up at the blond hair she'd put up for tonight. "Do *you* ever let your hair down, Kia?" he murmured.

What was he really asking? Whether she'd dare go to bed with him? Somehow, somewhere, she had to find the strength to pull herself out of this. If Phillip were here…

Of course!

Stronger now, she planted a cool smile on her lips. "Phillip's really the only one I let my hair down for now."

He tensed, a muscle ticking at his jaw. "Phillip didn't seem himself tonight."

She knew what he was implying. That Lynette's presence had upset him. "He's been doing too much this week."

"Nothing else?"

Kia remembered the deciphering way Brant had

looked at her and Phillip after Lynette had left and she felt a flutter of panic. "Maybe being the center of attention tonight was too much for him."

"Perhaps."

Everything had been crazy since the accident, and with Phillip having been told he'd have a permanent limp, she knew Brant couldn't be sure that *hadn't* been the problem tonight. She was banking on that to save her from further interrogation.

The music ended, and her heart skipped with relief when he let her slip from his arms without another word. He escorted her back to the table, fortunately without touching her, but she still resisted the urge to fan herself as she took her seat. One more dance with him and she'd have gone up in smoke.

"Are you enjoying yourself?" Serena asked.

Kia smiled at the other woman and tried not to show how her pulse was bubbling like the fresh glass of champagne in her hand. What a question. How could she enjoy herself when every look sent her way told her that this woman's date wanted her with a passion.

"I'm having a great time," she lied, watching Brant sit down on the opposite side of Serena. "I just wish Phillip hadn't left so early." That, at least, was the truth.

Serena's eyes turned sympathetic. "He needs time to adjust."

Kia felt her throat close up. She didn't deserve Serena's sympathy. Or anyone else's, for that matter. She was such a fraud. "I know," was all she could manage.

After that, talk around the table turned to other

things. Her heart took the chance to settle back to its regular beat as she listened to the discussions going on around her. They were all such nice people.

She glanced at Brant, his dark head tilted toward Serena while she spoke to him. Well, *nearly* all of them were nice. She couldn't exactly call Brant Matthews "nice."

It didn't apply to a man with probing eyes and an inscrutable expression, a man whose body coiled with barely controlled sensuality but bordered on an unfriendliness that belonged to an archenemy.

Thankfully the music started up again, this time playing rock and roll, and Simon asked her to dance. Desperate to forget thoughts of Brant, who was now asking Serena to dance with him, she willingly went with the older man to the dance floor, where he showed her that being middle-aged still made him capable of some daring moves.

"He'll be paying for that tomorrow," his wife teased to Kia when she returned to the table with Simon after only one song.

Kia smiled, but before she could catch her breath, Bill Stewart grabbed her hand and insisted on a dance, too. She figured out then that they were making sure she was having a good time even without her fiancé.

When she eventually got to sit down, she saw Simon about to get to his feet again. "No more," she gasped, reaching for the jug of ice water. They were killing her with kindness.

"Oh, but—" Simon began.

"No more," Brant said firmly across the table, the look in his eyes reminding them all who was boss. "Kia looks tired."

Kia didn't want to agree with him, but she didn't want to dance again either. "I am a little," she smilingly apologized to Simon.

"That's okay," the older man said with obvious relief. "I wasn't sure I had another one in me anyway."

After that, the music got even louder, until it became more impossible to talk. It wasn't long before the older couples decided to call it a night.

"Would you ladies like to go home soon?" Brant said, encompassing both her and Serena with his question. "It's nearly midnight."

Rather than going home with Brant, Kia would have sat here all night if she knew she hadn't been inconveniencing Serena. "That's up to both of you."

"I'm ready when you are," Serena agreed, giving a delicate yawn followed by a self-conscious laugh. "I have an early appointment in the morning anyway."

"No sleep-in for you then," Kia teased.

Brant quickly finished off his drink. "Right. Let's go," he rasped, getting to his feet.

Startled by his tone, Kia got to her feet, too, followed by Serena, who didn't seem to notice and continued to talk while they made their way through the tables to the exit.

Kia listened even while she wondered why Brant's face looked like thunder. Had it been her mention of sleeping in tomorrow morning? Did it remind him of being in bed? Of making love? She must have reminded him that he *wasn't* about to get any sex tonight. Not from Serena. And certainly not from *her.*

Of course, he would still have plenty of other woman friends who would willingly sacrifice themselves for his pleasure. He only had to make a phone call and it would be his.

But she soon forgot all that when they reached the front of the hotel and were discussing where they lived while waiting for Brant's car to be brought around. It appeared Serena lived closest.

"Then we'll drop you off first, if you don't mind," Brant said as the gray Mercedes glided to a stop in front of them.

Serena smiled shyly. "Of course I don't mind," she said, and before Kia could do a thing about it, Brant was holding the back door open for Serena and she had slid onto the backseat.

Kia was tempted to slide in right next to her, but as if he knew, Brant took her by the elbow and walked her to the front passenger door.

His touch made her shiver in the balmy night air. Soon she'd be alone with a man who had no need to touch to get his way. A man who had perfected foreplay with just a look. Perhaps it was as well she was an "engaged" woman now.

Three

Kia consoled herself on the way home that at least her presence wouldn't give Brant the opportunity to seduce the innocent Serena. Not that she really thought he would now, not after the brotherly way he'd been treating the younger woman all night.

Then she remembered her father and all the young women who'd passed through his life and she knew that some men just couldn't help themselves.

Five minutes later, she watched from the car while Brant walked Serena to the front door of her house. The security light had come on at their approach and Kia saw everything clearly. She breathed a sigh of relief when Brant gave Serena a smile and a quick peck on the cheek, then strode back to the car.

"Was that chaste enough for you?" he mocked as he started the engine.

Chaste? A kiss from this man could never be considered chaste. Not for her, anyway.

She forced a cool smile. "I didn't think you knew what the word meant."

He smiled grimly as he pulled out from the curb. "I could say the same about you."

"Me?"

He glanced sideways, his eyes boldly raking over her. "Sweetheart, you *ooze* sex appeal. Why do you think young Danny was falling over himself?" Obviously seeing her surprise, his eyes narrowed. "Surely Phillip's told you how sexy you are?"

Sexy? No, Phillip had never told her that.

"Yes, of course," she lied.

"You don't sound too sure."

She stiffened. "Of course I'm sure. It's just that…" *Think.* "Well, since the accident we've been concentrating on him rather than me."

He appeared to consider that. "He's going through a tough time right now." Once more his gaze slid over her, almost contemptuously this time. "But if any woman can make him think like a man again, it's you."

She didn't appreciate the comment. "You've missed your calling. You should be doing talk shows."

This time he laughed. A deep, rich sound that made her catch her breath and confirmed why women of all kinds wanted him. She didn't even *like* him and *this* was her reaction.

Luckily for her, they came to some night roadwork and Brant had to slow the car and concentrate for the next kilometer. After that, except for her directing him, they both remained quiet until they reached her street.

"It's the house at the end," she said as they came around the corner into the leafy cul-de-sac.

A few moments later he pulled into the driveway and cut the engine. "You live here by yourself?" he asked, his eyes going over the ground-level house nestled amongst the lush garden. It was obviously too big for one person.

"I live by myself, yes, but the house has been divided into two. The owner lives in one apartment and I live in the other."

It was a bonus that June didn't drive, so Kia got to use the garage at the far end of the driveway. But why, oh, why hadn't she driven herself tonight? If she'd known Phillip would leave early and she'd be stranded with Brant, she would have insisted on taking her Porsche.

The Porsche Brant thought Phillip had bought for her.

He opened his door, letting in the late-night sounds of a tropical summer. "I'll walk you inside."

She'd known he would. Her front door was actually around the back of the house, so it wouldn't be possible to dismiss him easily. The minute he saw her walking down the driveway alongside the house he'd be out of the car and following her anyway.

"It's around the back." She moved to get out of the car, but her long dress proved difficult, and before she knew it he stood beside her, offering her his hand. For a moment she hesitated. Already her pulse was skittering all over the place. What would his touch do to her?

Having no option but to appear unruffled, she held her breath and put her hand on his. Her skin immediately tingled from the contact, but surprisingly his fingers didn't close around hers. His hand remained open, palm up, allowing her to grip him as she chose.

Is this how he lets a woman make love to him? At her own pace?

That thought spread the tingle through her body as her fingers closed around his hand and she pressed her palm against his, using his strength to bring her to her feet.

He stepped back before their bodies could touch further, making her grateful for small mercies.

"It's this way," she said huskily and hurried forward, the path illuminated by small garden lights mingling through the palm trees, the clicking of her high heels in competition with a chorus of green tree frogs.

But when she came up to the door, it was standing open. She began to frown, then gave a soft gasp as realization hit. Someone had broken in.

"Oh, my God," she whispered in disbelief.

"Stay there." Brant strode the few feet to the door, swearing softly when he tread on some broken glass. He reached inside for the nearest switch, flooding the kitchen with light.

Kia came up behind him and they both stood there looking around. At first it appeared as if nothing had happened but the glass on the floor showed that someone had smashed one of the panels on the door.

"Careful," Brant warned, stepping over the mess, then helping her while she lifted the skirt of her long dress with one hand and gingerly stepped over the glass.

Kia's heart was almost jumping out of her chest. "Do you think he's still here?" she whispered.

Brant peered toward the darkened hallway, his expression hard. "If he is…" He pulled his cell phone out of his jacket pocket. "He's going to regret it."

Kia shivered as he dialed the police and spoke quietly for a moment. She almost felt sorry for the robber if he was still here. He'd be in for a shock if Brant got hold of him.

He swore as he ended the call. "They've had a busy night. They could be a while."

Kia's stomach churned with anxiety. She'd hate to think what would happen if she were here alone. For the first time, she was glad of Brant's presence. "What now?"

He reached over to grab a knife from the block on the sink. "I guess I'm going to play the bloody hero," he muttered, stepping toward the hallway, but he stopped when he saw her face. "What's the matter?"

"You're not going to use that, are you?"

He grimaced. "It's only for protection. Come on. Stick with me."

Kia needed no second bidding. She stuck like wallpaper while they went from room to room, switching on each light, her knees knocking with relief when no one jumped out at them.

In the loungeroom they discovered her laptop and DVD player missing, plus a small antique clock, along with other knickknacks. Her bedroom appeared un-touched, thank God. She'd hate to think of some stranger handling her personal things. Perhaps fondling her silky bra and panties…

She shuddered, and Brant put his hand on her forearm and turned her to face him. "Are you all right?"

"Yes," she murmured, though she knew she wasn't. She couldn't seem to stop shaking.

"Shhh," he said, starting to massage her arm in a comforting gesture that made her drop her gaze to his hand on her, suddenly wanting to lean into him and let his strength wrap around her.

She looked up and all at once he was staring into her eyes.

"Kia?" he growled, and she opened her lips slightly despite a silken thread of warning in his voice. He was going to kiss her…. She wanted him to, dear God, she did.

Just then the sound of crunching glass came from the kitchen and a male voice called out, "This is the police. Everything all right in there?"

Brant immediately stepped back. "About bloody time," he rasped without looking at her and left her side to stride down the hallway. "We're here, Constable," he said more loudly. "We were just seeing if there was any damage."

Kia stood there for a moment, fighting intense dis-appointment. Brant obviously hadn't suffered from the same frustration—or if he had, he hadn't shown it. He'd turned away from her so fast she'd almost got whiplash watching him.

Which only reminded her that's exactly what he'd

do if he ever got her into bed. He'd use her, then he'd walk away without a second glance.

Kia took a deep breath and straightened her shoulders. Now she felt strong again. She'd resisted him this far and would continue to do so. She'd been weakened by the shock of the robbery, that's all.

For the next ten minutes she sat at the kitchen table and answered questions for the two very nice policemen who'd responded to the call, while Brant leaned back against the sink and watched the proceedings like a judge in a courtroom. He certainly made the younger policeman uneasy, by the looks of things, though the older one didn't bat an eyelid.

"Probably an addict," the older policeman said now, giving a world-weary shrug. "Got to get their fix somehow. Just as well you were wearing that necklace, Miss Benton, and didn't leave it at home."

Kia gave a soft gasp as her hand went to the diamonds circling her neck. Then she saw Brant's jaw clench and the way his eyes burned her and she couldn't help but think he was somehow angry over Phillip giving her the necklace.

The policeman interrupted her thoughts by going on to suggest ways of tightening her security, including putting a bolt on the door and getting a dog.

"Oh, but we do have a dog. I mean, the lady in the apartment next door has a dog." Something occurred to her. "Oh, no. I wonder if he broke into June's place, as well? The house has been divided in two, you see." She swallowed. "Do you think you could check? She's not home this weekend, thank goodness. She went to visit her sister and took Ralphie with her."

"I'll go take a look around," the younger policeman said after getting a nod from his boss, then nervously looked at Brant before leaving the room, as if glad to get out from under such a strong presence.

The older policeman glanced at Kia. "Have you got someone to stay with you tonight, Miss Benton? Something like this can shake people up pretty bad."

"*I'll* be staying with her," Brant said before she could open her mouth.

She shot to her feet. She couldn't have Brant stay here. She just couldn't. "I can look after myself. I don't need anyone. I—"

"What if he comes back?" Brant cut across her.

The spew of words froze on her lips. Somehow she managed a short laugh. "He won't. He got what he wanted."

"Did he?"

She shivered and hugged her bare arms. "Stop it. You're scaring me."

"Well, you should be bloody scared," he said, straightening away from the sink. "You've got a door with a broken lock and no one close enough to hear you scream." His jaw tautened, making him look dark and dangerous. "I'm staying."

How silly to feel relief. She should be more scared of Brant and her own attraction for him than of being robbed again. Only if the robber came back he might not only want to rob her. He might want more than that....

"I really think that's a good idea, Miss Benton," the older policeman coaxed, looking at her in a fatherly fashion, reminding her that they weren't alone.

She swallowed deeply. "Yes, of course."

Right then the younger policeman stepped back into the kitchen, interrupting them. "Everything's fine next door." He shot a look at his boss. "Sarge, that call we were expecting just came through."

"Right." The older man straightened and immediately put his notebook in his pocket. "We'll be in touch," he told them quickly, then was gone.

A moment's tense silence stretched between her and Brant, then she cleared her throat, determined to be as businesslike as possible. "I'll get the couch ready for you."

Brant's mouth twisted. "I doubt I'll get much sleep on that two-seater in your loungeroom."

She felt as if her breath cut out. *Was he asking to share her bed?* Over her dead body.

Well, maybe not her *dead* body, she mused, hurrying to the refrigerator to get a cool drink. "Isn't that the point? To stay awake and protect me?" She lifted out the jug of cold water, almost tempted to hold it up to her forehead to cool herself down. "Anyway, it opens out to a sofa bed. You'll have plenty of room."

He began loosening his tie. "Fine. I like being able to spread out."

"That must be a novelty for you," she said before she could stop herself.

The look in his eyes held a spark of eroticism. "You make it sound like there's a woman in my bed every day."

She feigned ignorance. "You mean there isn't?"

"Sweetheart, I'm not married. I only let a woman in my bed when I'm looking for some affection."

"That's what I said. Every day." She placed the jug on the bench and walked toward the hallway door. "I'll get you a blanket," she said before he could respond. She had to get out of that room or she'd strangle him with her bare hands. Either that or smother him with one of the pillows she was about to get him.

The ringing of the telephone next to him woke Brant with a start the next morning. It seemed as if he'd only just fallen asleep, having tossed and turned for most of the night, blaming the sofa but knowing it was because the sexiest woman alive lay in a bed not meters away from him, with only a thin wall between them.

So he didn't appreciate being woken now. "Yes?" he barked into the mouthpiece.

A moment's silence, then a man's shocked voice came down the line. "Brant!"

Brant's eyes flew open. "Phil?"

The other man sucked in a sharp breath. "What the hell? Where's Kia?"

"Look, it's not what you think," Brant growled, shooting to a sitting position and regaining his composure. "Someone broke into her place last night. I slept on the sofa so I could keep an eye on her, that's all."

"Is she okay?" Phil asked, anxious now.

"She was a bit shook up last night, but I'm sure she'll be fine in the light of day."

He looked up and saw Kia standing in the doorway. Her blue eyes were sleepy, her blond hair sexily tousled, not a bit of makeup on her beautiful face as she wrapped the sash of a silky blue creation around her waist. She looked so bloody gorgeous he had to stop himself from throwing the phone down and ravishing her on the spot.

"I'm glad you were there for her," Phil said slowly, dragging Brant's thoughts away from the woman in front of him. Phil still sounded depressed.

"Phil, I'm sure she would rather have had you here," he said, watching her eyes come fully awake at the mention of the other man's name.

"Is that Phillip?" she said, stepping into the room and hurrying toward him. In an instant Brant could feel her female heat coiling around him. Could hear the silky swish of her thighs. The soft gasps of her breath that came closer and closer. If he reached out, he might just be able to caress her.

Instead he held out the phone. "Yeah, it's Phil."

She snatched it to her and immediately turned her back on him. "Phillip? Did Brant explain what happened?" She gave a delicate shudder. "It was awful. I can't believe someone would do this." She listened for a moment, then said, "He broke the glass door. The police think…"

She continued to talk, but Brant had stopped listening. And he'd almost stopped breathing. She didn't know it, but with the morning sun streaming in the room he could see straight through her gossamer robe to the line of her buttocks. God, how he'd love to run his hands over them. They'd be so smooth to his touch.

Giving a silent groan, he leaned his head back against the pillows and closed his eyes. Dammit, he had to stop this. She wasn't worth the looking...the wanting....

"Brant?"

Did she have to say his name in such a husky voice? As if she was his lover, waiting for him to stir. The next thing she'd be reaching out to touch him....

"Yes?" His voice sounded rough, like the night he'd just had.

"Are you awake?"

"No. I always talk in my sleep," he mocked and opened his eyes. Disappointment rippled through him when he saw she'd moved out of the sunlight.

Her mouth tightened. "That's one thing *I'll* never find out."

"No, you won't, will you?" And suddenly it was the biggest regret of his life. His lips twisted. Okay, that and getting involved with Julia all those years ago. She hadn't been too innocent when she'd run off and married his brother.

He threw back the sheet and swung his legs over the side of the sofa bed, his black briefs his only covering. "Tell me. Does Phillip ever talk in his sleep?" he asked, forcing himself to remember who this woman belonged to...and what she was about.

Money.

She gave a light laugh. "Only to murmur sweet nothings in my ear."

An intense jealousy slashed through him. It should have been *him* who whispered in her ear. *Him* who lay beside her. *Him* who made love to her. That's what felt right. Not her and Phillip. Every minute he grew more certain of it.

He reached for his trousers. God, what was going on here? Why didn't he suddenly feel right about those two? There was something he couldn't quite put his finger on. Something important. Yet all he had was a gut feeling he couldn't shake. And a bloody hunger for Kia Benton that wouldn't stop.

"Would you like coffee before you go?"

At the crack in her voice he looked up and caught her appraising his bare chest and taut stomach. Despite being newly engaged, the look in her eye said she wanted *him.*

His muscles immediately tensed as he zipped up and asked the question that hit him from out of nowhere. "How come you didn't call Phillip last night?" All at once he found it interesting that she hadn't gone running to her fiancé after the burglary.

She'd been about to turn away, but now her eyelids flickered, as if the question startled her. "What? Er...I didn't want to worry him."

"If you were my fiancée, I'd *want* you to worry me."

She moistened those oh-so-enticing lips. "You know he was tired and in pain when he left the party."

"I'd still want to know if you were in danger."

Her chin angled. "Phillip's not like you, Brant."

No, he wasn't, was he? Phillip was a one-woman man. And that woman was Lynette Kelly, of that Brant was suddenly certain. Ever since he'd seen Phillip's reaction to his old girlfriend at the Christmas party last night, he'd had this deep nagging feeling. And what about Lynette's reaction to Phillip? They were both still in love with each other, no doubt about it.

Brant looked at Kia and wondered if she knew. Surely she'd noticed something amiss?

"Forget the coffee," he rasped as he quickly slipped on his shirt and made a grab for his jacket. He had to get out of here before he did or said something he'd regret. Phillip may be in love with Lynette, but the other man obviously wasn't prepared to do anything about it. And Kia must be thanking her lucky stars she'd found a man who didn't give a damn that he was being taken to the cleaners.

Ignoring the tight knot forming in his stomach, he sat down again and began putting on his socks and shoes. "I'll call a locksmith and get him to fix the door for you." What he should really do is get someone to lock *her* up. Only then would men be safe from her beauty and self-seeking ways.

"I'm quite capable of picking up a phone."

"I didn't say you weren't, but I can get it fixed faster. I have connections."

"What you mean is you'll offer him more money to fix it today?"

"The company can afford it."

She drew in a sharp breath. "Don't be ridiculous. I won't be letting the company pay for anything."

His mouth clamped into a thin line. Who was she trying to fool? This was a token protest at best.

"So you're going to sleep another night with your

door wide-open?" He stood up, ready to leave. "I could always come back and use your sofa again." It was a foolhardy threat. He'd never be able to handle another night without touching her. And he had better things to do with his time.

"I'll go to a motel."

His teeth clenched. "Fine and dandy. And when you get home, the rest of your stuff will have been stolen." Without waiting for a response, he started toward the door. "Someone will be round within the hour."

"Brant—" she warned, only to have the ring of the telephone interrupt her.

"Answer that," he said and left the house before she could get another word in. What he found interesting was that she hadn't mentioned staying at Phillip's place, when that would be the ideal solution. Perhaps she was holding out for a white wedding, he mused cynically.

Four

Later that day, when Phillip's attendant knocked on her door to pick her up to take her to the art exhibition, Kia had to take a calming breath before answering. She was furious with Brant over the locksmith he'd sent here. All the names she'd been calling him seemed too tame for the thoughts bubbling in her brain right now.

But instead of showing her feelings, she smoothed her hands down the front of her slim-fitting sleeveless dress and reached for the door handle. She wouldn't let Brant spoil her afternoon. She'd rather eat rat poison.

"G'day, Kia."

The breath caught in her throat. The man on the other side of the doorway emitted a sex appeal so potent it cracked through the air like a whip, invisibly wrapping around her body and almost pulling her toward him. Black trousers fitted his lower torso to perfection, a light gray polo shirt molded over his chest. He looked casual and confident. A man any woman would be proud to be seen with.

Anyone but her.

"Aren't you going to invite me in?" Brant said, stepping past her into the house without waiting for an invitation.

She spun around to face him. Of all the arrogant... "How dare you!" she managed to say.

He merely looked amused. "How dare I be in your house? You didn't mind me being here last night."

She glared at him. He made it sound as if they'd been making love all night. "I'm talking about the security alarm."

His forehead creased. "He didn't do a good job?"

"Yes, he did a good job, but that's not the point. He was supposed to fix the lock, not put in an alarm system." She'd thought the man had been merely checking security risks when he'd started going from room to room. By the time she'd realized he was doing the whole thing, he'd climbed on the roof and had half the place wired.

"I thought an alarm system would be better."

"*You* thought? Where do you get off ordering an alarm for *me?*"

"I told you. The company will pay for it."

"It's not the money," she said through gritted teeth.

His eyebrows lifted with cynicism. "Really? Then what's the problem?"

"This is *my* home, Brant. *My* private life. You're interfering in it. You've no right to even be here, let alone tell someone to install an expensive piece of equipment like this. Heck, it's not even technically my house."

His shrug belied the hard gleam in his eyes. "Don't make a big deal out of this, Kia. You're Phillip's fiancée now. He wants you to be safe."

She tried not to wince. "Phillip knows about the alarm?"

"As you're now his fiancée, I suggested it and he agreed. We all know it's quite common for criminals to return to the scene of the crime. You either had to get an alarm or move."

She flashed him a look of disdain. "Oh, really. And where would you like me to live?"

"How about with your fiancé?"

She gulped and quickly spun away to turn off the air-conditioning. Anything not to look at Brant. "Phillip and I haven't discussed that yet."

"That's what Phil said."

Relief rushed through her. "There you are then." She remembered the security alarm and glared at him. "Anyway, you and Phillip have no right to tell me what to do or what to put in my own house. And as soon as he gets here, I'll be making that quite clear."

"Then you're going to have a bit of a wait," he said, his gaze seeming to watch her reaction. "He's not coming. He rang and asked me to take you to the exhibition instead. He said he wasn't feeling up to it today."

Her stomach knotted. She didn't want to go to the exhibition with Brant. Damn Phillip for being selfish enough not to turn up. She was beginning to think taking the easy way out was a weakness he couldn't control.

"Why didn't he phone me himself?"

"He said he'd tried a couple of times but kept getting the busy signal."

She bristled with indignation. "Because the alarm was being connected to the phone line, that's why." She waved a dismissive hand. "Oh, it doesn't matter. I'm not going without Phillip."

His eyes narrowed. "Phil said one of our clients invited him to the exhibition."

"Er…yes…" She licked her lips. "But it just wouldn't be the same without Phillip. I'm sure they'll understand."

"*They* may, but *I* won't. This is a work assignment, Kia. Think of it as payment for the security alarm."

Her mouth tightened. So there *was* a catch to his free and easy statement of "the company will pay for it."

"Perhaps I should go by myself…on behalf of the company, that is. There's no need for you to waste your Saturday afternoon." She didn't want to deprive some poor besotted female of his company either.

"I wouldn't think of it as a waste. I'd like to see the exhibition, too. Early Australian art fascinates me."

It fascinated her, too, but she didn't want to say so. Yet could she spend hours with him and survive the draw of his attraction? She swallowed. It looked as though she wasn't getting a choice. But after she put in an appearance for their client, she'd make sure it was the quickest walk around the gallery on record.

* * *

An hour later she and Brant strolled through the art gallery by themselves after they'd shared an afternoon tea of pineapple scones, finger sandwiches and a delicious tropical fruit platter. Brant had been his charming self with their client and the others. A couple of times she'd even let her guard down and surprised herself by actually laughing at some of his witty remarks.

Of course, being witty and a womanizer was what he was about. That's how men like him got women into bed, and if the looks some of the other women were giving him were anything to go by, he'd have had plenty of offers today if she hadn't been around. Yes, he knew exactly how to charm the panties right off a woman. She stiffened. *Not this woman.*

"I like this painting of the early settlers," he said now, his deep voice bringing her out of her thoughts. "I saw a print of it years ago, but the brushstrokes and paint textures are nothing compared to the original." He turned to look at her. "It's very evocative, don't you agree?"

She fumbled for words when she saw the piece of work he was referring to. "Um...yes."

He arched a brow. "You sound surprised?"

A thrill raced through her, but she managed to shrug as if it were no big deal. "It's my favorite painting."

"And you didn't expect us to have the same tastes, right?" He paused, his blue eyes darkening. "I think we'd have a lot in common if we looked closely."

She moistened suddenly dry lips. "Yes. Phillip, for one thing."

He gave a slightly bitter smile. "Ah, Phillip. We'll always have him in common, won't we?" He turned back to the painting. "Tell me. Why is this your favorite?"

Obviously he wanted to keep things on an even keel, and she was only too happy to oblige. Yet she couldn't help but feel a burst of excitement that he found the imagery of the painting as touching as she did. Perhaps there was more to him than met the eye.

She turned to the painting and let her gaze wander over the picture of their pioneer ancestors, losing herself in its sheer vibrancy and color. "I'd say it's because it personifies the Outback spirit. That it's possible to overcome any obstacle, no matter how big or daunting."

"So you like challenges?" he pounced.

She drew in a shaky breath. Always the predator. He just couldn't help himself. "*Some* challenges," she admitted.

"I like certain challenges, too," he drawled, his eyes intense. "If somebody tells me I can't have something, then that's when I want it."

And he wanted her. He had no need to say it out loud. The wanting poured from him like a familiar scent.

She plastered a smile on her lips. "Then you'd better get used to disappointment," she quipped, knowing her first instincts about him were correct. She hadn't misjudged him. Not in the slightest.

A few hours later the two of them sat at an outdoor café not far from the exhibition, sipping at fruit daiquiris. The pre-Christmas festivities were still continuing, and people were out in force and in holiday mode, enjoying a stroll along the sail-shaded Smith Street Mall, listening to a busker play her guitar, watching a mime artist perform.

Brant couldn't have cared less where they were or who was nearby. His concentration was solely and fully on one person. Kia looked as beautiful as always, with her blond hair pulled back in a French knot, and wearing a lemon-colored dress that displayed the elegant line of her neck and showed off her tanned shoulders and arms.

But something else about her today set his pulse spinning like a top. Watching her talk to the others at the gallery, he'd glimpsed an innocence in her lovely eyes that had been at odds with the knowing look in them, as if she couldn't quite hide the sweet beneath the spice. Yet *sweet* was hardly a word he'd expect to use about Kia Benton.

He swallowed some of his drink, then decided he didn't need any more intoxication right now. Apart from a brief time last night and again this morning, he'd never really been alone with her like this before. It had gone to his head—no, his *body*. His state of constant arousal was killing him.

And she knew it. That's why she wasn't quite facing him as she sat sipping her daiquiri, her body turned slightly toward the crowd.

But she was only fooling herself. There could be a brick wall between them and the attraction would still seep through. Didn't she know there was no stopping it? Not unless they made love and got it out of their systems, and then he had the feeling it would probably only intensify.

"Tell me more about your father," he said, suddenly interested in what made her tick.

She raised a wry eyebrow. "Why?"

He gave a smile. "Are you this suspicious of everyone or is it just me?"

"Just you," she said, her lips curving into a sexy smile that was as unexpected as was her words. God. She was lovely, with her smooth cheekbones, perfect nose, eyes that could dazzle a man with just one look and a deliciously tempting mouth.

She put her glass down, and when she looked up again her face had sobered. "There's nothing much to tell. My father thinks he's one of the beautiful people. He can't stand being around someone who isn't."

Brant frowned. "You're still his daughter."

Her slim shoulders tensed. "The only reason he wants me around is because he thinks it's good for his image."

All at once something occurred to him. "Good Lord. Your father isn't Lloyd Benton, is he?"

If it were possible, she tensed even more. "The one and only."

Now he knew where she was coming from. Lloyd Benton owned the biggest fleet of used-car yards up and down the east coast of Australia. He was constantly in the newspapers with some young thing hanging off his arm—usually his current wife but not always. The man gave *sleaze* an added dimension.

"*He's* your father?"

She raised her chin in the air. "I won't apologize for him."

"I don't expect you to."

No wonder she didn't seem to hold men in high regard. Well, *some* men. He freely admitted that men like himself, who took one look and wanted to take her to bed, would only confirm her low opinion of the male species. Dammit, suddenly he was seeing another side to this woman that he wasn't sure he wanted to see.

"It certainly explains a lot about you and Phillip."

She tensed. "If you mean I want to marry someone who doesn't have to bed every beautiful woman he meets, then you're dead right. Phillip's a nice man." Her gaze dropped to her glass, then up again. "He'll be a wonderful father and a faithful husband."

"You didn't say you loved him." And he found that interesting. *Very* interesting.

"That goes without saying."

"Does it?"

"Yes."

And perhaps it was all an act. Perhaps working on people for sympathy was how she wormed her way into men's beds...and their hearts. Perhaps it was all about paying back her father for being so weak.

"What about you?" she said, catching him off guard. "Are your parents still alive, Brant?"

He had no wish to talk about himself. "No. They died when I was eighteen."

Sympathy flashed in her eyes. "I'm sorry. Any brothers or sisters?"

His jaw tightened. "A brother. And before you ask, he's younger than me by a couple of years." He looked at his watch and stood up. "Come on. Let's go. It's getting late."

For a moment, surprise mixed with hurt appeared in her eyes, then cynicism took over. "Got a date, no doubt."

"No doubt." He didn't tell her he was getting together with his two best mates for dinner, though Flynn and Damien would no doubt find it amusing that they were to be his "date" this evening.

Not that he'd tell them. The three of them had grown up together on the same street in this town—had shared everything from stories of their first kiss to their first million—but Kia Benton was one thing he wasn't about to share with his rich and successful friends.

"Phillip Reid, how could you!" Kia exclaimed the next day as she swept into his study. She'd been phoning him on and off since returning from the art exhibition yesterday. He hadn't answered, but she suspected he'd been at home. He'd been feeling low so she'd given him a reprieve, but now she had a few words to say to him whether he still felt bad or not.

He looked up and winced. "What can I say, Kia? I'm sorry."

She stopped right in front of his desk. "I don't like being used," she said through gritted teeth.

His dark brows drew together. "I wasn't… I didn't mean…"

"Yes, you did." She slapped the box containing the diamond necklace down in front of him. "Don't try and fool me, Phillip. You gave me this because you knew Lynette was going to be at the party. And then you had Brant dance with me so she'd see who you'd brought as your partner. And to top things off, you tell everyone we're engaged and leave me high and dry to field all sorts of questions."

He looked thoroughly shamefaced and embarrassed. "I really *am* sorry. I didn't mean for it to go so far."

She was nowhere near ready to forgive him. Not after what she'd been through. "And yesterday? What happened to coming to the art exhibition with me?"

He swallowed hard as he leaned back in his wheelchair. "I'm sorry. I just wasn't up to going out." Then he looked confused. "Didn't Brant take you? He said he would."

"Yes, but I'd rather have gone by myself," she said sourly, preferring not to think about how much she'd enjoyed herself. She had to remember Brant could charm *any* woman into having a good time.

A speculative look came into Phillip's eyes. "Are you upset because I didn't go? Or because Brant did?"

Kia tensed, then forced herself to relax. "It's awkward spending time with one's boss," she said, avoiding a direct answer.

"You don't mind spending time with me."

She shrugged. "You're different."

"Look, if there's something between you two—"

Somehow she managed to hide her panic. "Don't be an idiot, Phillip. And, by the way, what's the deal about my security alarm? I don't remember giving either of you permission to put one in my place."

Phillip frowned, falling for the diversion. "It was the only thing to do, seeing you're my...er...fiancée. Brant would have been suspicious otherwise."

Her teeth set on edge. "Engaged or not, I am *not* some feeble female who can't take care of myself," she said with more bravado than she'd felt the other night after the robbery. "And if Brant thinks he—"

"So this *is* about Brant?" Phillip said, pushing his wheelchair back from the desk, looking very much the all-knowing male now that the heat had been taken off him.

She realized she'd given too much away. "Phillip, will you stop this. I don't know what's come over you today."

He wheeled his chair around the desk and toward her. "He gets to you, doesn't he?"

She gave a hollow laugh. "Of course not."

"And I've gone and spoiled it for you by telling everyone you're my fiancée." He stopped a few feet in front of her and thumped his hands on the armrests in helpless anger. "Hell. This is all such a bloody mess."

"That's an understatement." She just wished he'd stopped to think things through before making drastic announcements like they were engaged. "The question is, what are we going to do about it?"

He looked up at her, his expression thoroughly wretched. "I'm not sure."

"This can't go on, Phillip."

"I know. God, we were just supposed to be a couple for *one* date."

Sympathy started to soften her. "Phillip, you didn't know Lynette's father was going to be at that dinner."

"Yeah, but I knew he shared the same business circles. Dammit, I shouldn't have asked you to continue with the charade after that. It wasn't fair of me." He looked down at his leg and his lips twisted. "Pity the accident got in the way and ruined everything. But this…" He gestured at the plaster from toe to thigh. "I *know* Lynette. She would've convinced herself that I needed her. And then she would have convinced *me*. I couldn't let that happen." He took a shuddering breath. "She deserves better than a cripple for the rest of her life."

"Oh, Phillip." She crouched down in front of his wheelchair. "Don't say that. A limp does *not* make you a cripple."

He took a deep breath. "Sorry. I'm just full of self-pity today."

"Look," she said, thinking hard. "Let's wait until after Christmas, then we'll make an announcement that things didn't work out after all."

His eyes lit up, then drooped just as quick. "But your name will end up being mud. No one will care about the details, especially not the press. They'll just know you broke off the engagement during a bad time for me." He grimaced. "I'm sorry, Kia. I never meant for any of this to happen."

She squeezed his hand, trying not to think about all this being made public to the people of Darwin. "Let's ride it out, Phillip. In the meantime, we'll carry on for another week until Christmas. I heard you tell Mary that you were going home to Queensland for the holidays anyway. That'll give us some breathing space."

Intense relief surged across his face. "Good idea."

All at once Kia couldn't help but think that Brant would never let anyone else sort out his problems for him the way Phillip was doing here. Brant would have taken charge and done what he had to do. Actually, on second thought, he would never have gotten himself in this situation in the first place. Brant relied on no one except himself. He needed no one.

Just like her.

"Don't let him get to you, Kia."

She feigned ignorance. "Who?"

"Brant."

She pretended to be unconcerned. "I wish you'd stop implying that there's something going on between me and Brant. There isn't. End of story."

Is it? Phillip's eyes asked, but she promptly looked away. She wasn't about to tell him she suspected he was right.

The next week leading up to Christmas proved difficult for Kia. Not only was she extremely busy tidying things up at work so that she could enjoy their two-week closure over the holidays, but Brant seemed to sense something amiss between her and Phillip. She had the funny feeling he was homing in for the kill.

Then, just as she thought she might be able to relax, the airline phoned at the exact moment Brant walked into her office. They were checking to see if there was anything else they could do to assist Phillip on his trip to Queensland tomorrow.

Kia tried to sound as if she were talking to a client. She didn't want Brant to know she wasn't joining Phillip at this stage. "Thank you, but I believe everything's under control."

"What about on arrival in Brisbane?" the woman persisted on the other end of the line. "Can we arrange transport from the airport?"

"That's kind of you, but there will be someone to meet him," she said, then could have kicked herself when the look in Brant's eyes sharpened.

"That's fine then. But please let us know if there's anything we can do."

"Thank you, I will." Kia hung up, swallowed, then planted a polite smile on her face. "Can I help you, Mr. Matthews?"

His mouth thinned. "You can't keep calling me 'mister' for the next twenty years."

She kept a reign on her temper. "Who knows where any of us will be by then?"

"You'll be married to Phillip, of course."

She'd forgotten that was what he'd think. "Yes, of course."

"Who was on the telephone just now?"

Her heart thumped as she quickly began to tidy up some papers. "Oh, no one you should worry about."

A pair of hands flattened on the desk in front of her, stilling her. "That was someone from the airline, wasn't it?"

She drew a shaky breath and looked up into blue eyes that were riveted on her face. The caress of his warm breath on her cheeks stirred her senses. "Yes."

"So you're not on the same flight as Phillip?" he demanded, shooting each word at her with the precision of gunfire.

"No."

"Are you catching another flight?"

"Yes." To Adelaide.

"To Queensland?"

She lifted her chin in the air and decided she'd had enough of this. "I'm not going to Queensland. I'm spending Christmas with my family in Adelaide."

He leaned in that little bit closer. "So you're not spending Christmas with your new fiancé?"

She resisted shrinking back in her chair. "Not this year, no."

"Why?"

"What do you mean why?"

Anger flared in his eyes as he pushed himself back from the desk and straightened. "It's usual for an engaged couple to spend Christmas together."

"We're not a usual couple." She realized what she said too late. "I'd already made other arrangements," she pointed out as she slowly began to breathe again.

An odd glint appeared in his eyes. "I'd have thought you wouldn't want to let him out of your sight."

"I trust Phillip," she said, slightly puzzled by his question. It wasn't as though Phillip would be out nightclubbing every night. Now if it was Brant who was her fiancé…

"But do you trust Lynette Kelly?" he purred.

Shock ran through her. Had he guessed that Lynette still had feelings for Phillip? Did he know things hadn't really been settled between them?

"Lynette and Phillip are no longer an item," she said coolly, and before he could say anything further she handed him a piece of paper. "I believe this belongs to you, Mr. Matthews."

His face hardened. "Kia, I swear if you call me Mr. Matthews one more time…" He trailed off as he opened the slip of paper. His head shot up. "What's this?"

"A check for my security alarm." She'd rung the man who'd come to her home only to find out the bill had already been paid.

Cynicism entered his eyes. "Forget it. You paid for it by coming to the art exhibition, remember?"

Yes, so why did she deserve that mocking look in his eyes? "I'm sorry, I don't see it that way. Not even as Phillip's fiancée."

"My offer was non-negotiable." He ripped it in two.

She got to her feet and walked to a cabinet too close to Brant to get her purse. "Fine. I'll write another one and give it to Phillip."

"No need for drama, Kia. Let it go."

"Mr. Matthews, if you think you can do what you like—"

He captured her arm with his warm hand, sending a slew of shivers racing over her spine. "Listen, if I did what I'd really like—"

"Is everything all right in here?"

Kia drew a ragged breath before she looked up to see Phillip had wheeled to the office door and was looking at them in concern. She stepped sideways and Brant dropped his hand.

Somehow she planted a stiff smile on her lips. "Yes, everything's fine. I was just reminding Mr. Matthews that you're going to Queensland tomorrow."

"The name's Brant," Brant snapped and stormed out of the office.

Phillip raised his brows as he looked at Kia. "Sure you don't want to come with me tomorrow? It might be safer."

Kia shook her head. There was no place on earth safe for her. Not another state. Not another country. No, she'd just have to polish her armor and pray that Brant had better things to do on Christmas Eve than harass her.

And if she believed that, then maybe Santa Claus really did exist.

Five

Kia saw Phillip off at Darwin airport the next morning, then returned to the office to finish up some work before doing some last-minute Christmas shopping. She found Brant in Phillip's office, riffling through some papers on his desk.

He looked up when she appeared in the doorway, and his eyes darkened when he saw her. "You're back," he said as if she'd returned just for him.

And suddenly she knew she had. Despite all the attraction she *didn't* want to feel for this man, she still felt it. Her armor was paper-thin at best.

"Yes," she murmured, willing him to come to her. To pull her into his arms. To make love to her. Long moments crept by, and she saw the struggle on his face to resist doing that very thing.

He cleared his throat. "Phil's plane get off okay?"

Phillip. Her so-called fiancé wasn't gone half an hour and she was ready to fall into bed with Brant. Dear God, why did this man have such a hold over her? She hated it. She would fight against it...with every fiber of her being.

Her gaze dropped to the paperwork in his hands. "Can I help you?" she asked, injecting cool disapproval in her tone.

His face closed up. "I was looking for the Robertson file." He went back to searching through the papers. "Phil was supposed to do some work on it."

"He did. I just have to finish typing some notes, then you can have it. Give me an hour and I'll get it to you."

"Fine." He strode around the desk and came toward her, all business now. "I'll be in my office."

She stepped back and moved to her desk before he could come anywhere near her. He sent her a mocking smile as he passed by. Well, he could mock, she told herself as she sat down and opened up the file. It wouldn't get her into his bed any faster.

Or at all.

An hour later she hurried down the hallway to his office, determined to leave the paperwork with his PA, only Evelyn was nowhere to be seen. He must have heard her in the outer office, because a few seconds later he called out to bring it in to him.

She swallowed hard, not wanting to go into his inner sanctum when no one else seemed to be around.

"Kia?"

She straightened her shoulders and walked forward.

For all its luxury, she may as well have been walking into a prison cell.

"How did you know it was me?" she said.

He gave her a look that told her he always knew when she was around. "Bring it over here," he said, putting down his pen and leaning back in his chair as if she were about to put on a show and he didn't want to miss a second of it.

She hesitated. Her legs felt like jelly. Then she moved forward, and just as she'd known it would, his gaze slid over her blue tailored skirt and white silky blouse. She could see him mentally stripping the clothes from her body, piece by piece.

She was wishing that she hadn't discarded her jacket before coming in here. At least then she wouldn't have the urge to cover up the tight feeling in her nipples, and her arms wouldn't be goose-bumping in reaction.

She put the correspondence on his desk. The hint of sandalwood aftershave filled the air and stirred her senses. "I'll be leaving now. I want to finish some Christmas shopping this afternoon."

"When are you off to Adelaide?"

"Tomorrow morning."

"You'll miss Phil, no doubt?" It was a question, not a statement. Those eyes watched her like a cat stalking a mouse, waiting for her to make one wrong move. Well, she didn't much like cheese.

She pasted on a smile. "Naturally, but I'll be kept pretty busy. My mother loves to put on a bash at Christmas," she chatted on nervously, until all at once she saw a hint of bleakness in his eyes that clutched at her heart. She spoke before she could stop herself. "What about you, Brant? Any plans for Christmas?"

"So you remembered my name, eh?" Then he straightened in his chair. "A friend has invited me around for Christmas dinner, but I'm not sure I'll go yet. I've got too much work."

"What about your brother?" she said, curious to see his reaction again.

"What about him?" he snapped, his eyes turning colder than winter.

She swallowed. "I just thought—"

"Look, I don't want anything to do with my brother and that's the way I like it."

She took a step back. "Oh."

Tension filled the air and hung there for a few seconds before Brant appeared to make himself relax. Then he leaned over and took something out of the drawer in his desk. "I have a Christmas present for you."

Her heart jumped in her throat. "A…a present?"

He held out the small package toward her. "I gave Evelyn one, too. Can't let the best two PAs in town not know they're appreciated."

His tone held something biting, though she knew it was intended for *her,* not Evelyn. But she accepted the gift anyway. Phillip had given Evelyn a present, so what was wrong in Brant giving *her* one?

Then she met his eyes and she knew that everything *was* wrong about this. This wasn't because of her work. It was because he wanted her. This was a man wanting his woman and telling her in the only way he could.

Her hands shook as she undid the wrapping paper and lifted the lid on the small box inscribed with the top jeweler's name in Australia. She gasped when she saw the small medallion nestled on a velvet bed amongst the gold chain.

"It's not a diamond necklace," he said with cutting emphasis, "but it should keep you safe on your journey home."

"It's a St. Christopher medallion," she murmured, pushing his cynicism aside, touched by the charming gift. "Thank you. It's lovely. I'll make sure I put it on before I leave."

"Let me," he rasped.

Her breath hitched. Could she bear to have him touch her, no matter how briefly? Oh, how she wanted this. Was this one little thing too much to ask?

"Thank you," she whispered, her voice shaky.

He came around the desk and took the present out of her hands. "Turn around."

She did, and for a long moment everything in the room went quiet. Her heart skipped a beat. She could feel him standing there looking at her, his warm breath flowing over the nape of her neck, making her light-headed. If she leaned back, his arms would snake around her and then... *Oh, for heaven's sake, Kia, get a grip on yourself,* she scolded inwardly.

The package rustled and then the gold chain came

around her neck. The medallion lovingly touched the base of her throat, cooling her skin.

He placed his hands on her shoulders and slowly turned her around to face him.

"Merry Christmas, Kia," he said hoarsely, moving in to kiss her.

She lifted her lips. She had to. An avalanche could be coming their way and she'd still wait for that kiss.

His lips touched hers briefly. So brief that it should have been a chaste kiss. But every pore of her skin felt him there, acknowledged him, cried out for more.

He moved back and their eyes locked. Her throat seemed to close at the intense desire written in his eyes and the struggle within him not to take her.

He stepped back with a low sound in his throat that seemed to wrench from deep inside him. It broke the spell of the moment.

She drew in a shaky breath. "Merry Christmas to you, too, Brant."

A muscle knotted in his jaw as he walked back around to the other side of the desk. "I hope you get everything you want."

If ever there was a time for *not* getting what she wished for, it was now. When she wanted *him*.

She spun around and hurried toward the door, needing to get out of there.

"Have a good holiday, Kia…even without your fiancé."

Kia stopped to glance at him and saw the look in his eyes was harder than ever. She tensed. They were right back where they'd started. And that was fine with her.

"I intend to," she said coolly and left the room.

Kia normally loved being with her family at Christmas. Neighbors dropped by for a Christmas drink in the morning, and her sister, Melanie, came around for lunch with her husband and young son. The weather usually proved to be hot at this time of year, so a variety of seafood and salads was the order of the day, followed by an English-style trifle that her mother made to perfection. A treat her stepfather loved. All very normal and comforting. Usually.

So why did she feel as though something was missing this year? It was a nagging thought inside her that remained there throughout the day and began again when she woke on Boxing Day. She felt restless. As if she should be some place else but didn't know where.

It wasn't until a barbecue lunch in the backyard, where she was playing peekaboo with her six-month-old nephew, that she looked up and her heart dropped to her feet. The laughter died on her lips. And suddenly she knew what had been missing. *Brant*. He stood near the corner of the house, watching her, his eyes piercing the distance between them. Her family faded from her mind.

"Who's that?" she heard her mother say, and all at once Kia realized he *was* there. He wasn't a figment of her imagination. And here she was dressed in denim jeans and a stretch knit top, far from the businesslike persona she kept for the office and even for Phillip.

She handed Dominic to her sister and jumped up. "It's okay, Mum. It's one of my bosses. I'll be right back."

She raced toward him, her hand going to her throat as something occurred to her. Something must be wrong. Terribly wrong.

"Phillip?" she croaked as she got closer.

Irritation flickered across his face, then disappeared. "Relax. He's okay, as far as I know."

She moistened her lips. "Then what are you doing here?" It had to be something important if he'd flown from the north of the continent to the south, over three thousand kilometers.

"The Anderson project needs redoing. Phillip must have been having a bad day when he met with them, because he got all their instructions wrong. If we don't present them with another option by Thursday morning, we lose the account."

Kia remembered she'd been a bit uneasy about that particular project. She'd even said something to Phillip about it and gotten her head snapped off at the time.

"I've got a ton of work ahead of me and I need a PA."

She frowned. "What about Evelyn?"

He smiled without humor. "Remember that medallion I gave her that was supposed to keep her safe? It didn't work. She came down with a stomach virus yesterday morning. It looks like she'll be out of action for the rest of the week."

She grimaced. "Poor Evelyn." But why did she suspect he was pleased about this? Not about Evelyn being sick but about needing *her* as replacement.

Probably because he was enjoying ruining her holiday like this.

Her eyebrow lifted. "Why not hire a temp?"

"This project is too important, Kia. The company will still survive if we lose them as a client, but I'm not sure about Phil. How do you think he's going to feel if he finds out what's happened? He's pretty down at the moment." He had her with that and they both knew it. "No, I need you to come back to Darwin and help me out. I flew down last night and I've got a jet waiting at the airport now. I'll pay you triple time, of course."

She waved a dismissive hand. "I don't care about the money."

"Then think of it as repayment for the security alarm."

Her shoulders tensed. "You said that was already paid in full," she reminded him, though she still had every intention of paying off the debt herself, and in cash. "Or is this one of those debts that only seem to compound interest?"

A half smile crossed his face. "Perhaps."

"Kia, love," her mother's voice said behind her, and Kia froze. "Why not bring your boss over to meet the family?"

Kia leaned toward Brant. "Please don't mention Phillip," she whispered.

"What?" he muttered.

"They don't know about him." She saw his flash of surprise just before she swung around to face her mother to make the introductions.

But surprised or not, he soon recovered. Kia watched

him turning on the charm, but she knew he'd be asking some hard questions when they were alone.

"I can certainly see where Kia gets her looks," he told her mother with a warm smile that only seemed to be available for other women.

Kia mentally rolled her eyes, but she had to admit her father would never have married her mother if she hadn't been a looker. Her mother had the warmest of natures, too. She hadn't deserved to be treated so badly.

Marlene blushed with pleasure. "Thank you, Mr. Matthews."

He darted a wry glance at Kia that said *like mother, like daughter* for calling him "mister," then turned back to her mother. "Call me Brant."

Marlene nodded. "Well, Brant. Come over and meet the rest of Kia's family." She slipped her arm through his and began walking toward the others. "Have you had lunch yet?"

"Yes, but thanks for the offer."

"Then have a drink. It's Christmas, after all." She gave a warm smile. "Besides, we want to get to know Kia's boss." She leaned slightly closer to Brant. "We worry about her up there in Darwin by herself."

He smiled. "No need to worry. We're keeping a very close eye on her," he said, and Kia's heart lurched at the hidden meaning behind those words. Suddenly her jeans felt too tight and her pink top too skimpy.

"Oh, I'm so pleased to hear that." They reached the others. "Brant, this is my husband, Gerald." The two men sized each other up and shook hands. "And this is Kia's sister, Melanie. And her husband…"

Kia gritted her teeth as she watched the females succumb to Brant's charm like a line of dominoes toppling over. The men weren't so accommodating at first, but before long Brant had them eating out of the palm of his hand, too. Did this man know no bounds?

"So why have you come to see Kia?" her stepfather asked, and Kia saw that maybe Brant hadn't quite charmed the older man as much as she'd thought. She smiled at Gerald, loving him all the more for his protection.

"There's a major problem at the office and I need Kia's help. She's been working on the project with Ph—" He hesitated, then smiled at Kia. "She knows it by heart and I can't do it without her. I have no choice but to beg her to return to the office with me. Believe me, I wouldn't ask her if it wasn't important."

"Of course you wouldn't," her mother said. She glanced at her daughter. "Darling, are you still doing your studies?"

Brant's ears pricked up. "Studies?"

Kia groaned inwardly. "I'm learning Chinese."

"And she's doing very well, too," Marlene said proudly. "She's got quite a knack for languages and is already fluent in French and Italian."

Brant regarded her with a speculative gaze. "You really are a mystery at times, aren't you?" he said, but she could see a slight hardness back in those eyes.

He glanced at his watch. "We'd better be going."

She nodded. "I'll just get my things together." She left him talking to the others, a little regretful that she hadn't had more time to spend with her family. But, on the other hand, helping out in a time of crisis was a small sacrifice to make for the good of the company.

Then she thought of working alone with Brant when they got back to Darwin and she pushed aside a level of excitement that had nothing to do with the challenge of the project and everything to do with the man himself. She swallowed hard. Correction. This wasn't a small sacrifice. This was going to be a *big* one.

Her hands shook as she quickly showered before slipping into a floral-print shirtdress with a short-sleeved jacket that was easy-wearing for travel but stylish enough for the office. Not bothering with stockings, she stepped into high-heeled sandals that complimented her long, tanned legs. A light touch of makeup and a quick deft of her hand to twist her hair up and she was ready. For battle. For Brant.

"Perhaps you can explain something to me," he said once they were seated in the plush jet and were heading back to Darwin.

Warning shivers started going up and down her spine. "Like what?"

"Like why you didn't tell your family about Phillip?"

She tried not to flinch. "Oh. That."

"Yes. *That.*"

Her cheeks reddened. "I just want to be sure, that's all."

He straightened in his seat, on full alert now. "You're not sure?"

"Yes, of course I am," she said quickly. "It's just that it all happened so fast. I don't want my family to worry and I know they would."

A moment's pause, then he said, "Tell me. Do you love Phil?"

If she hesitated, she was lost. "Yes."

His jaw clenched. "When do you plan on telling them?"

"When the time is right. Thank you for not saying anything today. It would have been...awkward."

God, she didn't like lying, but what else could she do? If she told the truth, Brant would go all out to seduce her. She'd be putty in his hands and she had no doubt she'd enjoy it. But that would be just a physical release. It wouldn't be enough. She needed more from a man than a quick roll in the hay.

Besides, this wasn't just about her. She couldn't give the game away yet. How could she tell Brant the truth and dump all this on Phillip's shoulders without giving him any warning? She didn't think she was better than Phillip, but she couldn't do to him what he'd done to her. No, she'd have to wait until he returned to the office in another two weeks. She just hoped she survived until then.

"I'm sure they'd be happy for you," Brant said. "Phillip's a great catch."

"Yes." She ignored the cynical tone to his voice, not quite up to verbally fencing with him right now.

About to look away, something about him grabbed her attention and she was surprised to catch a bleak look in his eyes before his gaze dropped to the papers in his lap. An odd feeling of sympathy caught at her heartstrings. Was his coming to fetch her more than just the problem at work? Had he been feeling lonely, despite a "friend" inviting him for Christmas lunch?

"Did you have a nice Christmas, Brant?"

His gaze shot toward her. "Why?"

"I just wondered."

His smooth look made her wish she'd kept her mouth shut. "Yes, I was kept very…busy."

She winced inwardly. "I see." He was a womanizer, so he'd been with a woman most likely. She understood him only too well. He was just like her father.

Nine o'clock that evening Brant decided to wrap things up for the day. Exhausted, he eased back in his leather chair and flexed his fingers. He could hear the clack of the keyboard in the outer office and knew that no matter how tired he was he would still want Kia Benton.

Even today, when he'd caught her offguard at her mother's place, she'd made his stomach knot with desire. Hell, he could still remember how he'd felt when he'd seen her dressed so casually in those tight jeans that lovingly hugged her body. She'd looked so different. So carefree and friendly.

And when he saw her with that toddler in her arms…it was as if he'd been seeing a glimpse of the future.

His and Kia's future.

For the first time since Julia, he imagined actually being with a woman. Having more than just a physical connection. But not even Julia had roused the same level of yearning that had ripped through him today when he'd seen Kia.

But Kia was only out for one thing.

The woman needed money the way she needed air to breathe. Her assertion that she loved Phillip had sounded hollow to his ears, but even if he were tempted to forget it, he only had to remember that while her beautiful mouth might lie, the camera hadn't. The self-satisfied smirk she'd been wearing in that photograph of her and Phillip had said it all: Kia Benton had caught her man.

He straightened in his chair, disgust tightening his mouth. So how could he even think about Kia on a deeper level? It was all this damn Christmas stuff, that's what it was. It stirred too many memories of when he was growing up.

Not that he could complain about his childhood. His parents had been the best, practically adopting the other kids in the street. Many a time Flynn had taken refuge in Brant's house when his father had been too drunk to care. And Damien's parents hadn't meant to be so distant from their son, leaving the small boy starving for parental affection. Brant knew if it hadn't been for Barbara and Jack Matthews, his two friends may not have turned out as well as they had. It had bonded the three of them together.

Like brothers.

His mouth tightened. Unlike his own flesh and blood, who had stolen his fiancée.

He got to his feet and walked to the doorway, pushing

aside the thought of his younger brother, Royce, as he forced his mind back to the business at hand.

For a minute he stood watching Kia's fingers fly over the keyboard while she continued to type up the reams of paperwork needed to get the project back on track. He didn't know what Phil had been thinking, putting together a package like that. It had been totally wrong, full of errors and not feasible.

"You knew, didn't you?" he said, coming into the room. "That the presentation was all wrong?"

She blinked in surprise, then nodded. "I had an idea. I mentioned it to Phillip, but he thought he was right, so I left it at that." She shrugged. "He's the boss."

"And so am I. You should have come to me."

She arched a brow. "And tell you what exactly? That my boss wasn't thinking straight because he'd lost the use of his leg and now I was telling him he was beginning to lose his mind, too?"

"I admire your loyalty, Kia, but next time save us both some stress and just tell me about it. I won't go running to Phil, but I'll find a way around it. If Phil's not coping, we need to get him some help."

She sighed. "Yes, you're right."

He went to speak, to tell her how Phillip's judgment was sometimes suspect and had caused problems before, but then he remembered whose fiancée she was.

"Right. Let's call it a night. Would you like to get a bite to eat on the way home?" Suddenly he didn't want to go home alone. He had nothing waiting for him there.

And no doubt they'd still have all those sappy Christmas movies on television.

She began stacking papers. "No, thanks. The pizza was more than enough."

"We ate that hours ago."

She looked up with a rueful gleam in her eyes. "I'm still full from Christmas lunch yesterday."

That gleam hit him right in his chest. There was a warmth in her eyes whenever she spoke of her family that just didn't correspond with the cold, callous player he knew her to be.

He stared at her for a minute more, then spun around and went back into his office. He supposed even criminals had their good points.

Six

The next day Kia would have loved to concentrate on the job at hand, but with everyone still on vacation, just being alone with Brant in the executive suite left her scarcely daring to breathe. It was the reason she'd insisted on working from her own office at the other end of the floor. Away from him. Away from temptation. And out of the sexual firing line.

He'd seen right through her, but she'd still held her head high when she told him she felt more comfortable at her own desk. It had been the truth, after all.

"Bring me the next twenty pages when you've finished them," was all he'd said midafternoon, the glint in his eyes telling her that even a crucial project couldn't surpass this attraction between them.

"Aye, aye, sir," she'd snapped, spinning on her heels and leaving the room, but not before she'd seen the arrogance in his eyes. Okay, so he was the boss, but that didn't mean he had to "boss" her about. It only made her madder, and ever since, her fingers had been flying across the keyboard, wanting to finish the twenty pages as soon as possible so she could march into his office and slam them down on the desk.

And that's exactly what she did—in half the time it normally took. But to her amazement, when she got to his office, he was nowhere to be seen. The adrenaline that had given her fingers strength dissipated, leaving her drained and ludicrously disappointed. She sighed. The considerate thing for him to do would have been to tell her he was going out.

She placed the papers in the center of his desk and turned to go back to her office. A figure in the doorway made her jump. For a minute she thought it was Brant. Adjusting her eyes she realized it was Lynette Kelly.

Kia breathed in deeply, her heart not quite settling back into place. "Lynette, what are you doing here?"

Lynette blushed as she took a few steps into the office. "Oh, hello, Kia."

She looked so nervous Kia felt sorry for her. "Can I help you?" she asked gently.

"Er…I need to see Phillip. I called him at home, but there was no answer. I thought he might be here."

"I'm sorry. He's not." Lynette's face fell and Kia spoke before thinking. "He's gone home to Queensland for a couple of weeks."

The other woman's eyes widened. "Without you?"

Kia's gaze darted away then back. "I had to stay here. To work."

"Oh." Her shoulders slumped. She turned away. "I guess I'd better—" She spun back. "Kia, do you really love Phillip? I mean, like a woman should love a man? Please, I need to know."

There was such anguish in her eyes, guilt stabbed Kia in the heart.

"Kia, he needs me. I know he does. I love him with all my heart and I'm swallowing my pride in front of you and begging you to tell me the truth."

Kia couldn't stand Lynette's pain any longer. It just wasn't right to keep the other woman in the dark. She owed it to her—and to Phillip—to help straighten things out.

"No, Lynette. I don't love Phillip. Not in that way."

"Thank God." Lynette swayed, then quickly gathered herself, blinking back tears. When she'd recovered, a crease formed between her eyes and she looked confused. "So why did you get engaged?"

Kia told her the truth and explained how one thing had led to another. "I'm sorry for all the pain we've put you through, Lynette. I was just trying to help Phillip."

"Do you…?" Lynette swallowed. "Do you think he still loves me?"

"I know he does."

Hope filled Lynette's eyes and made them shine. "I have to go to him."

Kia nodded. Behind the other woman's delicate appearance, she sensed a strength of character she suspected would surprise Phillip. "If he gives you a hard time, tell him I said he's a fool."

Lynette quickly hugged her. "I hope you find someone for you soon."

"I'm not sure I want anyone," Kia said with a small smile. The only person who had ever really affected her was Brant. And he…well, there was nothing more to say there.

Lynette left the room, so happy she looked as if she were walking on air. Kia smiled as relief swept through her that she'd told the other woman of Phillip's love. It was in Lynette's hands now.

Just then, the hairs on the back of Kia's neck stood to attention. Even before she turned toward the connecting door she was certain Brant would be standing there.

And he was. He'd been in the small conference room the whole time. A fear such as she'd never known skittered under her skin. Primal fear. Sexual fear. She only had to look at the anger in his eyes to know he had overheard.

"Um…Brant. I didn't know you were there."

For a moment the air hung between them like a sheet of humidity.

"So the gold digger's conscience got the better of her, did it?" he sneered, leaning against the doorjamb, about as laid-back as a crocodile lazing in the sun.

She sucked in a sharp breath. "Gold digger?" *Was he crazy?* "Are you talking about *me?*"

"Too bad, sweetheart. You missed out on marriage

this time, but I'm sure you can find another man to fall for that innocent act."

"Wh-what?" She had no idea what he was talking about.

"Don't deny it. I saw your picture in a magazine. Even the journalist could tell a fortune hunter when he saw one. In fact, he remarked on how you'd hooked one of the Australia's richest bachelors."

Was she really hearing this? "That *journalist*—and I use the word loosely—has got it in for me because I refused to go out with him. He's just trying to make me look bad." She'd felt ill when she'd seen the photograph and the comment he'd made.

"Really?" Brant's eyes said he didn't believe her. "Even if that's the case, I heard you on the telephone. My ears don't deceive me."

She frowned. "Telephone?"

"That's right. When I came back from Paris I heard you bragging to someone on the phone about it being as easy to fall in love with a rich man than a poor one." His top lip curled. "The next thing, you were Phillip's shadow and engaged to him."

She tried to think. Then it hit her. "I was talking to Gerald...my stepfather. It's a joke between us. Good Lord. So this is why you've been a pig to me since I first met you? You thought I was marrying Phillip for his *money?*"

He made a harsh sound. "You were quick to take the diamond necklace from him."

"He asked me to wear it to the Christmas party. I

gave it back the next day. Ask him if you don't believe me."

Something flickered in his eyes. "The Porsche?"

"My father gave it to me. He deals in cars, remember?" Her heart twinged. "He likes his 'Barbie' to come with accessories."

For a moment there was a flash of sympathy, then his face hardened. "If you dislike your father so much, why take the car?"

"He offered and I thought why not? I figure the man owes me for all he's put me through. If he wants to give me a Porsche, I'm taking the Porsche. There's nothing wrong with that." She paused. "Anyway, if I wanted money, I only have to ask him for some…not that I would. He's got enough money to keep me in luxury for the rest of my life. Unfortunately it comes with a price."

A tic beat in his jaw. "Even if all that's true, you're obviously very good at conning people. You've been living a lie."

She winced. "For Phillip's sake."

"And for your own. You used him just as much as he used you."

Her chin lifted. He was so conceited. "Now why would I do that?" she said, then realized it was a challenge.

Suddenly he turned and closed the connecting door behind him. "To keep *us* apart."

Her eyes darted to the doorknob where his hand still rested. "Us? There's nothing between us."

He strode across the room to the main office door.

"Lying again, Kia?" He shut that door too. Then he turned back toward her in the middle of the room.

Her knees began to shake. "Er…what are you doing?"

"What do you think I'm doing?" His voice flowed over her like liquid silk.

Her throat went dry. "You're playing games with me."

"No game, Kia. Far from it."

She straightened her shoulders. "Brant, stop it. This is ridiculous. You're my boss. I'm—"

"About to be kissed," he murmured, stopping right in front of her. He didn't touch her. Didn't reach out. He just stood there, looking at her. And what she saw melted every bone in her body. He was still angry, but oh, God, he wanted her.

She licked her lips. "Brant, I—"

"I'm so angry with you right now I'm either going to swear or kiss you."

She tried to step back.

He grabbed her arm to prevent her from moving, his touch shooting desire to every region of her body. "And then I'm going to take the clothes off that delicious body of yours and taste all of you."

She felt the room twirl around her. "I don't know if this is a good idea."

He pulled her closer, his pupils darkening. "I've waited too long already."

A ripple of anticipation ran through her as she watched his head lower…watched those lips come closer…and when he touched her, she could no longer deny him or herself. Every moment from the minute she'd met him had been rushing headlong toward this kiss. Ever since her first look at him in this very office, nothing else had mattered, nothing but wanting to feel the consuming pressure of his lips on hers, as they were doing now.

At last.

The kiss still took her by surprise. She expected him to plunder and ravish her on the carpet, but he didn't, and she soon forgot all about his anger as the velvet warmth of his mouth stirred every nerve ending on her lips, before he used his tongue to slide inside her.

And there he stayed, exploring the soft, sensitized recesses of her mouth until she thought she might fuse with him. But she wanted him closer. She wrapped her arms around his neck and cupped the back of his head to hold him to her. It felt so good to be like this with him. This was where she belonged. If only for a short while.

Raising his mouth from hers, he gazed deeply into her eyes, so deep that she suddenly worried he might see the real her. Not the outside person but the inside person. The person who didn't know how she was going to handle this man.

"What's the matter?" he said, watching her.

"Um…nothing." Her gaze darted down to his chest, lowering her eyelids, briefly covering her face from him. She wanted to remain like this and not let him see her thoughts. She needed to keep something of herself to herself.

And then he took her arms from around his neck and put them at her sides. He lifted her chin, holding her gaze. "I won't let you hold back from me," he warned softly.

She took a shaky breath. "You won't *let* me?"

"No." He reached out and undid the top button of her dress, and suddenly she didn't have the strength to argue with him. She stood there and let him undress her. She *wanted* him to do it. *Wanted* him to undo all the buttons and feel his touch on her skin. *Wanted* to give all of herself to him.

His hands were sure and never missed a beat as they slid down from one button to the next, opening the material wider, more fully. For him.

She could see the pulse in his neck thumping wildly and she wanted to reach out and run her finger over it. Touching him would be like throwing a match onto kerosene.

He pushed the material off her shoulders and let it slide down her arms, down her body, to the carpet. She heard him groan as she stood there in a lacy bra, bikini panties, no stockings, and high-heeled sandals. For a moment she wished she'd worn them. It may have put up a barrier.

But who was she kidding? Nothing was going to stop this. She didn't want it to stop, God help her.

"I like the color peach on you," he murmured, his eyes flaring with hot desire. "It flatters you."

She moaned and whispered, "Touch me," and he suddenly swung her in his arms, carrying her over to the large mahogany desk. With one hand he swept the papers aside, then planted her in the middle of it. Her stomach somersaulted as he stood looking down at her.

"I've fantasized you like this for weeks," he murmured,

reaching out to twine his fingers in her hair, loosening the blonde strands at the nape of her neck. "And this," he said, lifting her hair up in his hands, then leaning forward and burying his face in her locks, inhaling deeply.

She stilled, breathing in the mingled scent of his body heat and aftershave as it soaked into her pores…until the soft peck of his lips moved to her ear, to her jawline and finally her mouth again.

Eventually he broke off the kiss. "Here, let me," he murmured, his fingers sliding under her bra straps and slowly pushing them off her shoulders.

She trembled when his palms caressed the bare skin there before slipping around to her back to undo the catch. Her bra fell away, and suddenly she was naked from the waist up. She wanted to hide, not from him but from herself. She didn't know if she could let herself go like this.

"Beautiful," he said in a gravelly voice, teasing her breasts with his hands until her breathing quickened even more and she had to close her eyes from sheer pleasure.

His head lowered, his mouth closing over one nipple, and she gasped, her breasts surging at the intimacy of it all.

"Brant!"

He pulled back, his eyes searing a path over her. And then he moved and his lips followed that same path, kissing down the center of her, teasing her belly button with the tip of his tongue before stopping at the top of her thighs.

He inhaled deeply through the thin lace, and she

almost dissolved. She'd never done anything like this before. Never *let* a man do this to her. She'd had one lover in high school and nothing since.

He pushed the material to one side. "I have to taste you," he said, his fingers seeking her, opening her to him. He placed his mouth against her, and she cried out his name as his tongue darted out to taste her, explore her, tracing the shape of her, teasing the small part of her that suddenly felt as if she were about to explode.

"Oh, Brant," she moaned again. She closed her eyes as something powerful inched up inside her with every touch of his tongue. It felt so good…so right…so exquisite.

"Ooh!" She exploded with one more stroke, going up in flames like a bushfire sweeping through her, burning everything in sight, leaving nothing of her unmarked. She would never be the same again, never forget what it was like to have this man touch her like this.

And when she opened her eyes, Brant was leaning back in the chair, watching her with such possessive satisfaction that her breath caught in her throat.

Her heart gave a triple beat. She wanted to look away, only she couldn't. There'd been too much between them all these weeks. Too much longing. Too much wanting each other. They'd earned this moment between them.

Brant spoke first. "Here, let's get you dressed," he said brusquely and gently closed her legs.

"Oh, but…" She could feel her cheeks growing red as he passed her bra. "I mean…um…aren't we going to…?"

"Make love? Not yet." He stood up and helped her off the desk as intense disappointment swept through her. She went to turn away, but he held her still. "My place. Seven o'clock."

She blinked. "To-tonight?"

"Yes." He ran a finger across her lips, his eyes a mixture of need and still-deep anger. "No more waiting. For either of us. And I can't do everything I want to do to you in the office."

She swallowed, suddenly panicked by the magnitude of it all. He overwhelmed her. He made her feel things she didn't want to feel. Made her do things she *wanted* to do.

"No, I can't. I—"

"I've put my stamp on you now, Kia. You can't deny that."

She sucked in a shaky breath, very much aware he was right. "Brant, this was just a…brief interlude."

"It was a prelude," he insisted, putting his hand under her chin. "You were ready for me a minute ago," he reminded her, and she almost dissolved again.

"Yes, well…" She cleared her throat. "That was then. This is now."

His eyes darkened dangerously. "Kia, we should have been lovers weeks ago."

Her shoulders tensed. She could see his anger over Phillip still simmering beneath the surface. "Even if you hadn't thought I was with Phillip, it doesn't mean—"

"Yes, it does," he cut across her. "Have no doubts, Kia. We *would* have been lovers. You're only fooling yourself if you think otherwise."

To prove it, his hands slid around her waist and brought her close. Her body immediately arched against him, her near-naked curves tucking in against his hard contours. Heat rippled under her skin and jolted her mind into the realization that once again he was right. She pushed herself away, and thankfully he let her go, but the smoldering look in his eyes said it all.

Trying to maintain her composure, she hurried around the desk to get the rest of her clothes, feeling exposed in more ways than one. His gaze remained on her, watching her every move, and she silently shuddered as she dressed as fast as she could.

"Kia."

She did up the last button, then looked up at him. The hunger in his eyes sent a tremor through her.

"You owe this to yourself," he growled, challenge in his voice.

Kia made her way back to her office on shaky legs and collapsed onto her chair. She couldn't believe what had just happened. Had she really let herself be taken in such a way? No man had made love to her with his mouth before, though she knew it was an aspect of lovemaking that most couples enjoyed. Dear God, now she could see why.

What she hadn't expected was to come apart in Brant's hands quite the way she had. Where was her control? Her self-respect? She'd known she was a challenge to him. That he only wanted her body. So what had she done? She'd handed herself to him on a platter, that's what.

Or a desk, she corrected, feeling a blush rising up from the tips of her toes. How could she hold her head high now? Suddenly she knew she had to get out of there. She'd earned the right to leave early…in more ways than one.

Jumping to her feet, she grabbed her handbag and headed for the door. If she remained here alone with Brant, he might be tempted to take up where they'd left off and not wait for tonight.

Tonight.

You owe this to yourself, he'd said.

He was right, yet how could she turn up at his place when he thought she was a gold digger? Had thought it from the start. A woman who was mercenary enough to use men for her own advantage. That hurt.

So why did her heart turn over at the thought of *not* making love with Brant?

Brant tossed the pencil on the desk. He needed to get these reports out, but his mind kept dropping back to Kia. Could he accept she wasn't a gold digger? Her answers had made sense, but isn't that what con artists did? They conned you into believing what they wanted you to believe.

And all these weeks she'd been living a lie by pretending to be involved with Phillip. Had even let herself become engaged to him. Just as Julia had lived a lie. Until she'd run off with his own brother.

Hell. He thought he'd been hearing things when Kia had told Lynette she didn't love Phil the way a woman should love a man. She'd lied to *him,* dammit. He'd asked her straight out if she loved her fiancé and she'd said yes.

Why? Because she knew he'd have her in bed in no time, that's why. She wouldn't be able to help herself. She'd wanted to make love with him, too.

Yet how different she'd been to the experienced women he usually bedded. Women who proudly strutted their stuff. Women who took the initiative, the way he liked. Women who hadn't shattered in his arms as Kia had. Her passion, her innocence in this way, convinced him she hadn't been with a man or come alive under a man's mouth in years. That was something in her favor. Surely a gold digger wouldn't hesitate to use her body to get men to fall in love with her? Oh, hell. He just didn't know what to think anymore.

What he *did* know was that she'd been perfect. Had tasted better than perfect. It's the reason he'd held himself in check and not taken her fully as he'd ached to do. He wanted to love her slowly, take his time, make up for all those weeks of aching. Tonight he'd brand her with his body and make her his.

When he opened the door to his penthouse that evening, Brant almost forgot to breathe. The soft blue material of Kia's dress bared her tanned shoulders and arms and fell lovingly over the length of her body to just above her knees, in a simple design that would have looked plain on another woman. Yet on her it looked stunning. She couldn't look unattractive if her life depended on it.

He stepped back to allow her to enter. "Relax. I'm not going to ravish you on the spot," he said, even if the thought was more than tempting.

She moved past him in a cloud of perfume that was endlessly alluring, then stopped in the middle of the room and faced him, the light of battle entering her eyes. "That's a relief," she quipped, a becoming flush staining her cheeks.

He closed the door, knowing he could always count on her to be defiant even in the most difficult of circumstances. And this had to be the most difficult for her ever. But her uncertainty didn't change a thing. They would make love tonight.

"Take a seat while I pour you a drink." He gestured to the black leather sofa. "Gin and tonic, right?"

"Extra large."

"Oh, no, you don't," he drawled. "I don't want you to forget a moment of tonight. *I* certainly don't intend to."

She moistened her lips. "Brant, I think this is a mistake. I shouldn't have come."

"It isn't a mistake. It's called being grown-up. It's about being adults over a situation that we both clearly need to address."

Her chin rose in the air. "I thought it was more child-like when you give in and take what you want."

"Ah, so you admit you want me," he said as he poured the drinks at the bar.

She glared at him. "I think we should leave things as they are. My being here will only complicate matters."

He picked up the glasses of liquid and walked toward

her. "A complication I'll willingly embrace, if you'll pardon the pun."

She ignored that as she accepted her glass. "How do you know I won't be faking it? After all, I faked the engagement and you never knew the difference, for all your extensive experience."

"I suspected something was amiss."

Her mouth set in a stubborn line. "I did it for a reason. To help Phillip."

"And to keep me at arm's length."

"It worked."

"And now it doesn't. Accept it."

Her blue eyes lit with anger. "Look, you said yourself that I'm a gold digger. If you want a woman tonight, why pick on me? Wouldn't any *body* do?"

His amusement deserted him. "No," he said tersely. No other woman in the world would do. It was the reason he hadn't returned any of his women friend's calls. Why he hadn't made love in weeks now. The reason he'd thrown himself into his work even harder. And why he'd been so bloody snappy with everyone lately. It just hadn't been humane that the one woman who turned him on had been involved with his business partner.

He expelled a breath he hadn't realized he'd been holding. Yes, she *had* been involved with Phil. *Had* been untouchable. *Had* been out of reach.

But she was no longer.

He nodded at the sliding glass doors. "Let's go out on the balcony. We can have dinner out there."

Her shoulders stiffened. "I'm not hungry."

"Then perhaps we should give dinner a miss?"

She immediately stepped forward and strode past him to the balcony, her set mouth telling him what she thought of that idea.

"I figured that would change your mind," he murmured, following her over to the railing, where she stood looking out over the spectacular sunset view of Mindil Beach and Darwin Harbor. It was glorious out here at any time of year, but during the beginning of the wet season, like now, he loved watching the incredible lightning displays that lit up the sky most nights.

Yet tonight the only thing he wanted to light up was the woman standing next to him. He turned to look at her. The evening sun reflected on the delicate contours of her face, giving her a special glow, making her look more beautiful.

"Do you have to look at me like that?" she said in a throaty voice, a blush creeping into her cheeks.

"Yes," he said huskily. Right now he didn't think he'd ever get enough of looking at her.

She swallowed hard. "You're not making this any easier for me."

"Nothing worthwhile is ever easy."

She turned to face him, her expression growing resentful. "That's the attraction, isn't it, Brant? You couldn't have me, so you decided you wanted me."

"I admit I like a challenge." His eyes dipped to her parted lips. "But wanting you wasn't a decision I chose to make. I took one look at you and knew the decision had already been made for me."

"How nice," she said with false sweetness.

He smiled. She could fight herself all she liked, but it wouldn't make one speck of difference. She would be in his arms tonight. And in his bed. He was sure of that.

"Shall we eat?" he said and took great pleasure in placing his hand under her elbow to lead her over to the small dining table in the middle of the balcony. Her shiver was from desire, he saw it in her eyes, and it sent a hunger for more than food racing through him. But he could wait. He wanted to savor her first.

They dined on prawn cocktail as an entrée, followed by a grilled lamb with zucchini and tomatoes that his housekeeper had made. Brant watched in amusement over Kia's attempt to go slow as she chewed each mouthful as though it was the last food she'd ever eat.

"This is very good," she said, taking another tiny bite of the lamb. "Did you cook this yourself?"

He shot her a mocking smile. "Do I look like a cook?"

She stiffened. "I don't think there's anything wrong with cooking. Lots of men like to do it."

"And lots of men like to make love," he said, purposefully seductive. "How many men have made love to you, Kia?"

She almost choked, then recovered quickly. "How many have *you* made love to?"

"I don't find men attractive. Now women, that's more my style."

Her eyes filled with derision. "I guess it's more an art form than a technique with you then."

He leaned back in his chair, curious at her remark.

She pressed on. "I'd say you've had plenty of practice having sex."

"True. But I've always practiced safe sex, so you have no worries on that score."

"I'm relieved," she said drily.

"It's important, Kia."

She sighed. "I know."

"So, Kia." He paused and took a sip of wine. "How many lovers have you had?"

"One."

He arched a brow as the muscles at the back of his neck tensed. Could she really be as innocent as all that?

She shot him a defiant look. "Hey, you asked, so don't blame me if you don't like the answer."

His eyes narrowed. "I know your game. You think I'll back off if you tell me you're inexperienced."

She placed her fork on the table. "Actually, I don't care what you think. It's the truth."

His gut clenched. "Tell me about it."

"Why should I?"

"Because I want no more secrets between us, Kia. Not in bed, anyway."

She considered him for a long moment. Then she said, "I lost my virginity at a party when I was fifteen. It was the one and only time I got drunk and I gave it away to the first boy that looked at me because my father had just gotten married and didn't want his 'plain-looking' daughter at his wedding and I needed to feel loved. He didn't even ask me my name."

She said it so matter-of-factly that he believed her. He swore under his breath.

She shrugged. "I hardly remember most of it. I was just so lucky not to have found myself pregnant."

He scowled. "The boy didn't use protection?"

"I was too drunk to notice."

"But surely—" His jaw clenched, then he forced himself to relax. "I'll make a deal with you. We'll make love, but if at any time you want me to stop, I will."

Her throat convulsed. "You'd do that?"

Something softened inside him. "I want a willing female in my bed. I don't get my kicks from forcing a woman." Rising, he held out his hand. "I need you. Need to make love with you, Kia Benton," he said, deliberately saying her name, wanting her to know that he knew exactly who she was, unlike the boy who had stripped her of her virginity. "I promise you this won't be like your first time."

Seven

The evening breeze gently lifted the lace curtains away from the open window as Kia followed Brant into the bedroom. In a way, she felt like those curtains. As if she was lifting a part of herself, unveiling herself for him to see.

Yet it was a risky move to make, and for a moment she hesitated. Did she really want him to leap the boundaries she kept around herself? Today in his office she'd relinquished her body to him. But now, once his body was inside her, once he knew her so physically, what would happen to her emotionally?

Just then, he squeezed her fingers and she looked at him. The sheer depth of desire in his eyes made her shiver with longing. All her doubts disappeared.

"I want you, Brant," she admitted, unable to stop the words from spilling from her. She couldn't deny herself this. No matter what happened afterward, no matter what he thought of her, she would always have this memory. "I want you so much."

Heat flared in his eyes. "Then you've got me," he muttered, pulling her close.

She went willingly into his arms, the palms of her hands pressing against his chest, feeling his warmth and vibrancy through the material of his shirt.

"I have *never* had a more beautiful woman in my arms," he rasped, his warm breath flowing over her.

"You make me *feel* beautiful," she murmured. And he did. As if someone had waved a magic wand over her and turned her into more than she was.

She lifted her face for his kiss, and his mouth swept down and took possession of hers. And from that moment on she was his. Her need had been smoldering inside her for so long now. She needed this release.

His mouth moved against hers, silently telling her how much he wanted her. She reveled in it, opening her lips, letting him take whatever he wanted yet returning the favor. She wanted to be a part of him, so much a part of him that he'd never forget her.

The kiss deepened, lengthened. His hands caressed her spine through her dress, then eased down the zipper to stroke her bare skin, gliding up to the curve of her shoulders and provocatively pushing the material aside like a maestro playing their song.

He broke off the kiss and skimmed his lips along her

jaw. Hypnotized by his touch, she arched her neck, as his mouth continued to her earlobe and then proceeded down the smooth column of her throat. He planted a tantalizing kiss at the hollow of her neck and she gave a soft moan and slid her hands beneath the material of his shirt, not prepared to wait another millisecond to touch him.

Her head spun at the first feel of his warm flesh beneath her tingling palms. "Oh, my God," she whispered, the shock of his taut muscles running through her body even as she luxuriated in feeling the strong beat of his heart against her palms. Strong and fast.

"You're playing with fire," he said, shuddering, then stormed her mouth again in a kiss that sent her up in flames. At the same time he clasped her hips, grounding her against him. She'd felt his arousal once before when they'd danced together. This was different. This was her first full contact of him as a man. It stunned her. Delighted her. It made her ache for him.

He pulled away and in one swift motion tugged at her dress, letting it rush down her body and fall to the floor. But he didn't stop to stare, though she felt his gaze on her. Her bra vanished next. Her panties followed. Then he swept her up in his arms and carried her over to the bed, laying her out on top of the comforter.

And that's when he finally stopped to look down upon her. The intensity in his eyes sang through her veins, making her very much aware of being not only a woman but the woman he wanted.

"Tonight you're mine, Kia."

Her throat went dry. She wanted to deny it, but how could she deny something so intrinsically right?

"Yes," she whispered.

His hands went to his shirt and he quickly began to undress. It hit the carpet, followed by his trousers. It didn't take long before he stood beside her all naked and in full glory.

Her breath caught in her throat. He was absolutely magnificent, with a beautifully proportioned body that shot her pulse right off the chart. His broad shoulders topped a powerful chest that fostered wisps of dark hair and tapered down to lean hips and long, muscular legs. And to a commanding erection that magnified his masculinity tenfold.

He joined her on the bed and she surrendered to the moment, to herself, to him. She gasped when his lips moved to her breast and enclosed a nipple, pleasuring her into a mindless state even as his hand brushed over her hip and dipped to the junction at her thighs. His fingers slid between her feminine folds and ran around the small, sensitive nub in circles. Sanity began to blur as her world shrank to that one caress of his finger, to the sweet tug of his mouth at her breast.

But then, just as she was about to go over the edge, he pulled away, making her cry out in intense disappointment. "Don't stop!"

"Shh. This time we make love together," he murmured, reaching for a foil packet on the bedside table. He sheathed himself and poised at her thighs. She softened beneath him, ready to take him into her. *Needing* him in her.

"Open yourself to me," he said, nudging her legs farther apart, and she did willingly.

He entered her slowly, his eyes never leaving her face as her tightness confirmed what she had told him earlier. No *man* had ever filled her in this way before. Acknowledging this, his eyes bathed her with a tenderness that took her breath away. Then he filled her completely, gently, only stopping when he could fill her no more. His sensitivity made her heart roll over.

For one long moment they stayed still, each studying the other, connected in both body and spirit. It was the most profound moment Kia had ever experienced. She sensed it was the same for him.

As if in silent agreement, he took a deep breath and slowly began to withdraw. Then he moved forward and filled her again. He took another breath and withdrew as far as he could without separating their bodies. He kept repeating the motion, and she lifted her hips to take more of him into her, feeling something building, something so electric she had to close her eyes.

"Look at me," he said hoarsely, and she moaned but she did what he told her, finding it incredibly erotic when he mesmerized her with his eyes and began to move once more. He picked up the pace, and that rush of heat turned into a whipcord of male muscle, stamping her with each thrust of his body, taking everything she had within her. She offered it up to the one man in the world worthy of everything she had to give.

"Brant!" she cried as he rasped out her name in a strangled tone that said he couldn't hold on much longer either.

He kissed her then. A deep, deep kiss that was followed by a final plummet of his body as she arched against him.

They reached their climax together, holding themselves as one, in total sync at this precious moment in time.

Kia spiraled down to a hazy aftermath with a series of lingering kisses before he rolled over and held her in his arms for a few moments.

Then she watched his long, lean length disappear, as he rose and headed toward the bathroom. She lay back and closed her eyes. She had to, otherwise when he came back he would see something that had just hit her.

She had fallen in love with him.

Shock ran through her. She went hot, then cold. *She loved Brant Matthews.* She would love him until the day she died, even knowing she would never be enough for him. Dear God, this couldn't be…yet she knew it was, felt it in her heart.

The bed sank on one side and she scarcely dared to breathe. Brant was sitting beside her, waiting for her to look at him.

"Kia?" he murmured, tenderly pushing some strands of hair from her face.

She had no alternative but to look at him and pray that he didn't see what was so obvious to her now. How had she not seen this coming?

Her eyelids lifted, and her breath hitched in her throat at the look in his eyes. It was all-knowing. All male. Full of sexual satisfaction.

And he had no idea she loved him.

Thank God. She could breathe easier now and enjoy

their time together. That's all she'd let herself ask for. That's all she'd let herself want. It would be over soon enough. And if he ran true to form—as her father did with his women friends—having gotten what he'd wanted from her, she wouldn't be seeing much more of him after this anyway. She shivered. Already that thought cut through her heart.

"Did I hurt you?" he murmured.

"No." But he would. When he dumped her.

His shoulders relaxed, his mouth curving with sheer sensuality. "Woman, that was the best sex I've ever had."

Yes, that's all it came down to with Brant. She tried not to show her hurt. "Me, too."

"For all intents and purposes, you were a virgin." He leaned forward and gave her a long, slow kiss, then looked into her eyes. "I'm honored I was the first *man* to sleep with you." He kissed her again briefly, then leaned back, an odd look in his eyes. "Why?"

Her breath stopped and she realized he saw more than she'd thought. She licked her lips. "Because I…I mean, you…" She shrugged. "Well, what woman wouldn't want to make love with you?"

His mouth twisted. "Flattery will get you everywhere," he mocked, but she had the feeling he wasn't happy with her answer.

But if he expected a declaration of love, he was going to be disappointed. Maybe that's what his other women always provided, but she wasn't about to copy them. She swallowed hard at the thought of all those other women who would come after her. She couldn't bear to think about it. And she wasn't going to wait around for him to throw her away like some piece of garbage that was past its use-by date either.

Panicking, she sat up, almost knocking him out of the way. He put his hands on her shoulders, stilling her.

"What's the matter?" he said with a scowl.

"I'm going home." She tried to push him away, but he kept his body firmly in front of her.

Surprise came and went in his eyes before they flared with anger. "I won't let you run out on me, Kia."

"*You* won't let *me?*" she choked out. Did he think because he'd made her his own she would leave her brains at the door?

"I've already had one woman who mattered run out on me. I'm not going to let you do the same. Not yet, anyway."

She gave a soft gasp. A woman *who mattered* had run out on him? And she was in the same category? But what did he mean by mattered?

"Are you saying that I'm…that we…?" She tried to find the words to say it. "Is there something more between us than I think, Brant?"

He stood up, and she saw he had wrapped a white towel around his lower half. "You bet there's something between us. And we're going to see it through to the end."

The end. She shouldn't be surprised by his choice of words, yet she was. How could she love this devil of a man? Fate had certainly played a sick joke on her.

"Don't tell me what to do, Brant."

"If I told you everything I wanted you to do, you'd run for your life."

She got to her feet, wrapping the sheet around her as she did. "I don't need to run. I'm leaving anyway."

"I don't think so," he warned ominously.

Her heart jumped in her chest. "You can't stop me."

Can't I? his eyes said arrogantly. "Then you have nothing to lose by coming over here and kissing me like you mean it. Do that, and I'll even hold the door open for you on the way out."

She moistened her suddenly dry lips. "And if I don't?"

"Then I'll come over there and kiss you, and we'll see where it leads."

"What a choice," she muttered.

She swallowed. One kiss. Could she kiss him this one time and get away with it? She knew she would melt in his arms again. She knew she would want more. But hadn't she always prided herself on her strength of will?

Without stopping to think further, she pulled the sheet tighter and closed the distance between them. Then she went up on her toes and quickly kissed him on the mouth before turning away.

He grabbed her arm and spun her back toward him, his eyes holding a faint glint of humor. "Like you mean it, I said."

Somehow she'd known he wouldn't let her get away with that chaste peck. "Oh, but I did mean it like that," she mocked, even as a thrill raced through her. This time she'd give him exactly what he wanted and more. Then she'd walk out that door, put everything back on a business level and hope to God she could cope with knowing she'd fallen in love with a man who thought *woman* was a synonym for *sex*.

Her heart beating at full speed, she moved back toward him. In the split second before she put her lips to his, she saw his eyes darken and she realized she'd never once instigated a kiss with him. The other two Christmas kisses had been him coming to her, not the other way around. She felt thrillingly provocative.

She placed her mouth to his and began a kiss that gave him all the love she had inside her. Her stomach quivered even as she let her tongue slide around his mouth, then briefly dip between his slightly parted lips. She heard his groan deep within his throat, so she repeated the action, this time her tongue sliding over the top of his, tasting him, loving him.

The clean male scent of him exuded an attraction she found difficult to deny, and her arms slid up around his neck and cupped the back of his head, holding him to her, deepening the kiss. The sheet slipped down between them, and she felt the muscles of his chest tighten against her bare breasts. She rubbed herself against him, the feel of curly male hair teasing her nipples.

Suddenly he broke off the kiss with a guttural sound that made her think he had almost reached his limit. Then he swung her up in his arms and strode toward the bathroom.

"You're heading the wrong way," she murmured,

not really caring right now that she was supposed to be leaving and not coming back.

"No, I'm not. I know exactly where we're going."

They made leisurely love in the spa surrounded by tropical plants that gave a dreamy quality to the setting. Kia responded to Brant's instructions and sat on his lap facing him, with him inside her. It was an incredible experience. And the most brave. Face-to-face like that, she had to stop herself from crying out she loved him.

Then they made their way back to the bed, and she reveled in taking her time to explore his male body before he growled her name, rolled on top of her and made love to her all over again. Exhausted, they fell into a deep sleep.

The ringing of the telephone next to the bed woke them during the night. Kia groaned and pressed her cheek against Brant's bare chest, wanting to hold on to the euphoria, hoping the noise would go away so she could go back to sleep.

Vaguely she was aware of Brant reaching out an arm to pick it up. She heard the deep rumble of his voice as he answered it. Then, the next thing she knew, he'd jerked into a sitting position, throwing her off him.

"What the hell?" she heard him say as she lay on her back and came fully awake. "My God! Julia?"

There was silence for a moment as the person on the other end of the phone responded. Then Brant's gaze skidded to Kia and darkened. "Yes, I have company," he answered in clipped tones. He listened. "Now?" He looked at Kia again, then away. "Okay. Give me half an hour." He hung up and turned back to her. "I've got to go out for a while. Something's come up."

Yes, and her name is Julia.

"Don't worry, I understand. Totally."

His face hardened as he swung his legs over the side of the bed. "I didn't ask for your understanding."

That hurt. "Aren't you lucky I gave it anyway?" she snapped, throwing back the bedclothes.

"You don't have to leave."

Did he think she would wait for him to go to this woman, then come back to bed and make love to *her?*

"I don't want to stay."

A long moment crept by as she gathered her clothes from the floor.

"Then I'll walk you down to your car."

"Don't bother." She looked up and caught his eyes going hungrily over her naked body. A quiver surged through her veins and she wondered if she could stop him going to this Julia.

Then she realized what she was thinking and her lips tightened. Did she really want to compete with another woman? No, she'd had enough of watching her mother fight for her father's love.

Brant pulled on his trousers. "Nevertheless, I insist. It's late."

Yes, far too late, she thought, glancing at the clock and seeing it was two in the morning. It had been a mistake to make love to him. A beautiful mistake at the time but a mistake nevertheless.

In a damning silence they finished dressing, then he walked down with her to the underground car park.

"Call me as soon as you get home," he ordered, holding the car door open for her. "Use my cell phone number. I want to know you're safe."

She squashed the spark of warmth at his concern. He was only protecting what he thought was temporarily his. "I'll be fine."

"Call me," he warned, his dark gaze holding hers. "If you don't, I'll call you."

She didn't respond as she started the engine and drove out of the car park without looking back. Which is exactly what she'd have to do where he was concerned anyway. Walk away and not look back.

She was halfway home when something occurred to her. Was this Julia the woman who had "mattered"? Without a doubt she knew that she was. And obviously Julia *still* mattered or Brant would still be in bed with *her* right now.

Kia didn't call him when she got home. Worse, he didn't call her, and that made her heart sink more. Obviously she wasn't as important to him as Julia.

Kia got no sleep for the rest of the night and by morning she felt exhausted. Not even her usual shower, followed by a breakfast of sliced mango, nor a cup of coffee, could make her feel the slightest bit better.

If only she didn't love Brant. It would all be so much easier if he was the kind of man she thought might eventually love her in return. Only he wasn't. And he never would be. A leopard didn't change its spots. A womanizer didn't become trustworthy. The word *faithful* wasn't in his dictionary.

Phillip rang as she headed out the door. She'd decided to go to work early and get some of the paperwork typed and on Brant's desk before he came in. He was bound to be late, if he turned up at all.

"What do you think you're doing sending some woman to seduce me?" Phillip joked, his tone so heartbreakingly light that Kia had to smile.

"And did Lynette succeed?"

"Let's just say she surpassed all expectations." There was a slight hesitation. "How can we ever thank you for all you've done, Kia?" he said softly.

"Just be happy. That's all the thanks I want."

"We will. And we want you to come to the wedding in two months time. We would have scheduled it earlier, but I have to see one more doctor, then I'm all hers."

Kia knew she wouldn't want to go to the wedding. How could she bear seeing Brant in a social situation? Worse, with Julia by his side.

"I'll put it in my calendar."

"Speaking of calendars, aren't you supposed to be spending Christmas with your family in Adelaide? Lynette told me you were in the office yesterday."

She tried to think quickly without worrying him. "I did spend Christmas at home, but I got away early." She gave a light laugh. "Too much noise. Too many people. You know how holidays are."

"But you didn't have to go back to work so soon."

He paused. "Or is there a problem at the office I'm not aware of?"

"No, of course not," she assured him quickly. "I just popped in yesterday to pick up something I'd left behind, and Brant was there and needed something typed so I stayed."

A moment's silence, then he said, "Remind me to give you a bonus. Of course, most women think working with Brant would be bonus enough...." He trailed off suggestively.

"No doubt."

"I'll have to tell him, you know. About me and Lynette." He sounded worried. "You'll be open season after that."

She pretended to be unconcerned. "He already knows. He overheard Lynette and I talking yesterday."

"And?"

"And nothing." Time to go. "Phillip, I have an appointment and I'm running late."

"Oh, damn. I've just realized something. Word's bound to get out about you and I breaking up." He swore. "And I can't get back there just yet to help you."

"I'll manage." Phillip's idea of helping would probably make the situation worse anyway.

"But you're going to bear the brunt of it, Kia. Some people might think you dumped me because of my limp," he reminded her.

She pushed aside thoughts of what that journalist would say and knew there was only one answer. "Not if we're honest with them." Holding back the truth from everyone was of little value now anyway. "It's the best way to go."

He drew in a long breath. "Yes, you're right."

"Look, I really must be going."

"Kia?"

She stiffened. "Yes?"

"Are you sure you're okay?"

"Of course I am, Phillip. Thanks for asking. I'll talk to you soon." She quickly hung up so he wouldn't hear the catch in her voice. She couldn't bear that anyone else knew her feelings for Brant. As far as she was concerned, loving Brant was something so private, so personal, she couldn't share it with another soul.

Eight

Kia stepped out of the elevator at ten past eight and was tempted to tiptoe to her office just in case Brant was at his desk. But that would be acting like a coward, she decided, straightening her shoulders and striding down the hallway. The empty offices were quiet.

She reached Brant's door and glanced inside, her throat aching with defeat when she saw the room empty. Had she really thought he'd be at work? Dear God, how could he make love to her last night, then go to another woman? Her heart squeezed in anguish. It was morally wrong. So why was she surprised? Just because she loved him didn't change what he was.

Swallowing hard, she forced herself to continue to her office. She was beginning to have a new appreciation for the turmoil her mother had gone through with her father. She loved her mother dearly, but she'd never really understood how a woman could stay with a man who cared for her so little. She'd even sometimes thought of her mother as weak when it came to her father. Now she knew it had taken a special kind of blind loyalty to stay with him as long as she had.

An hour later Kia stretched, rose from her desk and went to stand at the window. She looked down at the sun-shadowed street below. The world continued to turn, but inside she felt dead, as if her heart had shriveled into a rock. She had to forget Brant, but she couldn't even summon the energy to do that right now. He still hadn't arrived. He was still with—

"Kia?"

She spun toward the sound. The heart she thought dead leaped to life. Brant stood in the doorway, dressed in a fresh set of clothes that made him look clean and vital and so disturbingly handsome that her knees turned weak.

She lifted her gaze to find him watching her with a knowing intensity that made heat surge into her cheeks. His look said she couldn't hide from him. That she was *his*.

Then reality kicked in and her stomach clenched tight. Physical closeness wasn't enough. It would never be enough. Her feelings for him ran too deep.

"I didn't think you'd be here so early," she said coolly, determined to keep her distance.

His eyes narrowed. "Why not?"

"I thought you'd be…preoccupied."

He started to close the gap between them. "Preoc-cupied with what?" he said silkily. "Or should I say *whom?*"

She managed a shrug. "With Julia, of course."

He stopped right in front of her. "Ah...you mean *in bed* with Julia, don't you?"

Did he have to rub it in? Was he getting some masochistic pleasure from pointing this out?

Her chin lifted. "Look, if you want to sleep with other women, that's fine. Just don't expect me to like it. Or to accept it. I won't share any man." She saw something flare in his eyes. "Julia's welcome to you," she ended in disgust.

There was a lethal calmness in his eyes. "So you're telling me to choose between you and Julia?"

"No, I'm telling you to choose between me and any other women you want to sleep with, *including* Julia."

"I don't take kindly to ultimatums. And I don't explain my actions to anyone." His arrogant gaze slid over her, pausing a moment on the swell of her breasts. "But for you, dear Kia, I'm going to relent on that last one. I did *not* sleep with Julia last night. The only woman I slept with was you, and then we got very little sleep, as I recall."

She wanted to believe him. Oh, how she wanted to. But how could she forget those nights listening to her mother's hushed accusations and her father's denials. Denials that had always proven to be lies.

She met his gaze with steely-eyed determination. "Very clever, Brant, but unlike some women, I don't believe everything I'm told. You say you didn't *sleep* with Julia. But you didn't deny having sex with her."

A shadow of anger swept across his face. "That's because I *didn't* have sex with her."

"I've heard *that* one before," she said, turning away.

He grabbed her by the shoulder and spun her back. "Listen. I am *not* your father."

She sucked in a sharp breath, stunned by his perceptiveness. Was she so transparent? Or did she subconsciously wear her thoughts blazoned across her back?

His hold tightened. "Kia, you once said you wouldn't apologize for him. Well, I'm not going to apologize for him either. Your father is a shallow man without integrity. Do you really think I'm like him?"

Her mind reeled in confusion. She'd never even considered the possibility that he *wasn't* like her father.

His jaw clenched. "You either believe me or you don't. It's your decision."

She stared up at him, trying to assess if he was telling the truth. If he was, then she'd have to reverse her opinion of him. That wasn't an easy thing to do.

She saw the strain in his eyes and etched around his nose and mouth. Suddenly she knew that if she didn't believe him, then it would be the end of them. He would shut her out of his life for good without a single regret.

And it was *that* very thing that made her admit he had a deep sense of personal integrity, unlike her father. She just hadn't let herself see it until now.

"I believe you," she said softly but firmly.

His chest rose and fell, but it was the flash of relief in his eyes that made her heart constrict. It overwhelmed her to know he really cared what she thought of him.

His fingers loosened on her shoulders. "Thank you," he said with a casual sort of dignity that was at odds with the arrogance just beneath the surface.

All at once she knew this was no longer just about her believing Brant.

"And now you've got to believe something about *me,*" she said, taking this chance, knowing this was important to her. "I'm telling you truthfully that I'm *not* a gold digger, I've never worked anyone to get either money or marriage out of them and I'm not with *you* for money or marriage." She lifted her chin with clear determination, her heart slamming against her ribs. "You can choose to believe me or not."

He studied her face for more than one heartbeat, his eyes not leaving hers for a second, but she saw the jolt of surprise in them, the assessment of her words, a decision and finally the admiration.

"I believe you," he murmured, pulling her into his arms, holding her close, which was just as well because her knees had given way. The knowledge that he was seeing her as the person she was for the first time made her feel gloriously thankful.

He leaned back. "And for the record, just in case you think you're like your mother because you believe me like she did with your father, you're *not.* So you have no need to feel guilty."

She frowned. "Guilty?"

The sensual spread of his mouth made her heart hammer against her ribs. "For wanting me."

Her frown disappeared as her lips began to twitch. "Who said I wanted you?"

"I seem to remember a few whispered pleas in my ears last night," he murmured, lifting her hands and placing them around his neck. She didn't resist.

"Hey, that was me begging you to let me sleep."

"Oh, really? Perhaps we should repeat it tonight and see." His warm breath caressed her cheeks.

"Not tonight," she teased. "I'm busy."

"You'd better not have a date," he growled.

"I want to wash my hair."

"I'll wash it for you."

"Will you do my ironing, too?"

He chuckled and pulled her closer. "We can come to a compromise. Wear non-crushable clothes. Better yet, wear no clothes at all. It'll make for a very interesting evening."

Just the thought of how interesting it could be made her feel very sexy. "My place or yours?" she asked throatily, amazed at how easily she'd slipped into the role of seductress.

"Mine," he murmured, nuzzling her neck. Then he gave her a quick, hard kiss and let her go. "I've got a meeting in an hour with one of the Anderson executives. We'll continue this tonight. I'll pick you up at seven."

She was melting so fast she had to keep some independence. "I can drive myself."

"Fine, but don't plan on leaving early." He gave her

a smile that sent her pulse spinning. "In fact, I doubt I'll let you leave at all."

At seven-fifteen Kia found herself once again standing in front of Brant's penthouse. It was hard to believe she'd been here twenty-four hours ago, and even then she'd sworn to herself it was a one-off thing. Talk about making the same mistake twice. Talk about being a woman weakened by love.

When he opened the door, it was like opening the door to her heart. Everything inside her reached for him, enveloped him, made him hers. It was the oddest feeling, yet it felt so right.

He didn't say a word. He just stepped back and let her pass, then kicked the door shut with his foot, his hand sliding around her arm and turning her to face him. She had no idea how long they stood gazing at each other.

"Come here," he finally murmured and tugged her toward him. She went willingly, and his lips found hers, and she simply gave herself up to him and his touch. He made her feel whole. As if her world had been split in two until this moment and now the top and bottom half of her heart had been sealed with love. Her love for him.

Overwhelmed with emotion, wanting him, needing to touch him, she broke off the kiss and began undoing the buttons on his shirt, stripping it from his broad torso as he stood and watched her with a look in his eyes that seared through to her soul.

"Too much," she whispered, not just about him standing in front of her but about her feelings for him.

"Yes," he said brusquely, watching her as she placed her hands on his hair-roughened chest. She skimmed her palms over him and heard him groan, loving the feel of him and the scent of him. She inhaled deeply against his skin.

In one smooth motion she reached for his trousers and pulled down the zipper, freeing him. His erection was all male and challenged her to touch him more. He rasped her name as her hand slithered around him and gripped him, moving over his hard flesh, rousing his passion, rousing her own even more.

"Not yet," he muttered, grabbing her hand and moving her back from him. Then he stripped the clothes from her body with a quickness and hunger that astounded her before swinging her up in his arms and carrying her to bed, where he lay her down, then sheathed himself.

In one quick motion he entered her. And just like that she came. No slow crawl toward orgasm. No indulgent inching to reach the pinnacle of pleasure. Just a powerful, all-fulfilling climax that made her shudder and cry out his name.

And when she caught her breath, he was looking down at her with another one of those arrogantly satisfied looks on his face that somehow didn't offend her this time. It made her feel very womanly.

And in a womanly way, she lifted her body slightly, nudging him farther into her.

"Too much," he growled, repeating her words, and he began to move. Slow at first, then faster and faster, the muscles in his neck growing taut with strain. He allowed her to have one more glorious climax before groaning her name and plunging deeper into her, burning them both in a downpour of fiery sensation.

It was a long, long moment before either of them could breathe, let alone move. Brant was the first to stir, and all at once Kia didn't want him to leave her. She wanted to stay right here, like this, forever. She tightened her arms around his back and held him close against her. She heard the rumble of his voice, but her fingers couldn't seem to unlock themselves.

"Kia?" he repeated, giving a low, masculine laugh against her neck. "As much as I love being inside you, you've got to let me go sometime."

His words finally penetrated. Her fingers loosened. He was right. She was making a fool of herself.

He lifted his upper body away from her, his eyes sexily amused yet strangely serious. "What was that all about?"

She forced a slight smile. "Just faint with hunger. I haven't eaten much today," she admitted. She'd been too nervous to eat.

"Then you need food, woman," he teased. He gave her one brief, hard kiss, rolled off her and headed to the bathroom. She hardly had time to think before he was back carrying a white bathrobe.

"Here," he said, tossing the robe toward her, his gaze sweeping over her naked body with male appreciation before he disappeared.

She could get used to this, she decided as she stood

up and wrapped herself in the fluffy material, enjoying its warmth in the air-conditioned apartment, burying herself in its male scent.

Her eyes widened as he came back into the room wearing nothing but a pair of well-pressed jeans. Jeans, for heaven's sake. Brant Matthews in jeans? And black ones at that. Normally he dressed as the consummate businessman. In jeans he looked what he was—the ultimate female fantasy.

He caught her staring and his eyes smoldered back in return. "If you want me on the main menu, you only have to say so."

A delicious shudder heated her body. "Actually, I think I'd like to keep you for dessert."

"That can be arranged."

They ate dinner in the small, intimate dining room. Or perhaps it seemed intimate because of the casual way they were dressed—her in his bathrobe, him in jeans.

Or maybe it was the look in his eyes. She tried to keep her cool, but that knowing look heated her cheeks and made her want to follow him like a lamb back into the bedroom.

Suddenly panicked by her loss of willpower, she said the first thing that came to mind. "Tell me about Julia," she heard herself say, then bit back a groan of dismay, not meaning to bring up the other woman again.

Or had she? Julia still played on her mind. Oh, not because she believed Brant was having an affair with her any longer, but there was something there, something still not quite right.

His eyes hardened as he put his coffee cup down. "She's my sister-in-law."

"Your what! Why didn't you tell me? Why did you let me believe she was—"

"One of my women?" His mouth tightened. "She *was* one of my women. Then she ran off to marry my brother."

"What! Oh, Brant, I'm so sorry."

"Don't be. It ended up for the best."

She frowned, not so sure he really believed that. It obviously wasn't for the best that a woman who had mattered had left him for the one person in the world he should have been able to trust, his brother. He wouldn't be bitter about it otherwise.

"So why is she contacting you now?" she asked, almost afraid to hear the answer. Did the other woman want Brant back? Is this what all this was about?

His piercing blue eyes contrasted sharply with the shrug he gave. "She wants help with Royce. He can't handle the fact that Julia and I were once an item and he's developed a drinking problem over it. Julia asked me to speak to him and make him see sense."

A swell of relief filled her. "Did you?"

"No."

She stared at him in astonishment. "He's your brother, Brant."

"I know."

A shiver skittered under her skin. "Surely that means something?"

"Does it?"

This, more than anything, showed her exactly how

he would treat her when the time came. And come it would. When he tired of her.

Dear God, it stunned her to know how much she'd been fooling herself. Just because she'd admitted Brant had more integrity than her father didn't mean he'd suddenly turned into Mr. Nice Guy. When he wanted her out of his life, he'd take the appropriate measures to do exactly that. No exceptions.

Well, maybe one.

Julia.

"You're a coldhearted bastard," she muttered, her heart twisting painfully inside her.

His eyes turned as unreadable as stone. "Feel free to think what you like."

"Oh, I will," she said, holding his gaze, determined he knew she didn't appreciate this side of his character.

For a moment silence hung angrily in the air.

Then he said, "Tell me one thing, Kia. Do you think if you went to your father right now and told him how you feel about him, it would change the way he thinks?"

She frowned. "What's my father got to do with this?"

"You're asking *me* to go to my brother and change his mind. It's a similar situation. And it won't work."

"But how do you know unless you try?"

His eyes bored into her. "Did you try with your father?"

She blinked in surprise. "Yes, I did."

"And what happened?"

She blanched, remembering. "He wouldn't listen."

"Exactly."

She sighed. Brant had a point.

His eyes softened. "Look, my uncle was an alcoholic. It ruined his family even before he killed himself and my aunt in a car accident while he was driving drunk. So don't you see? I *know* I can talk until I'm blue in the face and it won't change how my brother feels. I *know* I can get his promise that he'll get help, and tomorrow he'll break it. No, he has to want to seek help for himself. Not expect his wife to fix it for him. Or me."

Kia heard the rough edge of emotion in his voice and knew he wasn't as cold as he made out. "You're right."

He stood and pulled her up into his arms, his eyes darkening. "I don't want to argue anymore. I want to make love to you. Let's forget the rest of the world tonight."

"But—"

"Enough," he murmured, undoing her belt to slide his hands inside the robe and over the bare skin of her hips.

Hypnotized by his touch, she tingled under his fingertips. Greedily she gave herself up to him and to whatever he wanted to do to her.

"You need another lesson in some loving, Ms. Benton," he said, nuzzling her neck beneath the collar of her bathrobe.

She gasped with delight as his hands slid up her rib cage and cupped her breasts.

He leaned back. "Good. That's lesson number one completed."

Her breath caught in her throat as he squeezed her nipples, his touch sending shock waves to every nerve center in her body. "Er…number one?"

"Always respond when I touch you."

That was easy. "What's...number two?"

"Always say my name when I'm inside you."

She moaned as his hands slid up to her shoulders. "And if I don't?"

"Then we start over until you do," he murmured, pushing the robe off her shoulders and letting it fall to the carpet.

She licked her lips. "I was always a quick learner."

His eyes devoured her. "That's too bad."

"Why?"

"I was looking forward to teaching you the next lesson," he said huskily.

Her body was heavy with warmth. "Um...next lesson?"

"Lesson number three. How to get a man to kiss you all over."

She shuddered. And suddenly she wanted to know what *he* tasted like. What he would feel like against her tongue. "Do I get to reciprocate?"

His eyes darkened dangerously. "Only if you want to."

"Oh, I do."

"Then that'll be lesson number four," he murmured, rubbing a thumb across her lips.

"When do we start, teacher?"

"Now is as good a time as any," he drawled and pulled her closer.

Her mouth parted the instant his lips met hers and he kissed her with a hunger that shocked her. It was as if it had been years since they'd been together instead of a mere half hour.

He kissed a path down to her breasts, anointing each one with his mouth before going down on his knees and kissing her intimately through the curls at her thighs. His tongue flicked over the hot, moist core of her, and she gasped his name out loud, grasping his head to her as his tongue did marvelous things to her over-sensitized body.

"Come inside me," she implored, her hands pulling at his head to make him stop before she spilled over the edge. "Please, Brant."

He paused briefly. "Soon," he promised and returned to what he was doing, making her legs weaken as she melted around him, shuddering with intensity, suspended in time.

When he swung her up in his arms and carried her into the shower, her brain felt clouded, her body thoroughly seduced. He kissed her back to life and then led her into the bedroom.

"I want to please you like you pleased me, Brant," she murmured, following him down on the bed.

His eyes smoldered. "Are you sure you're ready?"

"Absolutely."

So he told her in explicit terms how a man liked to be made love to. She didn't need much encouragement as she kissed his chest, letting her mouth move all over him, and downward through the arrow of hair on his taut stomach, until she covered the tip of his erection with her lips.

"Kia," he growled her name as she began her own lesson in loving that had nothing to do with experience and everything to do with womanly instinct. She wanted him. *All* of him. And she almost got it.

Until he pulled her head up and away from him with a growl. "No," he muttered tightly, twisting to reach a condom on the bedside table. A few seconds later he rolled her beneath him and plunged inside her in one swift motion, quickly reigniting the fuse of desire inside her, plunging deeper and deeper until both of them shattered together in a sea of sensual pleasure.

Afterward she lay with her cheek resting against his chest. She had to ask, "Why, Brant? I wanted to."

He kissed the top of her head. "I know, but you weren't ready to take such a step, as good as you were."

"But…"

"Sweetheart, let me be the judge of that," he murmured sleepily.

Kia tilted her head back to look at the angular contours of his face. She loved the inherent strength in his features. That firm thrust of his jaw. Those undeniable lips. But she had to wonder exactly *who* wasn't ready for a full sexual commitment. The man who knew the score? Or the woman who supposedly didn't?

Brant waited for Kia's soft breath to tell him she was asleep before he opened his eyes and looked down at her naked body entwined with his. She was so beautiful. So bloody gorgeous.

And she was the only woman he hadn't let "go all the way." He wasn't sure why, but he did know he couldn't let her do what other women had done for him. Maybe because she'd asked first instead of taken. No other woman had ever asked. Not even Julia.

Not that it wouldn't have given him pleasure. It would have. Intense pleasure. But being with Kia wasn't about mere physical pleasure anymore. Deep down he'd known that all along but today when she'd stood her ground, forced him to admit she wasn't the gold digger he thought she was, something inside his chest had shifted. He just hadn't realized how profoundly she touched him. Yet it wasn't love. No, never that. He'd had one kick in the guts from a woman. He'd never let that happen again. Not even if she asked.

Nine

The next morning the telephone rang as soon as Kia stepped inside her house. Thinking it was Brant calling to tease her why she was late for work, she laughed softly and raced to answer it on legs that almost flew across the living room. For the first time she felt almost happy to be in love.

"How's my beautiful girl then?" a booming male voice came down the line.

The animation died on her face. Dear God, why did her father have to call now?

She forced herself to relax. "Hello, Dad."

"You sound disappointed. Not expecting anyone else to call, were you? One of your many boyfriends, no doubt."

"I've never been one for many boyfriends," she said

as calmly as she could. She wasn't like *him*. She didn't need adoration every minute of the day.

"A man friend then. Is it serious?"

"How are things, Dad?" Her feelings for Brant were private.

He chuckled. "That's my darling girl. Don't tie yourself down until you're at least thirty. Until then, have a good time. A really good time, if you know what I mean."

"Oh, I will." Kia's heart ached. Her father had really sunk to a new low.

"Anyway," he continued. "I'm in Darwin for a couple of days on business and I thought we might have brunch together today."

"Brunch?"

"Yeah. I want to see if you're still as charming as ever."

"And if I'm not?" she quipped to hide her hurt.

"Then I'll trade you in," he joked and laughed out loud as if it was the funniest thing in the world.

Moisture filmed her eyes and she squeezed her eyelids shut. Thank heavens he couldn't see her.

"What do you say then, darling girl? Coming to see your old man for an early lunch?"

She blinked rapidly and took a deep breath. He didn't really care if he saw her or not, so she should tell him flat out no. Then it occurred to her—if she went, she could dispel any lingering doubts that Brant was like him. He really wasn't, she knew that, but why not take this opportunity to put it behind her once and for all?

"Will Amber be there?" she asked. It wouldn't be a

pleasant lunch if the other woman attended. Not when her father's third wife was childishly jealous of her. Of course, Amber *was* half her father's age.

"No. I told her to stay in Sydney."

Kia's heart sank. So their marriage was on the rocks already. How sad. "Where and when?"

He named a restaurant in the heart of the city. She would have preferred to lunch at his hotel, but there was no chance of that. Her father liked to be seen when he was in town.

She laid the receiver on the cradle, then picked it up again, intending to call Brant and tell him why she wouldn't be in until later. Hearing his voice would be reassuring.

Then she remembered the invisible barrier he'd put up between them in bed last night and she stirred with sudden uneasiness. Perhaps it was best they both kept some distance.

Brant was just about to reach for the telephone for the tenth time when he heard the soft ping of the elevator door opening onto the executive floor.

Intense relief washed over him. It had to be Kia. Thank God nothing had happened to her. He'd already driven over to her place once this morning, to find out why she hadn't turned up at work after leaving his place earlier, and found no one at home. Her Porsche hadn't been in the driveway either. It had scared him silly, and that's something he didn't like to feel.

Bloody hell, he was going to demand an explanation, he decided, striding to the door, growing angry because she'd put him through this. He couldn't even think of an explanation that would satisfy him right now. Not unless...

His heart stopped, then began to thud like the deafening sound of tropical rain. Could she be seeing someone else? Was it possible so soon? Even Julia hadn't been quite that quick to run off with his brother.

With his gut tied up in knots, he reached the door...only it wasn't Kia coming toward him. It was Flynn Donovan.

Brant swore.

"That's a nice way to greet an old friend," Flynn mocked as he approached.

Brant grimaced. "Sorry, mate. I wasn't swearing at you."

Flynn's dark brows lifted. "Then who?"

"It doesn't matter." He planted a wry smile on his face, trying to appear nonchalant. "This *is* an honor," he said, turning back into his office and going to stand in front of the window. He glanced down at the street below, hoping to see...

"Is it?"

Realizing his friend knew him too well and had astutely picked up on some of his anxiety, Brant spun around. "What are you doing here, Flynn?" he said, gesturing for him to sit on the leather couch.

But the other man remained standing, his finely tailored suit reflecting the successful businessman that he was, the watchful look in his eyes one that no doubt his competitors in the boardroom had seen many times. "I've come to ask why you haven't been returning my calls. I thought we were supposed to get together over Christmas."

Brant gave a short laugh. "That's a bit hard to do when you were in Japan and Damien was in the States."

"I was back for Christmas, and Damien will be here tomorrow. But that's not the point. The fact is you've been avoiding us."

Brant walked to his desk and dropped down on the chair. "I've been busy."

"Haven't we all?"

Brant silently swore to himself, not liking being under the microscope. It was okay when he got together with his friends and they ribbed each other mercilessly about other things, but this was about Kia, and she was no joke.

"Well, I've been extra busy." He decided to throw Flynn a crumb to satisfy him for now. "You remember how Phil had his accident?" Flynn gave a nod. "He almost lost us a major account. I've been working double time just to set things right."

A sharpening look from Flynn said he'd taken the bait. "Anything I can help you with?"

"Thanks, no. I've got it all under control now," he said, relaxing a little, then darted a look at the door when he thought he heard the sound of the elevator.

"You seem kind of jumpy," Flynn said, and Brant realized his friend hadn't been fooled at all.

He shrugged. "I'm just waiting for Phillip's PA to arrive."

"Kia Benton?"

Brant sucked in a lungful of air. "You know Kia?"

"No, but I saw her at a couple of functions with Phil. She's a stunner. I wouldn't mind dating her for a bit. No wonder Phil—"

"Shut it, Flynn!"

For a moment there was silence.

Then Flynn spoke. "What's she mean to you, Brant?"

"Nothing."

Flynn's lips twisted. "Come on, mate. I know when you're lying through your teeth."

"We're lovers."

Another moment's silence. Then Flynn said, "Does Phil know?"

"No, but he wouldn't be too concerned if he did." Brant briefly explained the part about Kia pretending to be Phillip's fiancée. He left out the bit about him thinking she was a gold digger, which was just as well. If she was playing him for a fool, she'd regret it, he vowed, swallowing a hard lump in his throat.

"So this is about you bedding a beautiful woman because you thought she was out of reach and then she wasn't?"

"Yes."

Flynn gave a sardonic laugh. "Pull the other one, mate. I've known you all your life. There's more to you and Kia Benton than you're letting on. Am I right?"

Brant swore, hating being so obvious. "You're a son of a bitch," he said through half-gritted teeth.

"And how does she feel about you?" Flynn said, ignoring the tension coming out of his friend.

"How the hell do I know?"

"Perhaps you'd better do some fast talking or you might just find the lady will be snatched out from under you."

"Is that a threat?" Brant growled.

"Don't be stupid. All I'm saying is that she's a beautiful woman. She'd be a nice trophy for some men."

The thought of Kia being any man's trophy made him feel ill. "She wouldn't be interested."

"Really?" Flynn said in disbelief. "Let's see, a man could offer a woman like her riches beyond her imagination, travel across the globe, luxury like she's never seen before—and you're saying she wouldn't be interested? Get a grip, mate. Most women wouldn't be able to help themselves."

Brant stabbed his friend with his eyes, not appreciating having it spelled out like this. "When did you get to be so cynical?"

Flynn Donovan's eyes took on an odd glitter. "When I made my first million."

A couple of hours later Kia wondered how she'd ever thought Brant was like this man. The only thing the two men had in common was their gender. Brant may have a thing about commitment, but if he ever did fully commit to a woman, she knew it would be forever. And Brant's children would know they were loved for who they were, not for what they looked like. Brant was nothing like Lloyd Benton. Thank God.

It was a relief to get away from her father. Now, more than ever, she appreciated loving Brant. It was a privilege to love him, even if he would soon break her heart.

So she was surprised and delighted to see the gray Mercedes parked out front of her house when she got home just after midday, needing to collect some papers before going into the office. She parked in the driveway, almost falling over herself getting out of the car and into his arms.

Only, after a couple of steps toward him, she realized something was wrong. Her steps faltered. A sick feeling rolled inside her stomach. "Brant?"

"Where have you been?" he said in an ominously low voice.

"Wh-what?"

"I came around two hours ago to look for you."

"You did?" Oh, how she would have preferred being with him.

His eyes hardened. "Where have you been all this time?"

She stiffened, her own anger beginning to mount. If he'd asked nicely, she would have answered nicely. As it was, she didn't like his possessive tone. Or the implication that she belonged to him. She wasn't even sure where this was coming from.

She sent him a glare even as she squashed a queasiness rising inside her. "I didn't realize I had to get your approval to go out."

His eyes impaled her. "If I'm being faithful to you, then you can bloody well be faithful to me."

She gasped. "Faithful? Who said anything about being *un*faithful?"

"If you've got nothing to hide, then why not just say where you've been?"

"It's the principle of the thing, Brant. You don't own me. I'm not your puppet to say and do what you please. You wouldn't like me if I was." Her lips twisted. "I'm a challenge, remember? Or I *was*."

His mouth tautened. "You still haven't told me where you've been."

"None of your damn bus—" All at once, nausea swelled in her throat. She felt clammy. Her head began to swirl. She grabbed hold of him to balance herself.

"Kia?" he said as if from a long way off. "What's the matter?"

"I feel…sick."

"Damn," he muttered, swinging her up in his arms. "Let's get you inside."

She wanted to tell him not to move too fast, but he seemed to sense that. He was surprisingly gentle as he carried her to the door and logged in the security code she managed to tell him before carrying her into the bedroom.

He went to lay her on the bed, but she motioned for him to take her into the bathroom instead. Somehow she found the strength to push him out of the room in case she lost her lunch. Luckily she didn't, and after a short while she began to feel a bit better.

After splashing water on her face, she looked up and jumped when she saw him standing there with a towel in his hand. Gratefully she accepted the cloth and began dabbing it against her cheeks.

His gaze went over her in concern. "Feeling better?"

"A little."

"Let's get you to bed."

She began to shiver. "I'm okay."

"Yeah, I can see that." He gave her a hand into the bedroom.

"You shouldn't have stayed," she mumbled as he helped her lay down on the bed.

"Why not?"

"I can take care of myself."

He covered her with a light blanket, but his look told her what he thought of that comment. "Rest. I'll be back in a minute." He left the room before she could ask where he was going.

A short time later she was back in the bathroom. And this time she *did* disgrace herself but was too sick to feel mortified with Brant's hands on her head, holding back her hair. When she'd finished, she rinsed her mouth, then he carried her back to bed, where she lay against the pillows.

She closed her eyes for a moment, and the next thing she knew was Brant gently shaking her awake. "Kia, wake up. The doctor's here."

She groaned and opened her eyes to find Brant and a strange middle-aged man standing beside her bed.

"How do you feel now, Ms. Benton?" the doctor asked.

She tried to sit up but fell back against the pillows. "Like my stomach's seasick."

"I'd better examine you." He glanced at Brant. "Perhaps you'd like to wait outside?"

"Perhaps not," Brant said, an inflexible look on his face that said he wasn't budging.

The doctor arched a brow at Kia. "Do you mind?"

Her eyes darted to Brant. It wouldn't matter if she did. "No."

"Right. Then let's take a look at you."

He examined her for a few minutes, then put his stethoscope away. "There's a stomach bug going around. I'd like to rule out food poisoning, though. Have you eaten anything today?"

"She had breakfast with me," Brant said before she could speak. "And I feel fine."

The doctor nodded. "That's good. What about lunch? Did you eat together?"

Brant's gaze stabbed her. "No."

Kia wanted to groan. There was no getting around this. "I had something to eat in town," she said and saw Brant's shoulders tense.

The doctor frowned. "Hmm. Did you eat with anyone else? If you did, we'd better contact that other person and see if they're feeling okay. If they're not, we'll have to let the authorities know straightaway."

Kia glanced at Brant, who glared back in waiting silence. It was just as well she *wasn't* having an affair with anyone else. She'd be caught out otherwise. Not that she'd live to tell the tale.

"I had brunch with my father." She named the restaurant. "If you need to contact him, his cell phone number is written down near my phone."

"I'll call him now," Brant said, heading for the door, but not before she caught a glimpse of relief in his eyes. Her heart jolted painfully. He really *had* believed she was capable of an affair.

She was still mulling over that fact when he came back in the room.

"He's fine," he said, the unreadable look on his face telling Kia her father had been his usual irksome self but that Brant wasn't going to say anything about it to her. She swallowed a lump in her throat, suddenly overwhelmed by a strange feeling of relief. Brant truly didn't think any the less of her because of her father. In her heart, she hadn't been sure.

"Good," the doctor said, closing his medical bag with a snap. "I'll leave you something for the nausea."

"Thank you, Doctor," Brant said, then shortly after escorted the older man out of the bedroom.

A few minutes later he came back with a glass of water and a couple of the pills the doctor had given her. He helped her sit up while she took them, then laid her back against the pillows and tenderly pushed some blond strands of hair off her cheek.

Yet, oddly, his gesture brought to mind the time she had chicken pox and her father hadn't been able to hide his distaste at her appearance. Suddenly she felt self-conscious.

"I must look a mess," she said apologetically and tried to pat her hair in place.

He stared at her for a moment, then something flickered in the back of his eyes. "Never," he muttered, swinging away from her. He picked up the glass of water and took it into the bathroom.

Her heart jumped in her throat. She had the feeling he meant what he said. And if that were the case... No, she wouldn't get her hopes up.

He came back in the room, then straightened the light blanket over her. Suddenly he put his hand under her chin, making her look at him. "Why didn't you tell me you met with your father?"

Even feeling sick didn't stop the tingle that shot through her at his touch. "You're relentless, aren't you?"

"When I want something, yes."

She scarcely dared to breath. "And what do you want, Brant?"

"A straight answer."

She noted that's what he wanted from *her,* yet *he* wasn't giving any himself.

"You don't own me," she said quietly, feeling they were walking on dangerous ground. "Is that straight enough for you?"

He dropped his hand from her chin, then moved back from her, his expression inscrutable. "Get some rest. I'll stay and make sure you're okay."

"There's no need."

"Yes, there is." He left the room without further explanation.

* * *

Kia woke a couple of hours later and the nausea had gone, though she still felt a little headachy.

"I see you're awake," Brant said, lounging against the doorway.

She jumped in fright, then let out a slow breath as her gaze went over him. At least there was nothing wrong with her eyes. She could still appreciate how handsome he was. "You stayed?"

"I had to make sure you didn't collapse again."

"I didn't collapse the first time."

"No, but you would've if I hadn't been here to help you inside the house."

Her mouth tightened. "Perhaps if I hadn't been accosted in the driveway I would have been inside before I felt sick."

He straightened and walked toward her. "Don't hide anything from me, Kia. You'll find it's not worth it in the long run."

Suddenly she felt too weak to argue. Anyway, she couldn't tell him she loved him, no matter what. He wouldn't want to know. Not after his reaction last night when he'd held himself back from her. *That* more than anything proved he wasn't ready for a serious relationship.

As if satisfied that he'd gotten his message across, he walked over to the window and looked out. "I think we should go away for a few days."

She blinked in surprise. "Wh-what? With you?"

He turned to face her. "It had better not be with anyone else," he drawled.

The thought of having Brant to herself sounded wonderful. "Do you have a place in mind?"

"I have a house in the wilderness about an hour's drive south of here. I like to escape there every so often. It has enough luxuries to keep any woman happy."

Her bubble burst. How many other women had he taken to this house of his? "Sounds fine to me," she said stiffly.

His expression softened. "Kia, I've never taken another woman there, I promise. I want to get *away* from people when I go there."

Relief filled her. "When do you plan on going?"

"Tomorrow, if you're up to it. I have a couple of things to finish first, then we'll leave mid-afternoon. You just stay in bed and get yourself better. I'll swing by and pick you up around two."

For once, she would do what she was told. She didn't want anything spoiling these few precious days away with the man she loved. It would be moments like those she would always treasure.

The next morning Kia felt more alive than she'd ever been. All lingering nausea had disappeared during the night, and now she was ready to face the world. In fact, today she would *embrace* it. And for the next couple of days she would revel in her love for Brant. He need never know.

But first she'd drive into the office and leave a note for Evelyn, in case the other woman decided to pop in during the next week to check things over. Knowing

Evelyn and the way she took her job seriously, she would want to make sure there were no problems.

And deep inside, Kia couldn't wait until this afternoon to see Brant. Her heart was full of love for him. So full she was almost bursting.

Her steps light and buoyant, she stepped from the elevator and headed down the hallway to Brant's office. Not only were her steps light but her whole body—as though she could float to Brant's office....

"You've got it all wrong, Royce," Brant's voice warned from inside the office.

A feeling of apprehension shivered down Kia's spine and she stopped dead. Royce? Wasn't that Brant's brother?

"So you deny meeting Julia on numerous occasions?" the other man demanded with all the menace of a tiger about to pounce.

"No, I don't deny it," Brant answered, his tone firm. "But it's not what you think."

Royce gave a harsh laugh. "Yeah, right. I heard her calling you on the phone, telling you she needed you."

"To talk. That's all."

"At a hotel?"

There was a moment's damning silence, and Kia's breath caught sharply in her throat. She prayed there was some sort of mix-up. She waited for Brant to speak, to explain....

"There are other reasons for being at a hotel," he finally said, and Kia's heart sank at his detached tone. What other reasons? *Please, Brant, tell us.*

"I'm not a fool," Royce snapped, obviously unconvinced, too. "I took away your fiancée and now you want her back."

"Don't be so bloody stupid. Julia loves—"

"Stay away from my wife or you'll be sorry. I don't care if you *are* my brother."

Kia felt as though her legs had been cut from under her. Julia had been Brant's *fiancée?* They'd been *engaged?* Had been contemplating *marriage?* And Brant hadn't bothered to tell her.

A lead weight settled in the pit of her stomach. Dear God, it showed how little he thought of her. She was just another one of the harem. Oh, what a fool she was. An absolute idiot. Brant was no different than her father. She had believed Brant because she'd *wanted* to believe him.

She needed to get away. Be alone. She whirled around to leave, but then Brant spoke again. Her heart pounded. His voice sounded closer. He was going to come out of his office and at any moment he'd catch her eavesdropping.

"You're jumping to conclus—" He followed his brother through the doorway, stiffening when he saw her. "Kia!"

She swallowed, her gaze going from Brant to his brother. Somehow seeing Royce Matthews in the flesh made the accusations, the possibility of Brant's affair with Julia, more concrete. The younger man wore a business suit and looked rich and successful, and perhaps it was empathy, but in that split second she could see past the anger to the shadows under his eyes, to the bone-deep misery emanating from every pore of his skin. And she knew how Brant's brother felt.

Betrayed.

"Remember what I said, Brant," Royce warned, then strode past her and toward the elevator.

For a long moment Kia stared at Brant, trying to hold on to her composure. She heard the elevator door open with a whoosh, then close. And she knew this was the end for them. Utterly and totally. Anguish ripped her heart apart. The feeling was far worse than she'd expected.

Yet somehow, dear God, she had to face him with dignity. Experience with her father had taught her how.

She forced her expression to turn cool. "I have to get something from my desk."

Brant watched her in tight-lipped silence for a moment. "You should have phoned. I would have collected it for you."

"Perhaps it's better this way," she said pointedly and saw his gaze narrow.

Finding strength in her legs was difficult, but she managed it. She stepped past him.

He put his hand on her arm, stopping her. "What's the matter?"

She looked down at his arm, afraid to show him her eyes…and the pain that must be there. "Nothing."

"So you're all packed?"

"No." She shrugged off his hand.

"No?" he repeated, his tone hardening. "Why not?"

She looked up, unable to stop herself from spitting fire.

"I'm not going away with you, Brant. I've decided I've got too much self-respect to play second fiddle to Julia."

His jaw tautened. "I presume you heard Royce and I talking just now?"

"Yes."

"And you think Julia and I are having an affair?"

"That pretty well sums it up."

A sudden chill hung in the air. "Really?"

"I know what I heard." She went to spin away.

But he held her back. "What if I said you mean more to me than Julia ever did?"

A lump lodged in her throat. "Then why didn't you tell me about your engagement?"

A muscle flicked at his jaw. "It wasn't important."

"It is to me."

"Look, what Julia and I had—"

"Is none of my business," she finished for him. "Yeah, I get the point. I guess your brother does, too."

His eyes darkened. "Royce isn't thinking straight."

"Gee, I wonder why?" Her lips twisted. "Or maybe it's because of his *drinking* problem," she said with sarcasm.

His gaze stabbed her. "You think I lied about that?"

"How else could you hide your affair from me?"

Cold dignity descended over his face. "I'm only going to say this one more time. Royce *does* have a drinking problem, whether you believe me or not."

Oh, how she wished she could. But the evidence spoke otherwise. "Then why didn't you tell him that was the reason you've been meeting his wife?"

His jaw went rigid. "There's more to it than that."

"More?"

His eyes flicked away from her. "That's all I can say."

Because he was guilty. Guilty of loving his brother's wife. Just thinking about it squeezed pain through Kia's heart.

"None of this matters now anyway, Brant. It won't work between us. It's never going to work. I won't be second best."

Without warning, he grabbed her and kissed her hard. It was like kissing a stranger.

Until he softened it. And for a split second she turned boneless. The moment she did, he broke off the kiss.

"Does that kiss feel like you're second best?" he demanded, still holding her shoulders so she couldn't escape.

"Yes," she whispered. "That kiss was about *you,* not me."

He swore. "Kia, don't be so damn—"

"Let it go, Brant. Let *me* go. There's nothing more to be said." It was over. The end had come sooner than expected.

"Kia, it's not—"

Just then, the elevator doors opened and a female voice cried out Brant's name. Kia heard him take a harsh breath, and her head snapped around to see a slim blonde fly past her and into Brant's arms, her face pale.

"Oh, Brant, he was here, wasn't he?"

Brant's arms wrapped around the other woman even as his gaze flickered to Kia. She saw a flash of despair in his eyes, and a hot ache grew in her throat.

This man loved Julia so much he was willing to fight his brother for her.

Then he pulled back slightly and looked down at the exquisite features surrounded by a golden mist of hair. "Julia," he said softly. "We need to talk."

Tears glistened in Julia's eyes. "Darling, what are we going to do?"

Kia couldn't stand it any longer. These two people belonged together. She had to get out of there. Had to somehow put Brant out of her life. And her heart.

"Kia," he growled just as she was about to twirl on her heels.

She pasted on a false smile. "I won't stay, Mr. Matthews. I can see you've got your hands full."

Then she rushed toward the elevator. The last thing she saw before the doors closed was Brant leading the woman he loved into his office. Kia's knees buckled and she leaned against the elevator wall. She had never felt more devastated in her life.

Ten

Kia went straight home and packed a small bag, then tossed it in the car and drove off. She had to get away from here and she didn't care where.

She'd lost Brant. Lost him to the one woman she could never compete with. The one woman who had "mattered." He'd only wanted *her* body until Julia was free to love him again. He'd never wanted *her* heart.

But she'd given it anyway.

And Julia would soon be free. Brant and Royce would fight over her some more, but in the end Brant would win, of course. Then he and Julia would celebrate with champagne and caviar and they'd make love with so much emotion it would bring tears to Julia's eyes.

Kia swallowed a sob. The pain cut too deep to cry. She

just hoped Julia never found out what sort of man Brant really was. A man who loved one woman but thought nothing of sleeping with others to satisfy his sex drive.

Being at the northern tip of Australia, Darwin wasn't an easy place to leave on the spur of the moment, not with thousands of kilometers of desert between it and the southern major cities.

So for two hours Kia sat on Casuarina Beach and tried to think where she could go to lick her wounds. Eventually an approaching tropical thunderstorm made her look up, and she saw a billboard for one of the large hotels nearby. She made the decision to stay there for a few days instead.

She spent those days sitting on the balcony or walking along the beach, the breeze off the ocean providing a refreshing relief from the high humidity caused by the monsoon rains. In the evening she forced herself to eat in the restaurant and even managed to smile at people as if her heart weren't breaking and the food she was eating didn't taste like plastic. It all meant nothing without Brant.

But eventually she had to pull herself together and get on with her life. Tomorrow she would go home and pick up the pieces. She could do it. She had to.

But first she had to make her weekly phone call to her mother and pretend she was home and nothing out of the ordinary had happened. She was already overdue with the call.

"Darling, where are you?" her mother said the instant Kia spoke. "Are you okay?"

Kia's fingers tightened around the telephone. "I'm fine, Mum. Why?"

"We've been so worried. Brant's been looking for you and—"

She sank to the bed. "B-Brant?"

"Your boss, darling. Remember?"

Oh, she remembered all right. That's all he was to her now. One of her bosses. Soon to be ex-boss.

"He said you'd gone away for a few days but he didn't know where." Her mother paused. "We were really worried about you, sweetie. You never mentioned going away."

"It was a spur-of-the-moment thing, Mum," Kia said, feeling guilty for not calling sooner. Then she thought of Brant and her heart began to thump harder. "Do you know what he wanted?"

"He didn't say. I assumed it was another problem at work he needs your help with. He seemed quite upset about it, whatever it was."

Brant upset? He should be ecstatic now he was back with the woman he loved. She frowned. Or perhaps there really was a problem at work? Yes, that would be more likely.

"Anyway, darling, he asked me to call him the minute I heard from you. Where are you staying? If you give me the telephone number, I'll get him to call you."

"Mum, I'd prefer not to say," Kia said quietly. Brant would charm the information out of her mother if she told her. "I'm having a holiday and—"

"Darling, this isn't like you to just run off. I know

you're a grown woman and all, and some things mothers probably shouldn't know, but I'll always be here for you if you want to talk."

Kia blinked back tears. "Thanks, Mum. I know that. I just needed some time by myself, that's all."

A moment's silence ticked by. Then her mother spoke. "This isn't about work, is it? It's about Brant."

"Yes," Kia murmured. She took a shaky breath. "But please don't say anything to him. I'll call him shortly to see if there really is a problem at work. And I'll be going home tomorrow anyway. I'll call you then. I might even come down to Adelaide for a week after that." Suddenly she needed to go home. It would be for the best. Her mother, more than anyone, would understand her pain.

"Darling, you're always welcome here. You know that. Please call me tomorrow. I'll worry otherwise."

"I promise."

"And call Brant now. It may be important."

"I will." Kia hung up the telephone and stared at the wall. So he was upset, was he? Did he think she'd do something crazy just because he loved another woman? She wasn't that stupid. She was heartbroken, but life would go on.

Taking a deep breath, she picked up the phone again and dialed the number for his office. He answered on the first ring.

Just hearing his voice constricted her heart. Oh, God. How was she ever going to forget him?

"Kia?" he said when she didn't immediately announce herself.

"Yes." She swallowed hard then cleared her throat. "Yes, it's me."

"Thank God!" He paused. "Where the hell have you been?"

"On holiday."

He swore under his breath. "You've had everyone worried about you."

Anger hardened her voice. "They wouldn't have been if you hadn't called my mother."

"I had to see if you were there."

"Why, Brant? It's over."

"Don't be ridiculous. It's far from over. Not by a long shot."

She gasped. "If you think I'm going to carry on an affair with you behind—"

"Look, we can't talk about this over the telephone. Tell me where you are and I'll come to you."

"No," she said with a catch in her voice. In the flesh, he'd seduce her with more than words.

"Kia, I'm beginning to lose patience." He took a deep breath. "Please listen. This is important. I need to see you. I want to feel my arms around you and—"

"My God. Isn't one woman enough for you? Go to Julia, Brant. She'll be waiting for you."

"Dammit, there is no—"

"I'll come to the office tomorrow. Until then, just accept that I'm the one who got away. Goodbye, Brant."

"Kia, don't hang up. I'll—"

She carefully placed the phone in its cradle.

Whatever he'd do to her would have to wait until tomorrow. It still wouldn't change her mind.

At exactly noon Kia stepped out of the elevator and strode toward Brant's office. She'd come straight from the motel, dressed in a mauve knit top, white jeans and sandals. She'd never dressed so casually at the office before. Never even contemplated it. It was kind of freeing.

Just like the letter of resignation in her hand.

Of course, telling herself she should be feeling free was different to actually *feeling* free. That would come with time. Dear God, she hoped so.

For now, she had to face Brant and get it over with. Then she'd put one foot in front of the other and march out that door and out of his life.

She squared her shoulders just before she stepped in the open doorway, but it didn't stop the impact of seeing him sitting at his desk while he studied some paperwork in front of him. He looked so handsome. So…Brant.

For one precious moment she didn't think she had the strength to do this. But she had to. For God's sake— for *her* sake—she had to stay strong.

He looked up and their eyes met. And in that split second her heart cried out for him and all that she'd lost. She had come so close to finding happiness, utter fulfillment, only to lose all chance for both. The grief over that loss cut right to the center, the heart of her. She would never be the same, not even close.

"Kia," he said hoarsely, as if feeling that same pain. But that couldn't be. He would have to love her to suffer the same sense of desolation she felt. Yet she knew he didn't. He loved Julia.

Somehow, from somewhere deep inside her, she found the strength to enter the room. "I'm not staying," she told him in a firm voice.

His shoulders tensed. A mask came down over his face. "Why not?"

"I'm only here for one thing." She saw his eyes flicker over her, and her lips tightened. "No, it's not what you're thinking."

A muscle began to throb in his cheek. "And what would I be thinking?"

"Sex. That's all it ever was with you, Brant."

Those blue eyes bored into hers as he stood up and walked around the desk. "No. That's all you ever let yourself *believe* it was."

She stiffened. "So it's my fault, is it?"

He stopped right in front of her. "Who said anyone was at fault?" he asked quietly.

She gaped at him in disbelief. "Surely you don't think this is how a relationship should be?"

He reached out and cupped her chin, looking deep into her eyes. "Just because two people fall in love doesn't mean everything runs smoothly, sweetheart. But that doesn't mean they should end what they have."

She sucked in a sharp, painful breath and jerked her chin away. Dear God, was he enjoying the wounds he caused by his affair with Julia? "In other words, I should just let things slide along as they are? Boy, you really take the cake."

He seemed to freeze for a long pause. Then he said, "Kia, did you hear what I said?"

"No! I don't want to hear any more. I've come to give you this." She thrust the envelope at him.

Moments crept by as he stared hard at her, and she shifted uneasily. Then his gaze dropped to her hand. "What is it?"

"My resignation."

"You're not resigning," he said softly, taking the envelope and tearing it in half, just as he'd done with the check she'd written out for him over the security alarm.

She pulled out another envelope from her pocket. "I thought you might do that. You can tear this one up, too, but it doesn't matter. I've already sent one to Phillip in this morning's mail."

"You are *not* resigning," he repeated.

She gave a short laugh. "Unless you chain me to my desk, I won't be coming back."

"Chaining you to your desk sounds a bloody good idea right now," he muttered, grabbing her shoulders and lightly shaking her. "Kia, you say you listen, but you don't actually *hear* what I'm saying. I love you, Kia Benton. I'm not going to let you walk out of my life. I can't."

Her heart lurched in her chest. "Please don't do this to me, Brant," she whispered. "I can't be your mistress."

His hands tightened on her shoulders. "I don't want you for my mistress. I want you to be my wife."

Her mind spun in shock. His wife? For just a moment hope blossomed. Oh, yes, she wanted to be married to him so badly she ached with it. But did he love her, truly love her?

Then she remembered Julia, and that hope shriveled. There was only one woman he loved. A woman who belonged to another man at the moment. Kia's heart plummeted even further. Is that why he was asking *her* to marry him now? Had something gone wrong between him and Julia?

Regret and pain at what could have been flowed through her, cutting deep. "I'm sorry, Brant. I can't."

His head reeled back. "Why?" he rasped in a voice low and raw with something that sounded like need.

She blinked back tears. "You want me, but that's not enough. It'll never be enough for me."

"It's more than enough. For both of us."

"You're wrong. I won't be a substitute for Julia. I can't," she cried, spinning away. She had to get out of there before she fell apart. Before she let herself be taken on any terms.

"Stay."

His plea stilled her. Slowly she turned. Their gazes met for a long moment that seemed to last for eternity. She searched to the depth of his soul in those dark eyes, wanting to believe he loved her yet afraid to accept that the pain, the longing in his eyes, was real and not her imagination. She shook her head. No, she was too emotional to trust her judgment right now.

She was about to turn away again, to really go this time, but all at once she saw the anguish in his eyes and her legs refused to move. Brant wasn't a man to show his emotions and certainly not his vulnerability. Yet here he was showing that very thing. Hope and wonder bubbled inside her. Dare she believe? Could she believe in him? In herself? Her judgment?

She needed to stay rational. She needed to find out more about his relationship with the other woman before deciding. "What about Julia?"

The intensity of his gaze remained strong on her face. "She's already a wife. To Royce."

"But…you love her. You said things don't always run smoothly for people in love."

He took a step toward her and slipped his arms around her waist. "I meant *us*. I love *you*."

Yet something held her back, kept her from trusting him. An inner fear that she would still be second best, runner-up to Julia. He may think he loved *her* in a moment of madness, but for how long? Today? Tomorrow? For how many tomorrows would he love her? Would he secretly long for Julia, long to have her in his arms, even as he held *her?*

She just didn't know. She drew in a ragged breath, trying to think rationally, to get some clear focus. The only way she would get any kind of perspective was to have space to think about what had happened. She had to think about Brant's words of love. So much depended on her making the right decision.

"I need to think, Brant." She started to turn away, pain choking her words at the shock on that handsome face she so loved.

He stopped her, his gaze intense on her face. "You've got to believe, Kia. Trust in my love for you."

Something in his words got through to her this time. She didn't move, but suddenly she listened. Really listened.

A smile turned lovingly at the corners of his mouth. "Hear my heart, darling. Hear and learn." He put her hand against his chest. She could feel his heart thudding hard beneath it. And she could actually *hear* it as she looked deep into his eyes.

"You *really* love me, Brant?" she murmured, one inch from believing.

"You and no other," he said, his voice thick and unsteady. "I began to get an inkling when you were sick. You were going on about looking a mess, and I realized then I'd never tire of looking at you. That I would always find you beautiful, inside and out. No matter what."

Her knees wobbled. She felt weak and giddy all over. Finally she did believe.

Relief flooded her that she no longer had to fight her love for him. "Dear God, I've been wanting you so much. I…" She hesitated, still half-afraid to say the words out loud, as if all this would just disappear if she did.

His gaze filled with so much love she wondered how she ever doubted it. "I'm waiting."

She looked up at his strong, vital countenance, that firm mouth, those compelling blue eyes, that dark hair. "Oh, Brant, I love you, too."

He let out a slow, shaky breath that warmed her insides. "I know."

A soft gasp escaped her. "What?"

"Once I let go of the notion you were a gold digger…" His eyes apologized for ever thinking that. "I finally realized you weren't the sort of woman to get involved with a man unless your heart was involved, too. You see, I didn't listen to my heart either."

She moved closer, loving the feel of his hard body against her own. She'd never get enough of him. "Kiss me, darling."

His eyes darkened and he obliged her by doing exactly what she asked. And then some. Their kiss was so slow and deep it spoke more than words ever could.

When they pulled back from each other, she wanted to wallow in her joy. "Oh, Brant, I didn't know I loved you. Not at first. I thought it was just sexual attraction. It wasn't until we made love that it hit me."

His mouth curved into a smile. "You should have said something."

She rolled her eyes. "Oh, right. You would've disappeared off the face of the earth if you'd known I was serious."

He grinned and his love for her shone through. "Loving you isn't *that* bad."

"May I remind you of that in fifty years' time?" she teased, smoothing her fingers along his jaw.

"Definitely." He kissed her with a brief, hard kiss that still managed to touch her soul. "I have some other news. Phil's decided to stay in Queensland with Lynette and become a 'gentleman farmer'. I'm going to buy him out."

She nodded, knowing it was a good idea for all concerned. "It's best this way. As much as I like Phillip, he isn't a good businessman."

"You're right." His gaze held hers. "Now there's something else. About Julia..."

"You don't have to tell me. I trust you completely."

"Thank you, sweetheart, but I can tell you now anyway. I couldn't before because it was Julia's secret, not mine." He brushed a strand of hair off Kia's cheek. "She has a child. With a previous boyfriend. She had him when she was sixteen, and her parents forced her into adopting him out."

Her heart squeezed. To never see one's child...the pain of it. "Oh, poor Julia."

"I never knew and neither did Royce. It was only recently when the adoptive parents died in a boating accident that Julia found out where her son was. She came to me because Royce had started drinking and she didn't know what to do."

"Has she told Royce?"

"Yes, and he wants the boy. He's vowed to stop drinking. I know he'll do it, too. The first step is admitting he's got a problem. That was something my uncle would never do."

His brother's willingness to get his drinking under control was one good thing, at least. "How does Royce feel about you and Julia now? You'll always have a past together."

"Let's just say I convinced him I have other interests," he said, pulling her hips closer so she could feel his arousal.

Her breath hitched in her throat. "Uh...other interests?"

His gaze dropped to her mauve knit top. In one swift motion he stepped back, took hold of the hem and lifted it over her head, leaving her in her black bra and white jeans.

"Are you seducing me, Mr. Matthews?" she said huskily.

He ran a finger along the tops of her breasts. "Do you *want* to be seduced, Ms. Benton?"

"Hmm...no, I don't think so." Quickly she moved away and hurried to lock the door. Then she pocketed the key and turned to face him with a wicked smile. "This time I want to be the *seducer.*"

His eyes filled with a slow, sexy gleam that would always stir her senses. And her heart. "You realize this is an office, young lady."

"Oh, so that's what that big wooden desk is for. And that leather chair." She strolled toward him and slipped her hand in his. "Come and sit down, Mr. Matthews, and let me take note."

* * * * *

THE TYCOON'S HIDDEN HEIR

by
Yvonne Lindsay

Dear Reader,

Sometimes our lives are touched by the people in them without us even realising the long-term impact they have on us. I grew up half a world away from extended family but had the pleasure of the company of a grandmotherly neighbour who introduced me to reading romance when I hit my teens. Those books ignited a love of romance in me, a fire, that still burns as fiercely now as it did back then – a fire that compels me to write stories like the Knight brothers' journeys to love.

In one of my previous jobs I travelled as a sales representative through the central North Island of New Zealand. The winter roads can be treacherous, the isolation during the journey overwhelming – yet help can be just around the next corner in the road from a source as yet unknown. When I originally started writing *The Tycoon's Hidden Heir*, the third in my New Zealand Knights trilogy, I was motivated by the possible chain of events after a chance encounter triggered by a near-death experience. The what-ifs were mind-boggling.

I hope you enjoy Mason and Helena's story and that it keeps your love of romance burning bright.

With warmest wishes,

Yvonne Lindsay

YVONNE LINDSAY

New Zealand born to Dutch immigrant parents, Yvonne Lindsay became an avid romance reader at the age of thirteen. Now, married to her "blind date" and with two surprisingly amenable teenagers, she remains a firm believer in the power of romance. Yvonne balances her days between a part-time legal management position and crafting the stories of her heart. In her spare time, when not writing, she can be found with her nose firmly in a book, reliving the power of love in all walks of life. She can be contacted via her website, www.yvonnelindsay.com.

To Robyn Donald and Daphne Clair
for their support in the darkest hours,
for creating Kara School of Writing
for people just like me
and for sharing the joy when dreams come true!

Prologue

Twelve years ago…

Black, ice-cold water swirled around her, sapping the last of the heat from her body, the last of her will to survive. A tinge of irony touched her mind that she should die this way. Helena Milton, full of life, colour and crazy dreams, and powered by a get-go attitude to life that had alternately amazed and dismayed her quieter elderly parents.

Her parents—would they ever understand why she'd left? Why she'd agreed to marry Patrick Davies and settle for less than love? Deep in her heart she knew she was doing the right thing—for herself, sure, but most of all for them and for the sacrifices they'd made for her.

But she'd failed. An uncontrollable skid on the ice- and snow-strewn road had plunged her car through the bridge barrier and into the swollen river below. The river which now flumed with chilled water from the melting snow that came straight off New Zealand's central plateau mountains.

Helena lifted numbed frozen fingers to try the switch for the electric windows again. Futile. Not even her ever-weakened attempts to break the glass had any effect. With the doors jammed and the car's electrics out of commission she remained trapped. Helena closed her eyes again. What was the point in keeping them open when all around her was nothing but blackness?

A spark of anger lit briefly in her chest that she could die like this—alone and with her goals unfulfilled, no chance to earn her father's pride instead of being the object of his quiet disappointment. Defeat had an ugly, bitter taste.

Let go, whispered the little voice at the back of her head. *Let go.* She sagged deeper into her car seat, accepting the cold that penetrated to her bones, and let her mind drift. How long would it take, she wondered.

A new and different sound from outside penetrated the thickening fog of reluctant acceptance in her mind. She forced her eyelids up and scanned around her. Fairy lights on the road above. A crazed laugh, broken and weak, choked from her throat as some of her usual humour surfaced. Whatever happened to the white light at the end of the tunnel everyone talked about?

A dark figure loomed at her driver's window, a pale face pressed against the glass. Water foamed around the figure and against the window's edge. Helena felt the car shift slightly with the increasing pressure of the river's pummelling force. The man's lips moved but she shook her head slowly in response.

What was he saying? His arms raised and she recognised the outline of an axe clenched in his hands. He tapped it against the glass. Helena suddenly understood what he'd been trying to say. She threw herself sideways, into the deepening pool in her car, oblivious to the dice-shaped pieces of broken safety glass that showered her body.

The roaring growl of the water, muffled before, now crashed intrusively against her ears. Strong hands reached in to grab her by her jacket, her hair, anything that gave her rescuer purchase. Helena struggled to help him as he dragged her through the gaping window but she flopped uselessly as her limbs refused to obey. With one powerful lift he manoeuvred her slight frame free from the car. The shield of his body protected her from the hungry determination of the swirling current as he carried her to the bank.

The bank was hard, blessedly so. Helena relished each pressure point of discomfort as confirmation she still lived. She'd been so close to giving in. The concept that she was finally safe rejoiced through her mind. Now, all she wanted to do was sleep, except the man who'd pulled her from the car seemed determined not to let her.

"Is there anyone else in the car?" her rescuer shouted in her ear. "C'mon! Answer me, is there anyone else?"

Slowly, her lips formed the words, her voice weak. "No. Alone."

"Thank God. Are you hurt? Did you lose consciousness?"

She felt his hands, strong and capable, probe her scalp then skim her body as she shook her head. The cold air bit through her wet clothing all the way to her bones.

"Doesn't look like you've broken anything. Let's get you somewhere dry."

"My things? My car?" she managed to ask through frozen lips.

"Sorry, hon. Your car's heading downstream. First order of business is to get you dry and warm."

Her rescuer lifted her into his arms and strode toward what she now recognised as a large truck and trailer unit parked in a lay-by to the side of the road. A tiny smile pulled at her lips as she recognised the source of her earlier confusion. A long-distance trucker, his rig was festooned with driving lights.

"What's so funny?"

His voice was deep, young. Reassuring. She wanted to see what he looked like but the effort required to tilt her head and pick out his profile in the shadows cast by the truck's lights remained beyond her.

"Fairy lights," she whispered.

A deep chuckle rumbled through his body. "Sure, fairy lights."

He lifted her up into the cab of his truck then climbed in after her to settle her into the basic sleeping compartment behind.

"Do you remember how long you were in the water? What time you crashed?"

"J-just after nine…I think."

He flung a look at the clock on the dash. "About half an hour then. What the hell were you doing out on the road without chains? Didn't you see the warning signs?"

"D-didn't w-want to stop. I have to get to Auckland." The short speech took every last ounce of energy left within her.

"You won't be going anywhere tonight."

A sudden disembodied voice on the radio elicited a sharp curse from her rescuer before he responded. She tried to listen, catching only the words *accident* and *hypothermia* before drowsiness pulled at her with the strength of a super magnet. She began to slide into unconsciousness, rousing only as he shook her gently.

"Hey, don't go to sleep yet. You have to get those clothes off and get warm again. Can you manage?"

"N-no. F-fingers t-too cold."

She felt as helpless as a rag doll when he began to peel off her wet clothing, muttering under his breath as her limp limbs hindered the process and massive tremors racked her body.

"Shivering, that's good. You're on your way back."

Pain seared through her as circulation sluggishly resumed. "B-b-back? I n-never got where I was g-going."

He chuckled again, and Helena decided she liked the sound. It was deep and warm and made her feel alive again. Alive—something she'd taken for granted for far too long.

"I hate to tell you this, but we're stuck here for the night. I'd hoped we could make it farther up the line to a motel but the authorities have closed the roads in both directions until morning."

As soon as she was naked he laid her gently, almost clinically, on her side on the narrow bunk and tucked a down-filled sleeping bag around her body. She vaguely heard the sounds of his own wet clothing slap onto the floor. She couldn't stop shivering and the sleeping bag slid away from her body, exposing the length of her back. She barely felt the mattress dip as he lay down beside her but the heat that radiated from his body was seductively welcome. She sighed as strong-muscled arms gathered her close against the rock-hard plane of his chest and was asleep before he settled the sleeping bag around them both.

It was still dark when Mason Knight woke, disoriented, to find a warm, slender and very naked female body on top of his. The crush of her breasts against his chest and the tangle of her legs in his brought him to full aching arousal. Disorientation fled as he remembered the rescue from the car stuck in the rising river and bringing the driver to the truck to get her warm. Standard survival procedure, he reminded himself—get naked, get dry, get warm—but nothing in his survival training during his stint in the New Zealand army had prepared him for this particular scenario.

He willed his body into submission but one part of his anatomy stubbornly ignored him. Slowly and deliberately he poured images through his mind designed to quell even the hottest ardour—no luck.

He tried to shift his hips and roll her to one side against the back wall of the sleeper but she squirmed against him—the central core of her body so close to him he could feel the heat that now emanated from that private part of her. Shit. She'd freak out if she woke now, and he sure wouldn't blame her.

Shock jolted through his body as small feminine hands stroked feather-light across his torso, sending wild coils of desire tightening in ever-decreasing spirals. She rubbed her cheek against his chest, a sigh escaping her lips to brush over his sensitised skin.

"I need you." Her voice was husky and travelled through the velvet midnight darkness like a caress.

"No, it's just reaction to the accident. You're in

shock." In shock? *He* was the one in shock. "You don't want to do this."

"I need this. I need you." Her lips found one of his nipples and her tongue swirled around the sensitive flat disk, sending a raging hunger through his body that didn't want to take no for an answer. "Show me I'm alive," she whispered as she pressed her hips against his hungry flesh, a sharp moan punctuating her demand.

She rose up onto her knees—deft hands reaching for him, stroking his iron-hard shaft, her fingertips barely touching the swollen head, guiding him to the source of her heat—then she sank down onto him with a throaty groan that almost saw him lose control right there and then. A massive tremor rippled through her body as she took his full length deep within her and she stilled, her hands now resting on his shoulders. Then, she began to rock, slowly tilting her pelvis back and forth, maintaining the searing contact between their bodies, heat and moisture building between them like molten lava.

Mason trailed his fingers over her thighs and to her hips where he grasped a firm hold of her, silently encouraging her to up the tempo as his hips thrust upward to meet her every stroke.

This was crazy—he was crazy to let her do this—but somehow, in the anonymity of the dark night hours, it seemed as if it was the only right thing left in the world. To think that all her vitality, her heat, could have been gone forever. Yeah, he understood her need to affirm life—to feel life—right now.

Right. Now.

His climax hit him with the force of a runaway train and his fingers bit into her skin as he pumped against her. Her sharp cry of completion and the rhythmic pull of her muscles as they contracted around him prolonged the ecstasy even as she collapsed against him, shaking with the aftermath of pleasure.

"Thank you," she whispered, her head resting against his chest where his heart pounded so hard he thought any second now it would leap right from his chest. He cleared his throat to speak, but she raised one finger and pressed it against his lips. "Shh, don't say anything." And then, just like that, she was fast asleep again.

Aftershocks continued to quiver through his body. Mason hooked his arms about her and cradled her to him as he'd never held another woman before. In this timeless moment she was his woman and his alone. The overwhelming urge to claim her and protect her from the world came from out of nowhere—strong, feral, invincible. What the hell was he thinking? He didn't even know her name! Who was she? What kind of woman was she, that she could make love with such abandon to a total stranger then fall asleep in his arms as if she belonged nowhere else?

By the time the wintry-grey fingers of dawn crept across the sky he was no closer to finding his answers. Silent and careful, he eased her from his body, watching as she instinctively nestled into the warmth of the depression where he'd lain. He stifled an oath as his toes made contact with the near-frozen wet clothing abandoned on the floor and quickly reached for clean dry jeans and a sweatshirt from the locker above the bed.

A quick check on the radio confirmed the roads had been declared safe enough to reopen. It was time to go. He had a lot of time to make up and a wedding to get to in Auckland later that afternoon. His boss was much older than his bride-to-be and had been alternately ridiculed and lauded in the tabloids about his forthcoming nuptials. Either way, Mason didn't give a damn, but he did respect the man who'd given him his first job out of the army and had begun to teach him everything he knew about the transport industry in New Zealand. Mason considered it an honour to stand up for him when his boss's adult son from his first marriage had point-blank refused to have anything to do with the wedding.

The rustle of bedclothes in the sleeper drew his attention back to his immediate problem.

"The roads are open again," he said over his shoulder, reluctant to make eye contact.

"That's good. Is there a chance I can borrow something of yours to wear until my clothes dry out?"

"Sure, just check the locker. There's a spare belt in there somewhere, too."

"Thanks."

He felt her pause, as if weighing up the wisdom of bringing up last night. She'd obviously reached the same conclusion he had—ignore it and just maybe it would fade away. Every muscle in his shoulders clenched and he gripped the steering wheel with white-knuckled fingers as he listened to her pull on some clothes. The thought of his clothes clinging to the satin-soft creaminess of her skin had him rock hard in a split second. He fought the urge to turn around and watch her. Did her body clamour to repeat their nocturnal experience in the cold light of day as loudly as his did?

Apparently not. Eventually she came forward and plopped down into the passenger's seat in the cab and he got his first real look at her.

Hell, she barely looked twenty. Delicate fingers combed through tousled, long brown hair, hair that in the streaks of early sunlight reflected reddish lights of burnished copper. Delicate fingers that had held him last night, had guided him inside her body. His gut clenched into a fiery ball of want and he forced his eyes forward to the frozen landscape that stretched ahead of them, not willing to see what lay in her green eyes, not wanting to commit the pale heart-shaped face to his memory. But it was already too late. He would never forget her. Not her scent, not her touch—nothing.

"Thanks. For everything." Her voice was husky, hesitant, as if she found the words difficult to say.

"You're welcome," he ground out through teeth that ached, they were clenched so hard together. He forced his gaze back out the windscreen. It was clear she regretted her impulsiveness already. Okay, he could be a gentleman. He could ignore last night and the clawing need that the mere sight of her aroused in him. Somehow. "So, where are you headed?"

"Auckland, but you can drop me at the nearest town. I need to make a phone call first."

"That's it then?"

He heard her breath catch in her throat, just the slightest hitch, but quite enough to tell him she'd understood his question fully. Her answer was softly spoken but rang with finality as she turned to stare out the passenger window. "Yes, that's it."

Mason ran a finger inside the stiff white collar of his shirt and loosened his tie another blessed millimetre. All day he'd been plagued by last night's memories. Finally, while he was getting ready for the wedding, he'd resolved to try to find out who she was. The registration of her wrecked car would be a good start once it was dragged from the river. A few calls would do it. Then he would track her down—to see if they could make something more of the incendiary passion they'd shared. He'd never known anything like it. Like her. He wanted to know more.

He thought of what he'd gotten up to as a teenager to rile his dad and of the five years he'd spent in the army—of how he'd constantly searched for that one thing that would make his life feel like it had a purpose. The one thing to fill the void he himself couldn't define. For a brief time that void had been filled last night. He had to find her. He had to know if she was what he'd been looking for.

Patrick gave him a nudge as the opening strains of the wedding march drew the assembled congregation to their feet in unison. A hush settled amongst the crowd as the bride began her journey down the thickly carpeted centre aisle in Auckland's oldest and largest city church. All heads turned for their first look at the wife-to-be of one of New Zealand's wealthiest men and for the first time in his life Mason Knight nearly blacked out as his midnight lover glided down the aisle.

One

"It's quite simple, Helena. If you don't assign control of Brody's half share of the business to me within the next thirty days I will take every step to ensure the world knows exactly how you and my father met. Let's see how your precious son copes at school once everyone knows that juicy titbit."

He knew? How on earth had he found out? Helena's stomach lurched. Despite how careful she'd been to conceal her past, it was something she'd known could come out of the woodwork anytime in the last twelve years. That it should be from Patrick's eldest son, Evan, shouldn't have come as a surprise.

Her heart ached for Brody. He had only just settled back at his exclusive boarding school and had been troubled since Patrick's sudden death—easily upset and reluctant to leave her. Understandable, all of it, of course. She was already worried about how he'd cope at school during this difficult period of adjustment. If Evan spread his poisonous secret Brody's life would become a living hell. She would not let that happen.

But what on earth was she to do? Already entrenched in the company as marketing director, from the day of Patrick's fatal heart attack, Evan had exerted his power as new part owner of Davies Freight and taken over Patrick's chair and the decision-making processes that fell to the managing director. She'd been unable to stop him, and with the demands of dealing with Brody's grief, not to mention her own, she hadn't had the energy left to fight back in the boardroom. This week, she'd finally returned to the office, where she supervised the business's administration. It hadn't taken long to discover Evan had completely taken over.

Evan had never appreciated or understood his father's love of the cut and thrust of the industry, or his cautious plans for expansion. No, all he saw was an easy ticket to maintain his plush lifestyle and the quickest way to get rid of her. Of course, on paper, he could be seen to have gone through the motions—pitching new contracts, renewing old ones—but deeper analysis had shown the truth. If Evan was permitted to keep on his current path the business would be bankrupt within a year.

She'd grown up having to scrape together every penny. There was no way she would let that happen to her son.

A look of scorn slid across her stepson's face, making it patently clear that no matter how coldly polite he'd been to her while his father was alive, the gloves were most definitely off now. Helena's fingernails bit into her palms as she struggled not to whack him hard across his smug features. No doubt he hoped she'd do exactly that. With his connections, he could press assault charges and see her son removed from her care. Then he could do whatever he wanted with Brody's share of the company. Yeah, he'd like that all right, but it sure wouldn't happen this side of hell freezing over. Not while she still had breath in her body.

What scared her most was if Evan discovered the full truth he'd delight in ripping his much younger half brother to shreds. With the resources he had at his disposal she knew he'd have people digging for dirt on her—the fact he'd found out how she and Patrick had met was just one example of how far he was prepared to go to find anything to discredit her and help him reach his avaricious goal. She had to protect her son, no matter what, and at the same time to somehow find the courage to honour Patrick's last wishes to the letter.

Helena swallowed back the tears that threatened. When she'd met Patrick she'd been prepared to accept his help in return for her companionship in marriage. She'd never dreamed she would learn to love him. She missed her husband more than she could ever have imagined— his steady hand on the tiller of their world, his gentle encouragement to strive for her dreams, his unadulterated enjoyment in the child born within the first year of their marriage. He'd always boasted Brody had made him young again. Not young enough, unfortunately, to see the fast-growing boy much past eleven years old.

"So?" Evan's sneer jerked her back to cold harsh reality. "What do you say?"

"I can't answer you now, Evan. It's too soon."

"Don't underestimate me, Helena. You and the brat

are just a blip on my radar. I'll leave now, but remember I will have what's my due—one way or another."

Helena couldn't bring herself to rise from her chair to even see him from her home, couldn't trust herself not to resort to the old Helena and to fly at him, giving vent to her rage. No, if there was one thing she'd learned the hard way in the past twelve years it was to think first, act second. Evan knew the way out; she only wished he'd stay there.

The hollow echo of the front door resounded through the house and the tension slowly ebbed from her shoulders. God, she'd thought she was tough but it would take more than tough to see her through this. It would take a miracle. She drew in a deep breath and rose from the chair. There was work to be done, and plenty of it. First, she had to arrange an appointment—one she'd been dreading. She couldn't ignore Patrick's final instructions any longer.

Her heart twisted with regret that her sweet, generous husband had understood the reality of his eldest son's true nature, that he'd known that this situation would come to pass.

Half an hour later Helena let the telephone receiver fall back haphazardly into its cradle. Mason Knight was nigh on impossible to track down. She couldn't give up though, he was the one man Patrick had said would be able to help her, the one man he'd insisted she ask and, coincidentally, the last man on earth she wanted to seek out for help.

The secretary at his office had said he was out of Auckland and refused to give any further information, but Patrick had mentioned something about a holiday home on the Coromandel that Mason used as his bolt-hole when he needed to escape the city. She'd lay odds on him being there, so that's where she had to go.

A warning trickle of dread ran down her spine and for a moment Helena questioned whether she was doing the right thing. As intimately as they'd known one another that one and only time, the man was a virtual stranger. How would he react when she turned up on his doorstep and asked for help? Over the years he'd made it perfectly clear to her how much he detested her, and had avoided seeing Patrick when she too would be there.

Could she stand it if he slammed the door in her face and left her to deal with Evan on her own? And what of Brody?

There was only one thing for it. She had to get to the isolated Coromandel Peninsula address she'd found in Patrick's Rolodex. For a minute she rued the fact that Mason Knight couldn't have built his minipalace somewhere like Pauanui, a popular playground for New Zealand's wealthy and somewhere she was familiar with. But it was probably best not to have any chance of being recognised in his presence. It wouldn't take much mental arithmetic before tongues would start to wag and minds to speculate. She couldn't do that to Brody, no matter what.

Mason looked through the wall of floor-length glass that faced out to the ocean and drank in the wild beauty of the scene. He loved this place and not just because it was his own personal testament to the first million he'd ever made. He'd never grow tired of the sight of the native bush, as it hugged the hillside on its gentle drop toward the sea, or the sea's ever-changing mood. It'd been too long since he'd come here to recharge.

When he woken at 5:00 a.m., his mind still fogged with sleep, he'd known it was time to clear his diary and get away from the city, and all its demands, for the weekend. Okay, so it had taken some juggling, and a few extra grey hairs for his secretary, but he'd walked out of the office at two-thirty this afternoon without a backward glance. Now the weekend stretched before him, gloriously empty. His to do with whatever the hell he wanted.

He lifted a glass of red wine in a silent toast to the view then put it to his lips and relished the flavour of his favourite merlot—an indulgence he saved only for these stolen weekends here at his hideaway. His mouth twisted into a wry smile. Of course, Patrick had always teased him that the only thing to make a runaway weekend perfect was spending it in the company of a special person. But Mason had no such special person in his life. He had neither the time nor the inclination to weed through the gold diggers, the publicity seekers, the schemers.

Realistically, of course, he knew that not all women were like that—his sisters-in-law being perfect examples and hell-bent on putting what they believed were suitable marriageable candidates across his path. What was it about happily married people that made them want to see everyone in the same state, he wondered. It was like an epidemic over the past couple of years. His eyes rested briefly on the snapshot of his growing extended family taken at their last gathering. Who would've thought he'd be an uncle twice over by now?

Marriage. His lip curled slightly at the thought. While his brothers, Declan and Connor, didn't seem to have any complaints it certainly wasn't a state he was in any hurry to embrace. What he enjoyed now was the company of suitable escorts from his personal list. Sophisticated women who made no emotional demands on him at all. Cut-and-dried—just the way he liked it.

Mason strolled across the room to flip the light switch. It grew dark early this time of year. The wind was coming up. Good. He loved a howling winter storm. Nothing like it to blow the cobwebs from your mind and reenergize your soul. He had everything here he needed, and if the power went out, so be it. Nothing would mar the perfection of his all-too-infrequent time away from work, alone.

Buzz, buzz!

Mason froze. Nothing but the intrusion of an uninvited guest, he thought as the gate intercom's strident warning bounced about the high-raftered ceiling. Who the hell could it be? He hadn't even told his secretary where he was headed when he walked out the office door. Sure, his brothers or his dad would figure this was where he'd come if they tried to contact him at home, but they would respect his privacy. One thing was for sure: whoever was at the gate wasn't welcome.

Buzz, buzz, buzzzzzzzzz!

With a muttered expletive Mason put his glass of wine down on the heavy pine coffee table and walked over to the intercom console on the far side of the room. He leaned one forearm against the wall and depressed the Talk button with a dangling finger.

"Yeah, what?" he snarled into the speaker.

"Mason? Mason Knight?"

His skin chilled as he recognised the husky lilt of the woman's voice. How the hell had she tracked him here and, more importantly, why?

"Can we talk? I really need to see you."

"We have nothing to talk about, Mrs. Davies."

"Don't switch off. It's important, or you know I wouldn't be here. Mason? Please?"

Oh yeah, she injected just the right amount of pathos into her tone. Any other man would leap to her aid. Any other man but him. But then not everyone knew what a little schemer Helena Davies was, or how little she'd valued her wedding vows. He'd often wondered just how many times she'd cuckolded Patrick since that night and the thought still made his blood boil.

"It's for Patrick. Just give me five minutes," she finished.

Mason's heart gave a twist. Patrick Davies, the one man he'd admired unreservedly—until he'd married Helena. He warred with his desire to switch off the intercom, go out onto the deck and be buffeted by the rising wind and pretend he'd never begun this conversation. But despite Patrick's appalling taste in wives, he owed it to both the man and his memory to hear her out.

"Five minutes only. Come on up."

He hit the button to unlock the gate then strode through the house to the front door and threw it open to wait for her arrival. She didn't take long. He could hear the strain of the car's engine as the transmission dropped to a lower gear to climb the steep, unsealed private road. His whole body tensed as the taxi drove onto the flagstone-covered apron outside the house.

Taxi? He stifled a groan. Only Helena Davies would bring a taxi for the two-and-a-half-hour drive from Auckland to this spot on the Coromandel. The woman threw money around like there was an unending supply. He watched as she handed a fistful of hundred-dollar notes to the driver then alighted from the vehicle. His stomach tensed. She still looked good, he noted bitterly, although a bit paler and a bit thinner than the last time he'd seen her. In the dark emerald-coloured suit, buttoned just high enough to expose a hint of perfect creamy breast, and with her brown-red hair tightly twisted to the back of her head, she played the grieving widow well.

"A taxi, Helena?"

"And what's wrong with that? I've recompensed him, and then some." Her glittering green eyes met his gaze and clashed. Every nerve in his body went on full alert.

"Just seems a bit extravagant, don't you think? Especially when you can drive any one of Patrick's cars yourself."

"I don't drive anymore. Not since… Well, anyway, I never got my confidence back behind the wheel." Her eyes drifted away from his face and fixed on a spot somewhere behind him.

Acid burned low in his belly. Like he needed the reminder of that night right now.

The taxi driver swung through the circular turning bay at the front of the house and disappeared back down the drive. *What?*

"Hey, where's he going?"

"Back to Auckland." Helena's voice held an underlying thread of steel.

The tightness in his gut ratcheted up another notch as, in a few graceful steps, she closed the distance between them. Her perfume reached out to tantalise his nostrils—a bit sweet, a bit spicy. His body stirred with unwelcome interest. He hated that she could still do that to him.

"You said five minutes." He bit the words out as if he'd chipped them from stone.

"I lied."

The conniving witch. Rage boiled up inside of him and he ground his teeth together hard to keep the heated words he wanted to shout from spilling out. She hadn't changed a bit. Now her easy source of income was gone she probably thought she could move onto her next victim. He knew her type only too well.

"Enjoy your walk home." He spun away from her and stepped back inside, but he wasn't fast enough. The telltale waft of her fragrance followed close behind.

"So call me a taxi when we're done. I don't care. I have to talk to you."

"Oh, we're done all right. Now get off my property before I have you charged for trespass."

He was unprepared for the butterfly-like touch of her hand on his arm. His skin contracted sharply under the cool softness of her fingers and he shook himself free.

"I'm sorry, Mason. I shouldn't have tricked you."

"There are a lot of things you shouldn't have done, Helena. Marrying Patrick was only one of them."

She flinched as if he'd struck her and for a split second remorse lanced through him. His mother, rest her soul, would have been ashamed to hear him speak like that to a woman—even one like Helena—but the anger he'd borne toward her, and women just like her, took a firmer grip.

"Well, neither one of us is perfect," she murmured and shivered in the rapidly cooling air.

The storm he'd predicted started to make its presence felt in the darkened sky and heavy splats of raindrops hit the pavers outside in an increasing staccato. Damn, as much as he wanted to, even he couldn't make her walk out in this.

"You'd better come in," he said begrudgingly.

He held the door open for her to pass through, showed her through to the expansive sitting room that faced out to the ocean and gestured for her to sit in a chair.

Helena looked around the room, impressed with the luxurious comfort of the large open-plan living and dining area that had obviously been structured to take advantage of what must be a spectacular view of the water in daylight. He kept the place tidy. Aside from the half-full wineglass on the coffee table there wasn't so much as a dish left out on a bench. Even the wood stack next to the fireplace was arranged with military precision.

She sat, forcing the butterflies in her stomach to calm their crazy fluttering, as Mason lifted his wine from the table and took a deliberate slow draft. He set the long-stemmed glass back on its coaster and thrust his hands deep in the pockets of his black trousers. A slight sheen of the wine lingered on his lower lip and he swept it away with the tip of his tongue. Her eyes locked onto the tiny movement and, deep inside, her muscles clenched. She forced herself to drag her eyes from his lips, from his face, and stared out at the rain that lashed against the floor-length glass windows. Darkness encroached outdoors; solar-powered lamps began to glow gently around the periphery of the deck. She stared at the lamp nearest the window until the shape blurred into a watery ball of light.

It had been a long time since she'd felt at such a disadvantage. She hated the way he deliberately tried to dominate her—forcing her to look up to him, not offering her so much as a glass of water. If it was only up to her, and if she didn't need his help so badly right now, she'd have darned well started that walk back to

Auckland and damn the consequences. But this was Brody's future, his life, and she'd crawl over broken glass if that's what it took to get Mason to help her.

Where to start, where to start? She gathered her fractured thoughts. It had been so easy when she'd mentally rehearsed this scene in the taxi during the trip down. Now, face-to-face with him, it wasn't as easy as she'd hoped.

She let her eyes briefly rake over his body. Physically she couldn't discern much change from the dark-haired stranger who'd rescued her from certain death that night—he stood at six feet tall and beneath the dark soft cotton polo shirt he still had shoulders like a world-class rugby player. But now there was a hardness to his face, a remote look to his eyes, that had never been evident in the plethora of photographs Patrick had proudly shown her of his protégé.

"Is this going to take long?" His irritated drawl dragged her attention back to the present.

"No, I'm sorry. I don't mean to waste your time. It's just…I…"

"You what?"

She'd rarely heard less interest in a question. Helena reached to the soles of her feet and hauled up all the courage she could muster. "I need your help."

"And I'd want to help you—why?" His upper lip curled in derision.

Helena forced her fingers to relax their grip on the straps of her handbag. "Because it was Patrick's last wish."

She watched as he snagged the glass with his fingers and took another pull at the wine, the slight tremor in his hand the only giveaway that, oh yes, she'd struck a chord this time. It was a low blow, she knew, using his relationship with his old mentor now, but she had to use all the ammunition at her disposal. She knew Patrick's death had hit him harder than he'd shown at the well-attended funeral six weeks ago. There he'd been locked behind an aloof façade. Polite and friendly and not a sign of any other emotion. But to her, his grief had been stark in his dark eyes, in the pallor of his face and in the tight lines that bracketed his lips. She'd ached to comfort him but knew he'd spurn any empathy from her.

"Go on." His voice was steady, his eyes cold and flat.

Helena took in a deep breath. "He told me that if I ever had a problem with Davies Freight to call on you. To ask you for help. So I am. We need you. We're in trouble, Mason."

"You're talking crap. If there was anything crumbling at Davies Freight I'd know about it. Now, if you're finished, I'll call that taxi."

Helena bit back the sharp retort that sprang to mind and took a breath before continuing, "Hear me out, please. You'll have heard that Evan took over the managing director duties. You know that was never Patrick's intention. He always knew that if Evan assumed charge that he'd find some way to cut Brody out, to use any profit for his own means. It's what he's doing now. He's systematically bleeding the company dry. There'll be nothing left in a few months time. Nothing." Helena dug into her handbag and withdrew a typed sheet of paper. "It's why Patrick left specific instructions on his death to give you this."

She watched as Mason's eyes flew over the letter she'd been given by Patrick's lawyer after the will had been read.

"Anyone could've typed this. Even you. Why would he have wanted me to run Davies Freight?"

Helena watched as Mason discarded the letter to let it flutter onto the coffee table.

"I didn't make it up, you have to believe me. Patrick never expected to die so suddenly. He was fit, he was healthy—he expected to live for years more. To have the opportunity to start to groom Brody to take over from him in the future, the way he'd hoped you would until you set up your own firm. But you know how cautious he was. He wouldn't have asked you to do this if he hadn't thought it was important.

"You have to believe me. Evan's after blood. You know he's always been jealous of his father's relationship with me and with Brody. He wants to hurt us."

"Hurt you? C'mon, Helena. I think you're overstating things. Besides, wouldn't it be easier if you just stayed on Evan's side? It's the way people like you operate, isn't it?"

Helena ignored the hurtful inference in Mason's words. As difficult as it was, she had to school herself to be immune to his jibes, no matter how far they were from the truth. She sighed. "You don't know Evan like I do."

"And of course you know him *exceptionally* well, don't you."

Oh no, now he'd definitely gone too far. She leaped from her seat and met him face-to-face, shaking with anger. "Don't you dare suggest that! I would never... I could never..."

"Never?" Mason didn't move so much as a muscle, his voice low and filled with disgust. "You slept with me the night before you pledged yourself to a much older man. A man who could never keep pace with your physical needs. Why wouldn't you turn to someone else? Especially someone who stood to inherit equally with your own son."

"No! I loved Patrick. He became the hub of my whole world. I know I did wrong that night. But I wasn't the only one to blame. I didn't act responsibly, that's true, but I never heard you cry 'stop'. You can't possibly still hold that night against me."

"Can't I? I wasn't the one getting married the next day."

Tears burned in the back of her eyes but she wouldn't give in to them. Too much was at stake. Besides, he was wrong. Despite what she'd thought when she'd entered into her marriage she had loved Patrick. If she could have him back in a minute she would. She owed it to him—for everything he'd done for her, for the wonderful man he'd been—she had to get Mason to agree to help and somehow do it without giving Evan the chance to spread his malicious story and destroy her son's remaining security. She had to appeal to Mason some other way. Patrick must have known how he'd react. In his letter to her he'd been insistent she tell Mason the truth. But at what cost? She drew a steadying breath, deep into her lungs, and turned to face him.

"Please, Mason. Please help. I need your expertise and acumen. You're the only one who can make a difference now. This is Brody's inheritance we're talking about. His whole life lies ahead of him."

"So you're telling me you're not affected by this? You're only doing it for Brody? Your platinum card won't suddenly dry up without that astronomical salary Patrick paid you to decorate a desk at the office? I'm not a fool, Helena. The only person this will make a difference to is you. I'm sure Patrick left Brody more than well provided for."

"Of course. Patrick left both of us well provided for. But you know how much the business meant to him.

From Brody's birth he groomed him to take over one day. You can't simply stand there and let that slip from Brody's future. Besides, this isn't only about Brody and me. Any damage to Davies Freight is going to affect far more people than just me. You have to help."

"Have to? And why is that?"

A painful throb started in her head. She didn't want to do this, but Patrick's instructions had been explicit. She still hadn't even completely gotten over the shock of his letter herself, or the fact that he'd kept the truth hidden from her for so long. That he had, hung heavy in her heart. Gathering all her strength to her, Helena reached out and grasped Mason's forearm in a tight grip.

"Isn't it enough that Patrick asked for your help?"

He flung her a look of absolute distaste. "Through you? No. It's not. I think you overestimate your appeal."

Helena's fingers tightened as she hauled out the courage to say what needed to be said. "Then do it because Brody's your son."

Two

Your son. Your son.

The words echoed in his head, drowning out the roaring denial that filled his brain. Somewhere, deep inside, an intangible flicker leaped at the possibility, but then the heated brand of her fingers fought through the fog of shock to remind him she was there. A part of this—potentially a part of him through Brody—and he didn't trust her. Not so much as a millimetre.

She'd dealt with her grief in record time—it made sense she was on the lookout for her next cash cow, of course she'd look to pin something as outrageous as this on him. There was no way on this wide earth he was going to fall for that one—he'd seen firsthand how destructive a lie like that could be. He placed his hand over hers, peeled her fingers off his arm and dropped her hand.

"I don't believe you." He pitched his voice low and hard so she'd be in no doubt that he could be dissuaded.

She started and paled, as if he'd slapped her.

"You don't…?"

"You've wasted enough of my time, Helena. Now get out of my house." He banked down the anger. He simply wanted her to take her lies and her sexy body somewhere he'd never have to hear them, or see her, again. He stalked across the room, snapped up the handset of a cordless phone and began punching in a series of numbers. "You can wait in the front porch for the taxi."

"No."

His finger hovered over the last digit. "No?"

"I'm not going until you agree to help."

Fury clenched low in his belly like a tight fist. If he had to take her physically from the property himself he'd damn well do it. He dropped the phone back on the side table he'd snatched it from and began to walk toward her, his intent obvious in every step.

"I have proof that Patrick isn't Brody's father."

Mason stopped in his tracks. "Proof?"

"On his death he instructed his solicitor to make certain documents available to me, documents that prove he was incapable of fathering a child."

Mason choked out a humourless laugh and raised one brow. "And Evan? How do you explain him?"

"Adopted."

Sure he was. Was there no end to her lies? "Does he know?"

"Yes. I think that's partly why he's so bitter toward Brody. He thinks Brody is Patrick's natural-born son."

"And you, of course, know he's not."

"I do now."

"Why the hell should I believe you?"

She scrabbled in her bag, withdrew a letter-size envelope and handed it toward him. "Here. Read it yourself."

Reluctantly he took the envelope from her and lifted the flap to remove the folded sheets from within. He sat down on the long sofa facing her chair and began to read.

"So, this proves Patrick was infertile." He tossed the papers back across the coffee table toward her. "It certainly doesn't prove I'm Brody's father. How many other men have you slept with, or are none of them rich enough to pin this onto?"

"Brody is your son. You and Patrick were the only ones."

"You can't possibly expect me to believe that. You might have lost track of the details during your parade of lovers but I remember that night very, very clearly. You were no innocent virgin, Helena."

"Okay, you weren't my first, no, but there was no one else once I married Patrick."

He could neither help, nor wanted to prevent, the incredulous snort that escaped him. He'd been an unwilling audience to Evan's drunken boasts about how athletic his father's beautiful young wife was in bed. He knew she was lying right down to the delicately formed bones of her exquisite body.

A sudden flash of lightning split through the room, rapidly followed by a deafening rumble of thunder and an almighty crash outside. The lights overhead flickered, dimmed and brightened.

He had to get rid of her before the power went out altogether. Mason picked the phone back up and hit the

Talk button. Silence. He hit the button two times in quick succession. Still nothing.

"Problem?" Helena sat back on the chair and crossed her legs.

"Phone's out."

"So use your mobile."

"Can't. This is a black spot. No reception. I'll take you into Whitianga myself. You can check into a motel and get a taxi back home in the morning."

Helena watched in dismay as he grabbed a set of car keys from a softly glazed pottery dish on top of the dining table. That he meant what he said, she had no doubt. Reluctantly she picked up the papers from the table, pushed them back into her bag and rose to follow him through to the garage. If need be she'd come back tomorrow, and the day after that and the day after that until he'd agree to help.

Inside the garage, Mason flipped a switch on the wall. The ceiling light bathed a black behemoth parked in solitary splendour in the middle of the parking bay. She stared at the four-by-four, recognising in its strong powerful lines the personality of the man who drove it—yet, with the chrome running boards and highly polished mag wheels, enough of the daredevil showman who'd brazenly taken the freight community by storm to build the largest privately owned company in the country. The blip of the car alarm disengaging startled her as it echoed in the large area.

"Get in." Mason walked around the other side of the four-by-four, opened the driver's door and climbed up.

With as much dignity as she could muster, Helena opened her door and placed a foot on the running board to give her a lever up into the high leather seat. As she settled in and clipped her seat belt he put the key in the ignition and pressed a button on a remote on the central console. The wooden segmented door behind them slowly lifted open.

A long low-pitched string of expletives ran from Mason's mouth as he looked through the rearview mirror to the driveway. Before she knew what was happening he was out of the truck. What? She unclicked her belt and scrambled back down. Mason stood, just inside the doorway, hands on hips and with frustration and anger roiling off him in tangible waves.

She looked past him and out onto the softly lit forecourt. There, firmly planted across the drive, its tip entangled in dark wires, lay the solid trunk of a toppled pine tree.

"Is that what took the phone out?" Helena looked at the sorry excuse for a tree. It looked as if it should have come down years ago.

"Yeah, it was tagged for removal next week along with a few others. Stay here," he commanded.

"Is there anything—"

"Just do as I said."

Without another word, Mason went to a large storage cupboard along the back wall of the garage and flung open the door. He reached inside and pulled out a set of earmuffs, safety glasses and gloves and a mean-looking chain saw. Setting the saw onto the concrete floor he checked the petrol level, put on the earmuffs, then hefted the saw up again. For a split second, as he passed her, he met her gaze—accusation stark in his angry stare—before striding out into the driving rain. As if it were her fault the stupid tree had come down. Helena crossed her arms defensively in front of her body and fought back a shiver of cold. The temperature had dropped markedly with the onset of the storm.

In a half a dozen steps the driving rain had plastered his shirt to his body. She tried to tear her eyes away from him, from the outline of a supremely well-honed male, but failed miserably. About as miserably as she'd managed to convince him of the truth of Brody's parentage. It *was* her fault. If she hadn't come he wouldn't be out there right now. But she'd had to try—still had to. There was simply far too much at stake.

She should be helping him—after all, he wanted to get rid of her, didn't he? Another gust of wind whipped a flurry of needles and small branches to lash against him as he pulled on the gloves and started up the saw, immediately setting to work to remove the branch nearest him. Before she knew it she was out the door.

"Let me help," she shouted over the ragged noise.

Mason lifted one side of the silencers protecting his ears. "Don't be stupid, it's too dangerous. I told you to stay inside."

She ignored him and gripped a hold of the branch he'd just cut, and dragged it away to the side of the drive.

"Go to the garage and get yourself a set of earmuffs and safety glasses, you'll need them. And Helena?"

She paused and straightened.

"Don't get in my way." The words were nothing but a growl.

She gave a sharp nod to acknowledge his warning. Sure, she wouldn't get in his way, at least not while he wielded that chain saw with the dexterity of a seasoned professional.

From the garage cupboard she pulled out a pair of gardening gloves, although after trying them on she decided to do without. The way they fell off her hands would be more hindrance than help and right now it was more important to her to leave a better impression on Mason than that she'd arrived with.

The rain had soaked through her hair and ran in rivulets beneath the collar of her jacket, sending trickling shivers of discomfort down her spine. She mentally squared her shoulders and focussed on what she had to do. She slipped on the glasses and earmuffs and went back outside.

It was more difficult than she'd expected to clear the branches off to the side, especially in a suit and shoes better suited to a cocktail party than a logging operation.

Mason's eyes burned a hole through her back more than once as she staggered with another branch across the driveway. Through the earmuffs the softened roar of the saw bounced between the bank and the side of the house until Helena's head felt as if it was vibrating in unison with the noise. She pressed fingers, sticky with pine resin, over her earmuffs to seal off any gaps as Mason battled a particularly knotted piece of wood. He wielded the chain saw as if it was second nature to him, but then that's pretty much the way she'd noticed he managed everything in his life. A total perfectionist in whatever he did.

Any other day of the week Helena would have turned tail and left. The discomfort, the noise and the incessant rain would individually have been enough to persuade her to find sanctuary elsewhere. But she couldn't stop. She had to prove she was worth listening to and not, as Mason so clearly thought, just some grasping bimbo out to find her next sugar daddy. She bent to pick up the branch he'd finally worked free and jumped when Mason leaned forward and pulled one of the earmuffs away from the side of her head.

"Ready to give up yet?"

She looked up, raking his face for any clue that she'd satisfied him she wasn't just some pretty thing looking for an easy ride, but his features remained unreadable except for the flicker of heat in his eyes when they dropped to the gaping neckline of her jacket.

"Are you finished yet?" she countered, not daring to move.

Slowly, his eyes trailed back up to her face. "Not yet." His pupils dilated slightly.

Helena felt a brief surge of power. He might act as if he hated her, but he wasn't unaffected by her. At least not as much as he tried to portray. That telltale flare in his eyes had given her more control than she'd dreamed. "Well, then, I'm not finished either."

Despite all the activity, the cold evening air and her wet clothes combined to send a deep chill into her bones. She shivered as she bent to pick up one of the slices of the trunk. Mason reached out to stop her.

"What?" She stood up and put her hands on her hips.

"Go inside, you're wet through."

"It's okay, I can manage," she replied through gritted teeth, bending at the knees to get closer to the richly scented disk of wood.

Mason stood and watched her as she hefted up the piece. Holding it close to her body, she lurched over to where she'd stacked the cut branches. Then, he set to finishing off the remainder of the tree, although she noticed that he cut the slices narrower to make her job a little easier. Eventually he was done and, scooping up three disks to her miserable one each time, they finished clearing the driveway.

"What about that bit?" Helena gestured toward the

tip of the tree that had tangled in and brought down the phone line.

"I'll leave that for the phone guys. C'mon." He gestured toward the garage.

Helena hesitated a moment in the rain, which hadn't let up even the tiniest bit as they'd worked to clear the tree, then followed him back inside. She fought to combat the shivers that now cascaded through her body. The last time she'd come close to feeling this cold she'd been with him, too. Only then the outcome had been vastly different to today. She resolutely pushed away the memory of that night, of the lover who was as far removed from this aloof creature as a person could be.

From beside the passenger door of the truck she watched as he grabbed a rag from the cupboard to wipe down the chain saw and put everything away. She lifted a foot to the running board to climb back into the vehicle when warm hands slipped around her waist and lifted her back down. He only touched her for a moment yet it was enough to send a fire coursing through her body, radiating out from where his hands had rested against her sodden clothing. Fire blended with a bit of something else—something she couldn't afford to acknowledge or identify.

"Forget the road trip tonight."

"You mean it?" Relief coursed through her. The prospect of sitting in cold wet clothing even for the relatively short trip to Whitianga was anathema to her.

"I don't say what I don't mean. Clearing this mess took longer than I expected and we're both soaked through. By the time we get dried out it'll be too late for you to check in anywhere around here. I'll get you some dry things. You can stay in one of the guest rooms."

He sounded as though he'd rather endure a root canal without anaesthetic. Even so, Helena tried to say thank-you but he was already walking away from her. She followed him down the native-timber parquet floor hall to a separate wing of the house that she hadn't noticed on her arrival. He flung open a door at the end of the passage and walked through to another door that led into a large champagne-coloured marble bathroom and snapped on the faucet in the shower. Steam slowly started to fill the room.

"Don't lock the door," he said as he left her. "I'll find something for you to wear and drop it inside."

Helena could barely respond. The lure of warm running water called to her from the shower stall. With cold, stiffened fingers she tried to undo the buttons on the front of her jacket but they just wouldn't cooperate.

"Here, let me."

Warm hands brushed her fingers aside. She shivered as Mason deftly undid the buttons and peeled the tailored jacket from her body. Underneath, her simple black silk camisole clung to her skin, shamelessly exposing the fact she wore no bra. Under his gaze her nipples hardened and pressed against the dark silk. A flush of embarrassment flooded her cheeks.

"I'll be all right from here," she protested as he started to lift the hem of her camisole.

"You're so frozen you can barely move. Be sensible, Helena. Besides, it's not like I haven't seen you naked before."

His fingers brushed against her belly as he took hold of the bottom edge of her cami. The shiver that rippled through her body had nothing to do with cold—his touch scorched like a brand.

"Please, stop." Helena pushed his hands away and stepped backward. "I'll be fine from here. Truly." Blindly, she reached for a towel and pulled it in front of her.

"Whatever you say." He took a step back. "Come through to the living room when you're finished. I'll get the fire going and warm up something for us to eat."

Helena nodded and watched as he left the bathroom. She let go of the breath she'd been holding and swiftly shimmied out of her skirt and peeled off her clinging wet pantyhose and undies. She released her hair from the army of clips that bound it then gratefully stepped beneath the cascade of warmth thundering in the shower. Sheer bliss. She quickly lathered herself up and rinsed off. The stinging needles of the spray invigorated her and although her fingers and toes still felt cold she felt much better. Hungry though. She towelled off her wet skin, and arranged her damp clothes on the heated towel rail to dry, then picked through the mixed assortment of clothing Mason had dumped just inside the door while she'd been luxuriating in the hot water.

In amongst a couple of well-washed soft T-shirts and a pair of grey track pants her hand hesitated over a powder-blue merino wool sweater and a relatively new pair of woman's jeans. Was he sending her a message by including some other woman's forgotten clothing? Resolutely Helena selected a large faded sweatshirt and the track pants. There was no way she would wear another woman's castoffs—years of hand-me-downs from her parents' neighbours combined with the smart remarks from her classmates when she'd worn their old clothing to school had seen to that.

The sudden lance of jealousy that shafted her sideways at the thought of Mason with another woman came as an unpleasant surprise. It's not as if she had any say in his love life, she groaned inwardly, don't even think about it. She'd been a happily married woman herself for twelve years, so why did it suddenly bother her so much to think of another woman's clothing being left here?

With a determined push she shoved the blue sweater under the pile of remaining clothes and dragged on the pants and sweatshirt. The pants were far too large, but they were warm, and she wasn't beyond sacrificing a bit of dignity for warmth right now. She rolled over the waistband several times to try and pull them up a bit on her hips and turned up the legs. The sweatshirt hung almost to the top of her thighs. Well, she decided, looking in the large vanity mirror, she wouldn't win any fashion parades but then she wasn't here to impress anyone, was she. Lord, but her hair was a mess. She rummaged through the vanity drawers, searching for a comb or a brush. Her cheeks flamed as her hand brushed against an unopened twelve-pack of condoms.

"You okay in there?" Mason's voice at the door made her slam the drawer shut. Okay, she could go with the wild look for her hair for now.

Helena opened the bathroom door. "Yes, I'm fine. Thanks for the clothes."

He looked at what she was wearing and then the pile of clothes she'd dumped onto the vanity. If she wasn't mistaken the corners of his mouth lifted slightly for just a moment. She bit her teeth together to avoid verbalising the snaky comment that came unbidden from the jealousy that still twinged inside. He was letting her stay the night. There was no way she was going to do anything to jeopardise his reluctant goodwill.

"Come and eat then."

She followed him back down the hall to the sitting room where the aroma of warmed bread made her mouth water. Fire licked hungrily over split logs in the large stone fireplace and Helena bent to warm her fingers.

"Still cold?" Mason asked.

"Just a bit." Helena grimaced at the state of her fingernails and her hands. No sign now of the elegant manicure she'd had earlier in the week. But it was worth it to get this opportunity. If she hadn't already lugged so much of the tree from one place to another she probably would've hugged it for falling as it did and giving her the chance to stay longer.

"You'll feel better when you've had something to eat. Sit down."

When she was settled in the chair nearest the fire, Mason brought a tray with a bowl of a soup, filled with chunks of vegetables and meat, and several slices of warm French bread. They consumed their meal in silence. It was only as Helena placed her spoon back down in her now-empty bowl that he spoke.

"Thanks for your help outside."

"You're welcome. I don't like standing around while others do all the work."

Mason shot her a look of disbelief. Yeah, she knew what he was thinking. She was no better than a pampered poodle in his eyes. The truth couldn't have been further from his opinion. She knew all about the hard yards and what people had to do to make ends meet. Wealth and privilege hadn't always been tattooed on her forehead. And wasn't that what had put her in this situation in the first place?

Three

Helena held his gaze, defying him to contradict her statement. As their eyes locked in a silent duel, his pupils enlarged, the blackness all but consuming the darker brown iris. The only sound was that of the occasional hiss from the wood in the fireplace as flames consumed the logs and added to the heat escalating in the room. She could feel the throb of her pulse at her neck, and the answering beat from deep inside her. The beat that built in rhythm and send a curl of need to spiral outward from her core.

He hadn't spoken a word, yet in that look—no matter how much he abhorred her—she knew he still wanted her. And she wanted him back. Nothing had changed. The twelve years that lay between them yawned like a chasm—her marriage, their son. Each of them barriers to the desire that clawed with growing hunger and demanded to be assuaged. A log snapped in the fire-place, the sound giving her the impetus she needed to break the stare between them.

She gripped the sides of her tray and stood, making her way quickly to the kitchen. A small groan of discomfort escaped her as her muscles protested their sudden inactivity after the work she'd done outside.

"A bit too much action for you, Helena?"

To anyone else his enquiry would have sounded like no more than a tease, yet in the velvet stroke of his deep voice Helena could only hear contempt.

"Perhaps it's been a bit longer since you actually did 'the work' than you realised?" He deliberately baited her with her own words, twisting them to make her sound foolish.

"Perhaps you're right," she answered softly before moving over to the kitchen where she unloaded her tray and rinsed her dishes in the sink. "Being a good wife involves a different muscle group altogether."

The words had no sooner left her mouth before she regretted them. They were far too easily misconstrued, and in Mason's current frame of mind he would definitely have drawn the wrong impression. His next words only confirmed her fears.

"I can only imagine what you're referring to."

His voice came from right behind her, as steely and cold as a stiletto blade. Helena rotated her shoulders and took a deep breath. It wouldn't matter what she said right now, he wouldn't believe her. He was determined to think the worst.

"Not what you're thinking."

"Whatever you say, Helena. But then you have a habit of leaving out the important details, don't you.

Like being engaged to be married the day after you seduced a total stranger?"

"Mason—"

"Forget it. I don't want to trawl through the past. You made your bed, now you get to reap the consequences. I've been thinking about Brody. You say he's my son."

"He *is* your son."

"I want proof."

"I've shown you—"

"No." Mason crossed his arms in front of him. The black wool of his sweater stretched tight across his shoulders and over his upper arms. Her mouth dried at the latent power he projected, at the superbly sculpted masculine form that lay beneath the finely woven fabric. "Before I'll even consider another step, I want scientific proof."

"A paternity test?"

"Yes."

"And then you'll help us?" She clenched her fingers into fists, her broken nails pressing jagged lines into the palms of her hands. He had to agree.

"If you're telling the truth I'll look into what I can do."

"How soon can we get it done? Where?"

"That's what you'll have to find out when you get back to Auckland, won't you. And quickly, Helena. This had better not drag out any longer than absolutely necessary."

"I'll do whatever I have to, to prove it, Mason. You can count on it."

"Why doesn't that surprise me?" He arched a cynical dark brow and leaned forward, trapping her against the kitchen bench with one hand locked on either side of her hips. "Just get one thing straight in your mind. If I am Brody's father, that doesn't mean I agree to support *you* in any way. Not a cent. Do you understand me?"

Helena sucked in a breath, her nostrils flaring as she inhaled the scent of his woody cologne. To her shame she felt her breasts swell and lift, her nipples tighten and press seekingly against the cotton of her borrowed sweatshirt. Desire pooled low in her belly. "I don't need or want your money, but Brody needs a future. I'll do whatever it takes to satisfy your demands if it means my son's security. Whatever. Do *you* understand *me?*"

"Oh yeah, you're coming through loud and clear." He leaned a little closer. So close she could see the tiny rings of gold around the pupils of his eyes. "Maybe we should start that satisfaction right now."

"Wha—?"

He closed the distance between them. Every nerve in her body fired into attention and Helena felt the air shift as he brought his face to hers. She had a fleeting impression of darkness and heat before his lips were on hard on hers, consuming the startled cry that fled her mouth. She squeezed her eyes closed. She didn't want to think anymore. She didn't want to feel. But despite her wants, her body took on a life of its own, greeting Mason's plunder of her lips with a liquid heat that melted every last bastion of reserve.

His mouth pulled at hers, tasting, sucking, caressing her lips until they were sensitive and swollen. Suddenly she was kissing him back with a hunger she'd thought she'd never experience again. Mason's tongue probed between her lips, invading, taking possession. She met him on his own terms, deepening the kiss, permitting his invasion.

She was lost and helpless against the capacity of emotion that swelled within her. The rational part of her mind ratified his need to dominate her with the power of his passion, but as a tiny moan of desire rose from her throat, Helena admitted she had never wanted a man as much she wanted Mason Knight. She'd suppressed that need, had wrapped herself up in her husband and her son with an intensity that belied her behaviour during that one night she'd spent with Mason. Yet deep inside lurked a craving that hadn't diminished one bit in the past twelve years.

She knew what he thought of her, even understood it in a way. He would hate it that he betrayed his own desire for her in the tiny tremors that rocked his body, in the weight of the insistent erection that pressed against her. Helena lifted her hands with every good intention of shoving him from her, but instead her fingers assumed a life of their own as they dug into his shoulders, relishing the leashed strength of him.

Mason's lips broke away from hers. His breathing came in harshly drawn gasps as he rested his forehead against hers. His eyes were shut, and another shudder rippled through his body. Then, slowly, he pulled back and opened his eyes.

"You're a little rusty," he said in a voice that grated against her ears in scorn. "But it's a start."

A start? She stood, locked in shocked silence as he walked away. In the distance, down the hall, she heard a door swing open then click firmly shut. Then, nothing. Her mind whirled. Was he serious? Did he expect her to become his mistress? When she'd talked about his demands she'd meant for information and for proof of Brody's paternity—but not this, never this. She lifted a shaking hand to her face, her fingers pressing against her swollen lips. She could still feel him there; feel the impression of his body where he'd pressed against hers.

"No," she whispered. "Not again."

Pushing all thoughts of Mason Knight to the back of her mind, Helena automatically went through the motions of clearing up the kitchen and stacking the dishwasher. A minimum of investigation showed her where to store the trays and before long the kitchen was returned to its earlier pristine state. Unfortunately she couldn't say the same for her state of mind. No matter how hard she tried she couldn't get that kiss out of her head. She needed to talk this out with Mason, sort out what his expectations were and make her position quite clear. She'd be no man's plaything. She'd seen and heard more than enough in the past to know she'd rather walk over hot coals than debase herself like that again.

Her mind made up, she stalked down the hallway. Which room was his? A bar of light shone from beneath one of the doors and before she could change her mind Helena rapped sharply on the door and reached to twist the handle.

Mason heard her knock and schooled himself not to spin around at the sound of the door being opened. So, she'd come to him. Somehow, that didn't surprise him. He focussed on the dark vista across the bay, silvered by rain and moonlight, and drew in a deep breath before he turned to face her. A slew of emotions flitted across Helena's face. First, something akin to anger and determination, but it was closely followed by a hesitance that assured him—despite how his body had flamed to life only minutes ago, and still smouldered—he continued to hold the upper hand.

"What did you mean by that comment?" While the words were a demand, he observed, the delivery was sadly lacking. A telltale tremor in her voice confirmed she was still shaken by their kiss. As shaken as he was himself, no doubt, although there was no way she'd ever know that.

"Comment?"

"Don't play word games with me, Mason. You know what I'm talking about." She stared at a spot just to the side of his face, clearly unwilling to make eye contact.

"Why don't you tell me what's bothering you, Helena?" He swiftly crossed the room, coming to a halt to stand directly in front of her and forcing her to look up to meet him eye to eye.

"What you said—a start. A start to what?"

His mouth quirked at one corner. The million-dollar question. He lifted a hand and reached for a long tendril of her hair, rubbing its silky texture between his fingers, taking his time over his response.

"Well now, that all depends on you, Helena. As I recall we were discussing demands and satisfaction. Your demands. My satisfaction."

"Brody's your son. I shouldn't have to make any demands on you."

Mason let go the piece of hair and let his finger drop to the exposed prominence of her collarbone where the neckline of his sweatshirt dipped against her skin. She felt like satin, cool smooth luxurious satin, and held herself rigid as if his touch had frozen her in place. But beneath the fabric he could see what effect he had on her and he could hear the catch in her breathing as he traced a line to the top of her shoulder and round to the nape of her neck.

"Let's not discuss Brody just now. Not until I have the information I require." He slid his hand behind her neck, cupping it with his palm. "I'm curious about what you're prepared to do, Helena. What, exactly, you define as 'whatever it takes.'"

He lifted his other hand to cup her jaw and tilted her head gently upward toward his. His voice dropped an octave. "This, perhaps?"

He bent his head to capture her mouth with his again, to stroke his tongue against the seam of her lips, to draw the full swollen flesh of her lower lip into his mouth and plunder beyond it with a possessive sweep.

"Or maybe this?" He skimmed his hand from the back of her neck down her spine to press her lower body forward, into his, against the aching arousal that demanded to be assuaged.

"No," she whispered against his mouth.

"Be honest with me, Helena. Be honest with yourself." He kissed her again, holding her to him, feeling the taut resistance of her body as he tasted and suckled at her lips and exulting in the moment she surrendered her will to his own—when her body moulded against his as if she'd been carved from his very flesh.

He let go of her jaw and slipped his hand up underneath the waistband of her top to trace his fingers against the texture of her skin, slowly working the material away from her body until his fingers could splay across the warm globe of her breast. He plucked gently at the hardened nub of her nipple, playing the tender flesh until she sagged against his body and groaned deep in her throat.

Barely taking a second to release her lips, he swept the sweatshirt up and over her body. Both his hands spanned her tiny waist and skimmed over her rib cage, his thumbs trailing twin lines under the swell of her breasts.

He watched her face as he touched her; saw the glitter of desire in her eyes before they slid closed. Her parted lips were moist and swollen, an open invitation. He

should stop now. He should be repulsed by her eager-
ness to welcome his touch, his body. Instead, his arousal
escalated another notch. He felt her reach for the waistband of her pants, saw as she gripped the fabric with
fisted hands then pushed until the sweats fell in a pool
at her feet. Total surrender. Total capitulation. She was
his to do with as he wished.

Mason swept her small frame up in his arms and
placed her gently against the covers on his bed. As he
settled over her body he bent to kiss her lips, her cheeks,
her eyelids. Helena's arms wrapped around his shoulders, the fingers of one hand splayed against the back
of his neck, encouraging him to hasten. To take her lips,
to take her body.

But he would not be hurried. Every part of her face,
her jaw, her throat, fell victim to the relentless, but painfully tentative, attention he paid her. Attention he'd
dreamed of more nights that he could count. Attention
that had wound him in knots of frustration for more
years than he wanted to remember. He trailed his lips
and tongue down her throat, stopping only to nip gently
at the edge of her neck. The gasp of pleasure that
escaped her spurred him on his path and he bent his head
to capture one tightly budded nipple between his lips.
His tongue swirled with delicious intent around the
hardened peak, drawing it into his mouth and suckling
with a steady rhythmic pull. She squirmed against him,
silently urging him to press his body harder against hers.

He wore too many clothes. Mason lifted himself and
managed to divest himself of his shirt and unbuckle his
jeans. He clenched his teeth against the roaring torrent
of desire that threatened to swamp him as his body
finally settled, skin against skin—as her breasts flat-

tened against the hard planes of his chest. Protection, damn, he needed protection. He dragged himself away from her welcoming body to reach in the bedside cabinet drawer. If he didn't take care of things now it would be too late. Sheathing himself took only a moment but even then the time away from her heat was an eon.

Helena lifted a trembling hand to stroke his face, tracing the outline of his cheekbones, his jaw, committing every touch, every texture to memory. She shouldn't be doing this, but she wanted him with a fiery need she barely recognised in herself. She trailed her fingers over his lips before letting her hand drop to her breast where she repeated the caress across her aching nipples. His pupils dilated at her action, his chest shuddered with uneven breaths. She cupped her breasts with both hands—offering herself to him. Her skin, so sensitive now, it begged for him to touch her again. His eyes blazed over her, watching as she arched her body along the sheets. A primitive beat pounded through her veins, heightening her senses and her awareness of the man who watched her every move with the intentness of a panther stalking its prey. A piercing shaft of anticipation arrowed through her as he covered her body, length for length, driving a small whimper of sheer need to shudder from her lips.

Mason caught her face between his hands—forcing her to meet his gaze, defying her to break the contact. He slid inside her—slowly, completely—filling her with a sense of belonging that both terrified and soothed her. She drew him deeper inside, and took the groan wrenched from his very core as her reward.

He began to move, first slowly then in increasing tempo, fuelling the delicious tension that escalated within her. A fine sheen of perspiration broke out on her skin and her heartbeat accelerated, matching the cadence of their movements. Still, he held her with his eyes—still, she remained trapped. Drawn inexorably to him as if her existence depended on their ephemeral link. Helena gave herself over to the sheer volume of feeling that ebbed and flowed within and around her. Her sight began to glaze, her eyelids to flutter and a deep-throated sigh expelled past her lips as her climax approached. When Mason's hands let her go, she tilted her head back and lifted her hips to take him in as deeply as she could bear. Except suddenly her body was bereft of his heat, empty of his possession.

"No!" she cried. "Not now, please, don't stop now." Helena struggled to push herself up onto her elbows as Mason pulled away from her and got up from the bed.

"What's wrong?" Her voice, thick with desire, hung in the air between them as he watched her impassively. She fought to control her rapid breathing. A shiver rippled over her as the air caressed her flushed skin. Under his cool scrutiny Helena felt reduced to little more than a butterfly on a pin. Something bad had happened, something she didn't understand, and now she desperately wished she could cover her aching naked body from the emptiness in his gaze.

"There's nothing wrong." His answer was delivered at subzero temperature.

"Then why? Why did you stop?"

Mason bent to gather his clothing and yanked his jeans up his long legs and over his hips. "Because I can." He collected the sweatshirt and pants she'd worn earlier and tossed them onto the bed. The inference in his action was clear. Get dressed and get the hell out of his room. "And because now I know how far you're prepared to go."

Helena scrambled to cover her vulnerability, her skin still sensitised to his touch, her body still craving the release he'd denied them both. On trembling legs she sped across the carpet and through the door, the click of the latch behind her almost inaudible against the echo of her fractured breath as the reality drew home with terminal velocity.

Because I can. The words echoed hollowly inside her mind. In three words he'd reduced her to nothing but some *thing* to be enjoyed at his convenience. She'd allowed herself to be degraded to nothing more than what she was essentially fighting so hard to forget. It was as if she'd learned nothing in the past twelve years. Anger lanced through her body, followed swiftly by burning pain that billowed from deep within her chest. Helena pushed a fist against her mouth to hold back the scream that built inside, because she was suddenly frightened that if she let the sound go she'd never be able to stop.

In his bathroom Mason dispensed with the redundant condom—balling it up in tissue and flinging into the wastebasket with a guttural curse. He didn't know what he hated more at this moment—the fact that he'd made love to Helena, or the fact she'd let him. Made love, ha! He'd succumbed to a primal urge, nothing else—and if he kept telling himself that for long enough, he'd even begin to believe it.

He stepped into the shower stall, switched the water to as hot as he could stand and, resting his forehead against the wall, let the water pound against his shoulders.

He'd said no. It had seemed so important at the time

to be able to walk away—to resist her. To be in control. The victory should be pulsing through him, yet all he could feel was the acrid taste of failure compounded by intense clawing need. The compulsion to stamp himself on her body, her psyche, tormented him. Urged him to wipe away every memory she held of every other man— and there had been plenty of them, he was certain.

She'd responded to him so immediately, so intensely. A piece of him wanted to believe that her response had been for him, and him alone, but he knew her type too well. The painfully familiar nausea swelled inside him as he remembered the careful yet inappropriate brush of a hand, the kiss that lingered a little too long on his cheek and then later, in his room one night, the blatant offer from his father's much younger mistress. Yeah, he knew the type all right, and now he knew just how to handle her.

It helped that he had something over her—she needed his help. And then there was Brody. If the boy was his son he'd be doing him a complete favour to remove him from her influence, from the steady stream of men through the revolving door of her bedroom. No wonder she had Brody away at boarding school down country, she didn't have to be accountable for her behaviour this way. But not for much longer if the paternity test results validated her claim. Things were going to change.

Mason reached for the shower mixer and twisted it one-eighty degrees before lifting his face to the stream of water. He flinched as the spray flung cold needles at his body, almost to the point of pain, then snapped off the mixer when his blood had finally cooled to what approximated normality. It was a shame the same couldn't be said for his flesh. Damn her for having this effect on him, and damn him for letting her.

Four

Dawn slanted thick, pink streaks, laden with the threat of rain, across the sky, its light like a probe across her face. Even at her lowest, when she'd done things that had shamed her dreadfully, she hadn't felt this used.

Because I can.

Did he think he was so superior to her, so much stronger that he could use her and then just walk away? Of course he could. He held all the cards in this particular hand and he knew it.

Helena dragged herself from the twisted bed sheets and padded into the bathroom. God, she looked a wreck. She'd ended up going to bed in the tracksuit. Suddenly she couldn't bear to wear it a moment longer. She needed the reminder of his touch against her skin about as much as she needed a garden party right now. She slid out of the clothes—Mason's clothes—and kicked them across the floor. If only getting out of this situation were equally as easy. She plucked her underpants off the heated towel rail and pulled them on, swiftly followed by her camisole and skirt. The waistband of the skirt still felt damp and clammy to her skin, but at least she was wearing her own clothes.

Her clothes. Her decisions.

One way or another she'd deal with her problems, even if it included dealing with Evan. It had been Patrick's wish that she disclose the truth about Brody's parentage to Mason. She'd followed that wish to the letter. Now the ball was in Mason's court. She certainly wasn't going to stick around here and be a victim of his dictates any longer. The sooner she was gone, the sooner she could begin to garner the strength she needed for what she knew would be an arduous battle ahead.

Helena gathered up her handbag and let herself quietly out of the bedroom. The house was silent and still. Too still. She sucked in a deep breath, letting it out slowly to calm her sudden nerves then resolutely made her way down the passage. It wasn't until she'd picked up the cordless phone in the sitting room that she remembered the line was dead. How on earth would she get a taxi now?

There was nothing else for it but to walk down to the main road and hope she could get a ride with some passerby. However, at the front door Helena was stymied once again. Obviously Mason had brought his city habits here to the Coromandel. The front door was locked and a quick reconnoitre of the entranceway proved futile in the search for a key to let herself out the house.

The garage. What about the garage? The automatic garage door opener would have a wall-mounted control as well. She let herself into the garage and carefully closed the door behind her. Only a small amount of light filtered through the high windows in the wooden automatic doors and it took her a while for her eyes to adjust to the gloom in the garage.

The bank of switches by the door had been labelled by some organised soul. Mason, she didn't doubt. She knew he'd done a stint in the army. The way he kept things rigidly organised here at the house was no doubt a follow-on effect to his military training. Helena swiftly identified the switches that operated the garage door and the gate at the bottom of the private road. Her hand hovered over the switches hesitating briefly before depressing them. The garage door slowly opened.

It would be so much easier if she could simply drive out of here. Her stomach lurched uncomfortably as her eyes tracked across the garage to Mason's four-by-four. The beast was way bigger than the small sedan she'd lost to the river twelve years ago. Could she do it? Could she drive again?

She walked across the tiled garage floor and pulled open the driver's door, swinging up into the seat before she could think twice about it. Her hands shook as she laid them on the steering wheel. Fear washed over her in a sickening wave and Helena closed her eyes in a vain attempt to force down the choking nausea that pitched through her.

"You'll need these."

Mason's voice from just outside the open vehicle made her jump. From his fingers dangled a set of car keys. He was dressed all in black again today, the solid darkness lending a lethal edge to his appearance.

"I wasn't..." Her voice trailed off. She had no idea what she was thinking.

"Sure you weren't." He leaned across and inserted one of the silver keys into the ignition. "There you go."

He stood back and crossed his arms, silent challenge visible in his stance and the fierce expression in his eyes. She couldn't move. Couldn't bring herself to turn that key.

"What's stopping you, Helena?"

"I can't...I can't drive anymore." Her voice shook almost as much as her hands, and her stomach twisted.

"You used to."

"That was different. It was a long time ago."

"It's going to be difficult to run away from me if you don't."

She swivelled her head to face him. "I'm not running away. Not from you."

"Of course you're not. So go on. Do it."

There was a thread of steel to his voice, an underlying fury that both frightened and galvanised her into action. Helena reached forward and turned the key, bringing the four-by-four to sudden rumbling life.

"Still remember what comes next?"

Helena flung him a withering look. "Sure I do." She pulled the driver's door closed with a hollow *thunk* and selected Reverse to put the vehicle in motion. Her hands felt clammy on the wheel and her stomach was doing the kind of acrobatics that more appropriately belonged in a Cirque du Soleil performance. She backed out of the garage, spinning the wheel to turn in the parking bay so she could head off in the right direction down the drive. A quick glance in the rearview mirror confirmed Mason still stood in the garage, his arms crossed in front of him, his feet planted firmly on the ground.

She *could* do this. If only to show him.

Helena slipped the transmission into drive and held

her breath as the vehicle jerked forward. Another glance in the rearview mirror showed Mason hadn't moved an inch. She hooked up her seat belt then planted her foot firmly on the accelerator.

The truck fishtailed slightly as she took the sharp corner that turned from the driveway onto the private road that lead down to the main route back to civilization. Helena kept the momentum up, braking gently before she reached a blind bend in the road. Something wasn't right. A sea of mud, littered with small trees and debris, encroached on the unsealed surface. There was no way she could drive through all of that at this speed. She stomped on the brake and pulled the steering wheel sharply to the left.

She knew the exact moment the vehicle lost its grip on the loose metal road and, without losing momentum, felt the precise point at which the front edge of the bull bars connected with the bank, spinning her around, until with a muffled metallic wallop, the entire right side connected with the hard wall of earth that lined the road. The truck groaned as it settled back on its four wheels, rocking slightly in the process. The passenger door flung open.

"Are you okay?" Breathless, Mason climbed in and ran his hands over her chest and shoulders, frantically checking her for injuries.

"I... I don't think I'm hurt," Helena managed in a shaky voice as tremors shuddered through her.

"It's my fault. I shouldn't have pushed you."

"No. It's me. I chose to do it. I should've known better. I shouldn't have let you goad me into it." Helena felt her eyes flood with tears, felt the hot liquid spill over her lashes and track down her cheeks.

Strong arms wrapped around her shoulders and pulled her into the warm haven of Mason's body.

"Are you sure you're okay?" His broad hands cradled her head and gently ran through her hair, testing her scalp for any tenderness. He tilted her face toward his. "When I heard the crash I…" Mason shook his head, as if to dislodge the sharp lines of concern etched into his pale face. His thumbs reached up and brushed away the tears that rolled down her face.

"Don't cry, babe." His voice was strange, tight.

Helena felt the air shift between them as he brought his face to hers. His lips, when they touched, were hot, consuming. She softened against him, squeezing her eyes closed against the stark need she saw reflected in his gaze. She didn't want to think anymore. She didn't want to feel. But despite her wants, her body took on a life of its own, greeting Mason's possession of her lips with an answering flare of heat that melted every nerve ending. His mouth slanted across hers and she welcomed the power in his kiss. Tremors rocked his body like tiny after-shocks.

She wondered fleetingly if perhaps they were not all triggered by desire, but out of relief she hadn't been hurt—that somewhere inside he actually cared that she was okay. But as a tiny moan of desire rose from her throat, Helena knew she'd never be okay again. Not as long as she remained in Mason's arms. Not as long as she allowed him to feed the fire of her need for him— a need she'd denied for the last twelve years. A need ignited by a chance encounter a lifetime ago. She thought she'd learned to live without it, without wanting him. It hadn't been easy, but she'd made her choice and stood by it.

Mason lifted his head, resting his forehead briefly against hers before letting her go from his embrace. Without another word, he got out of the vehicle and stalked around to the front of the four-by-four. Helena watched in silence as anger, then resignation, flew across his face at the sight of the damage to the side of the truck.

"Pop the hood," he called in a clipped tone.

With a trembling hand Helena reached under the dash to find the necessary lever. She sighed in relief when she found the right one and the hood was raised as a visual barrier between them. She touched her fingers to her lips. Lord help her, would the wanting never go away?

Mason slammed the hood down with a heavy thud. He shouldn't have done it. He shouldn't have goaded her into driving when she was obviously not ready for it. By the same token, he knew she shouldn't have attempted to drive, especially something as powerful as what his brothers teasingly referred to as "the Black Beast." He could shake her for taking such a risk.

His gut clenched when he thought again of how badly she could have been hurt. The visual image that had imprinted across his mind when he'd heard the impact, of Helena's broken and bleeding body trapped in his wrecked truck, flared vividly. He shook his head and blinked hard to dismiss the all too graphic picture and took a deep breath. For reasons he didn't want to dissect, the thought of Helena coming to harm had frightened him so much that he'd flown down the drive like a 200-metre sprint champion. The relief that she'd been okay had been sharp, coming from deep inside.

He welcomed the anger that now followed— embraced it, as it gave him the opportunity not to examine his feelings too closely. Instead, it allowed him to focus on the physical damage to his truck and brought him some much needed composure. He was familiar with the cold tang of fury on his tongue when he thought of Helena. It was quantifiable. Justified. Worrying about her was not. Satisfied he'd reassumed control, he leaned back in through the passenger door.

"Hop out. I'll see if we can get the truck back to the house. I need to check if it can still make the trip back to Auckland." Mason extended a hand to help Helena climb across the front seats. He gritted his teeth when she rejected his overture of assistance. Fine, she wanted to manage without his help, so be it. Let's just see how long that would last.

He stood aside while Helena clambered gingerly over the seats. She was still as white as a ghost; her green eyes bright as emeralds in her pale face. His hands itched to draw her to him, to reassure himself once more that she was okay, but he suppressed the urge, focusing instead on the desire to give her a good shaking, which hadn't completely deserted him.

Nor had the desire to kiss her again. He was going to have to either get that out of his system soon, or learn to come to terms with it. And if the past was any indicator, he wasn't going to come to terms with it soon. He had to remind himself sharply of the reason why she'd invaded his haven.

Cursing under his breath, Mason climbed into the cab and settled behind the steering wheel. He turned the key in the ignition and heaved a massive sigh of relief when the engine turned over the first time. He eased the truck into gear and slowly drove forward, pulling away from the bank as he did so.

The scraping sounds against the side of his once highly polished paintwork was enough to bring tears to a grown man's eyes. Away from the bank, Mason slipped the truck into neutral and, leaving it idling, shoved and pushed against the driver's door until it could open enough for him to get out.

"Ah, hell." Mason shook his head again. Bare metal, crumpled and scratched panels. She'd made a fine mess. One of the wheel guards had buckled in and rubbed against the tyre. Knowing he needed to do something physical to relieve his suppressed anger and frustration— before it reached volcanic proportions—he burned up excess energy dragging the reluctant metal away from the rubber. The physical damage done to the truck could be repaired, but it wasn't going to be as easy to ignore the fire that still licked heatedly through his veins.

"Get in."

She flinched at his sharply bitten command, but at this precise moment he wasn't concerned with her mental fragility. The steam coming out from under the hood was beginning to tell its own story. The four-by-four would never make the trip back to Auckland and there was no way he was spending another night with her under his roof. He'd have to arrange alternative transport, and quickly.

Once she was settled he coaxed the vehicle back up the road and parked it in the garage.

"I need to climb up the hill, see if I can get a cell phone signal so I can make some calls. Why don't you make us some coffee." He gestured toward the kitchen, and was relieved when she gave a small nod.

Some time later, the aroma of freshly-brewed coffee tantalised his nostrils as he walked back to the sitting room. As he entered, Helena poured a mug of coffee and handed it to him.

"I'm sorry for what I did to the truck." She shook her head, not meeting his eyes. "After last night, I…"

A pang of remorse prodded Mason's conscience but it was short-lived. She'd come here without his permission. He couldn't afford any sympathy for a woman who'd barter her child—potentially *his* child—to preserve her lifestyle. What was it she'd said again? Oh yeah, *I'll do whatever it takes to satisfy your demands.* Last night had shown him just how far she was prepared to go. A curl of tension started low in his belly. No matter how hard he tried he could not remain immune to her. It was something he was going to have to handle. Last night had only whetted his appetite for more. Leaving her, as he'd done, had drawn its own satisfaction—and its own torment.

"Forget last night. The helicopter will be at the pad soon. Drink your coffee."

In confirmation of his words, the distant beat of rotor blades in the air approached the house.

"Helicopter?"

"It's the quickest way to get back to Auckland. Do you have a problem with that?" He downed his coffee in one quick gulp.

"No. No problem."

"Good. The sooner we get back the sooner you can find out when we can get the paternity test done."

"How am I going to do that without Brody finding out what it's for? I've been thinking about it and I don't want him to know that Patrick wasn't his father. He's been through enough already."

Mason bit back the retort that sprang to mind.

Typical. She wanted it all—his help with Brody and with Davies Freight, but no acknowledgement if her paternity claim proved to be correct. Why didn't that surprise him?

"We'll cross that bridge when the results come in. With respect to the testing, I'm sure you can use your imagination to find something that won't rouse his suspicions."

"He's a clever boy, Mason. He'll ask questions."

"Then you'll just have to be one step ahead, won't you. Get this clear in your head, Helena. Without proof, I'm not lifting a finger to help you. With that incentive you're bound to come up with something."

Five

The sound of the chopper overhead put an end to any further desire to battle the situation out with her.

"Come on." Mason led the way out of the house, snatching up his briefcase in the front entrance on the way. Beside the garage a path was cut in the bank, leading up to where a sleek black chopper, emblazoned with Black Knight Transport in gold along the side, had settled on the designated landing pad.

The pilot stepped down from the craft, opening the side door to usher Helena into a luxurious passenger compartment before ducking around the back to climb in on the other side of the cockpit. Mason secured his briefcase then settled himself in the pilot's seat.

Helena sat in the back, alone and feeling like a pariah. The journey back to Auckland could only have taken about thirty minutes, but it felt like forever, seated as she

was in splendid isolation. By the time the chopper set
down at Ardmore Airfield her stomach had tied in knots.
Mason opened the door to help her alight but, as before,
she refused his assistance. It was all very well that he exhibited such gentlemanly manners, but it was more than
she could bear to let her fingers linger in his hand—to
feel the hard, dry warmth of his fingers and not remember
how they'd felt as they'd driven the wild response from
her body last night. How he'd rejected her.

"Thank you," she managed through stiff lips. "I'll
call a cab to get home from here."

"A cab? I don't think so. I'll see you get home."

"A cab was good enough for me last night," she
reminded him tartly.

"I didn't believe I had a potential vested interest in
you then. Like I said, I'll see you home."

She bristled at his overbearing response but ac-
quiesced silently. What else could she do? She was
between a rock and a hard place, either at his mercy or
Evan's. She didn't know which was worse.

A shiny black late-model Porsche stood parked next
to a hangar, a tall, slim young man standing by it. Mason
walked toward it, lifting his hand to catch the keys the
younger man threw to him with a smile and a word of
thanks. When he noticed she hadn't followed, he
stopped and turned. The look in his eyes left her with
no doubt that if he had to pick her up and insert her body
into the vehicle he'd do it. With a tiny sigh she covered
the distance between them, hoping against hope that the
car could make the journey to her home in as short a
time as its smooth lines suggested. The sooner this
weekend came to an end, the better.

* * *

"What do you want me for, Knight?" Evan Davies stumbled a little as he rose from the chaise longue situated in the hotel lobby where Mason had asked to meet him. "It's Sunday night. I've got better things to do than discuss business with you." His words slurred slightly.

The strong smell of alcohol hit Mason square in the nose, but he bit his tongue. Evan's dissolute features aged him beyond his years. His excessive playboy lifestyle had caught up to him with a vengeance. It was hard to believe they were both the same age.

"I think you'll like what I have to say. Come upstairs. I've reserved a suite for our discussion."

Once in the plush suite, Evan went straight for the whiskey decanter on the sideboard in the main sitting room, pouring a generous serving before sinking into one of the large leather-covered sofas angled to appreciate the sumptuous harbour view.

"So spit it out. I haven't got all night."

"I want to make you an offer for your shares in Davies Freight."

Evan's short bark of laughter cut through the air. "You're kidding me, right? Black Knight Transport wants to merge with Davies Freight? It's a money soak hole. Why the hell would you want to buy it? Your distribution contracts outearn anything Davies Freight could bring you."

The information Mason had gleaned today had proven that the situation with Davies Freight was far worse than he'd imagined. The company was bleeding funds—badly. He had his suspicions about who was responsible. "I have my reasons." Mason remained standing, his fists pushed deep into his trouser pockets.

"One of those reasons wouldn't be about five foot four with come-to-bed green eyes and sexy chestnut hair, would it?" Evan's watery blue eyes narrowed speculatively. "You know she controls Brody's share of the company. Whatever you've got in mind, she's going to have to agree, too. I've tried to get that share off her already. She's not in a cooperative mood. Even telling her that it was our last chance to make some money off of dear old Dad's failing business wasn't enough to get her to sell. What makes you think you'll change her mind?"

"She'll agree." Mason's response was clipped.

Evan got up and refilled his glass, taking a big swig before tilting his head and eyeing Mason carefully. "You sound pretty sure of yourself. I wondered when she'd move on to her next conquest, especially when I disagreed with her about keeping Davies Freight going. Making the widow merry, are we?"

Mason fought the need to bite back at the other man's snide remark—to wipe the self-indulgent *knowing* expression off Evan's face. "What were you thinking of, Evan, offering to buy her out? You know the company is going to the wall anyway."

An expression of sheer hatred crossed the other man's features. "You want to know why? I'll bloody tell you. There's no way her whiney little brat is entitled to what should have been all mine. I want to sell the whole lot, but the stupid bitch won't let go of her baby's entitlement. I had a buyer lined up and everything. Of course he's gone cold on the idea now—he's not interested in half shares."

"I am. State your price."

Evan almost dropped his drink. He bent to put the glass down heavily on the coffee table in front of him.

"You want her that much?" he whistled long and low. "I'm impressed. She's good, but not *that* good, if you know what I mean." He winked and reached for his glass again.

Mason was a step ahead of him and moved the glass across the table, out of reach. "How much?" he demanded.

Evan sat back and announced a figure that would have had Mason laughing for weeks if he wasn't so firmly set on his path. "Done."

"Done? Just like that?"

"Just like that." Mason flipped open his cell phone and made a call. "Yeah, bring the contract up now. He agreed."

Before he'd even hung up Evan's sick laugh filled the room. "Boy, you really have it bad for her, don't you? What's she promised you, hmm? Extras? You know her type gets a lot more for extras. It's how she met dear old Dad, don't you know? Yep, there's a lot more to our darling Helena than meets the eye."

"What the hell are you talking about? They met in Wellington on a business trip."

"Is that what he told you? Yeah, sure. It figures." Evan smiled nastily. "She was an escort. You know the type—the higher you pay 'em, the lower they're prepared to go. Then again, maybe you don't. You've never had to buy the company of a willing woman, have you? Ha! Looks like you have now. I hope she's worth it, but from what I've experienced, I doubt it."

Evan's words fell like acid rain against Mason's skin. He was hard-pressed not to drive his clenched fist into the man's smug features. *An escort.* Suddenly her behaviour all began to make sense. How she'd seduced him that night in the truck. How she'd played the reluctant card on Friday night, yet still found her way into his bed. All along she'd played him with the oldest game in history.

A metallic taste filled his mouth and he realised he was biting the inside of his cheek. Damn her and all women like her. He wasn't falling for that again. Oh, he was sure they'd end up in bed again. There was a magnetic pull from deep inside his gut that drew him to her—no point in denying it. But there was one thing he was certain of—when it did happen it would be totally on his terms. Every step of the way.

The doorbell to the suite rang and Mason crossed over to open the door. His younger brother, Connor, head of the corporate law office for Knight Enterprises—their father's company—and the family's lawyer, stood with a briefcase in his hand, worry clear in his eyes.

"Are you sure about this, Mase? The figures don't look good. It's not a strong move for BKT."

"I know. I have my reasons. C'mon, let's get this over with."

Once the legal necessities were taken care of, Connor left and Mason turned to face Evan.

"Don't ever set foot near Davies Freight or Helena again. Do you understand?"

"Hey, you bought the company, not the dame. She's open to offers."

Mason stepped up to Evan, grabbed his shirt front in his fist, twisting it and drawing his clenched hand up under Evan's chin. He took great care to enunciate each word very clearly so there was no way Evan wouldn't get the message. "Stay away from Helena."

Beads of sweat broke out on Evan's pasty forehead. "Sure, mate. Whatever you say. I've about had enough of her anyway." He stumbled backward and fell onto the sofa as Mason released him.

Mason reached into his pocket and spun the room's key-card through the air. It landed against Evan's paunch. "Keep the suite for the night. It's all paid up. Anything else on the tab is your expense. Don't spend all your money at once."

He turned and stalked to the door. He wasn't spending another second in the same air space as this scumbag. He couldn't wait to be shot of the other guy, couldn't wait to wash the whole experience off his skin and out of his mind. If only getting Helena out of his system would be as easy. The satisfaction that he was now one step ahead of Helena's grasping greed should be overwhelming right now, yet still it remained beyond his reach. Instead, the sour tang of disappointment left a bad taste on his tongue.

By nine o'clock Monday morning Helena had the information she needed to set the paternity testing in motion. She'd spent time on the weekend searching the net and had been relieved to locate New Zealand's sole diagnostic lab for that area of work in Auckland. Armed with the data she took a taxi to work and, on her mental list of jobs for the day, made calling Mason her first priority. She was so preoccupied with her findings she didn't notice the buzz of activity at the ground-floor reception which coordinated the vast freight forwarding enterprise that made up Davies Freight; she missed the slightly frantic wave from Mandy, her receptionist. She flew up the stairs to the next floor, determined to tackle what stood firmly in her mind as her least favourite task to deal with today.

She noted with relief that Patrick's office door was closed as she made her way to her office. Evan must be inside, but the fact he had the door shut meant she needn't face his demands or his filthy double entendres right now—thank goodness. She slipped out of her jacket and hooked it onto the coat hanger behind her office door and sank down into her desk chair, finding comfort in the organised chaos that reigned across her desk and every available surface. Here was where she felt most alive. Most useful.

The business management degree she'd attained through part-time studies after Brody had been born was, next to her son, the thing in her life of which she was most proud. Patrick had insisted she continue with her studies when they'd married, giving her coaching and tips with her assignment work that had seen her graduate in the top ten percent of her class. Attaining her qualification had made everything worthwhile—even what she'd done to survive that awful year when she'd discovered her parents had mortgaged their home to put her through varsity. That in itself wouldn't have been so bad but when her dad lost his job teaching at the small country school where they'd lived due to a Ministry of Education downsizing, she'd been frantic to make the money back for them.

They'd sacrificed their retirement dream to see her enrolled into University without the hassle and financial pressure of a student loan, but the responsibility had lain heavily on her shoulders. When a friend had suggested she sign up at a modelling and escort agency to earn a few dollars, the idea had been a godsend. The money was good and she only worked when she could fit it in around her lectures and exams. Besides, it wasn't as if it was in any way taxing—she'd been no more than a pretty, conversational arm adornment for out-of-town businessmen. Until that last time, when her client decided to breach the terms of his contract with the agency and wouldn't take no for an answer. It had been that one final unpleasant incident that had blessedly led her to Patrick, who'd been staying at the same hotel where her client had made the ugly scene.

Patrick's calm command of the situation had despatched the other man in no uncertain terms and she'd spent the rest of the evening in his company, letting him coax her story from her and accepting his assurance that everything would work out okay.

Tears pricked at her eyes and she reached for the silver-framed family portrait, taken only weeks before his heart attack. He'd kept it in the library at home, the room which had doubled as his office. Since he'd passed away, she'd kept it here on her desk. It made her feel as though he was still there for her somehow. She reached out a finger to trace his features. She had so much to be grateful to Patrick for, and now she'd never be able to let him know.

Lost in her memories, the buzz of her phone startled her.

"Yes, Mandy?"

"Sorry to disturb you, Mrs. Davies, but you're wanted in Mr. Davies' office."

"Thank you, Mandy. Let Evan know I'll be right along."

Helena fought to quell the rising dread in her stomach. Dealing with Evan always made her feel ill. His dislike of her had been cunningly veiled during her marriage to Patrick, but since his father's death he'd been a thorn in her side and had made her life—and Brody's—as difficult as humanly possible. His vicious contempt, coupled with the lascivious way he always looked at her, made her wish she'd worn something with more coverage than the deep V-neck midnight-blue collarless blouse and matching tailored skirt which skimmed her knees.

Oh well, she sighed, there was nothing for it but to face him. The short distance between the offices was covered all too quickly. She hesitated a moment, smoothing her hands over her hair, which fell in a waving chestnut waterfall to her shoulders, and then her clothing to make sure she looked okay before rapping sharply on the door and letting herself in.

"You wanted me?"

"Good of you to turn up this morning. I trust you have a good reason for being so late," a deep well-modulated and all too familiar voice stopped her in her tracks.

Mason! What was he doing here? Her eyes raked the stony-faced self-made tycoon as he sat in his designer suit behind her dead husband's desk. If she'd found him remote—even for a moment—over the weekend, his demeanour now supplanted any such memory. He was as impassive and impenetrable as a Mount Cook face and, judging by the stern set of his mouth, just as dangerous.

"Surprised to see me? Good. This way we can avoid any false expressions of your questionable work ethic."

"There's nothing wrong with my work ethic. You don't even know what I do around here." Helena's spine stiffened in outrage. How dare he turn up at her company office and accuse her of not doing her job? What the heck was he doing here anyway?

"Ah yes, what you do around here. I've gathered some idea." He snapped closed the folder of bank statements he'd been perusing and leaned forward on the desk. "What kept you this morning?"

"I was finding out about the paternity testing—it wasn't something I wanted to do here at work." She crossed her arms in front of her. "God! I don't even know why I bother to answer you. You don't control me."

"That's where you're wrong." A smile stretched across his face and she was certain it had nothing whatsoever to do with pleasure.

"What do you mean, wrong?" A sick feeling of forewarning settled in her stomach, a lump ascending in her throat.

He swivelled round in the chair and rose to his feet, dominating her easily as he came around to the front of the desk. His proximity forced her to tip her head up to meet his black gaze. "I had an interesting time after I dropped you home on Saturday. A very interesting time indeed. You never told me that Evan was in the market to sell his shares in Davies Freight. Any particular reason you chose to not to let that snippet of information out during our…discussions?"

"I don't know what you're talking about."

"Of course you don't. Did he, or did he not, approach you on Friday to buy Brody's share of the business?"

"He did, but he never said anything about selling *his* share."

Mason rose one sceptical eyebrow, bringing Helena's blood to boiling point.

"What? What lies has he spun you?" Helena heard her voice rise in pitch, sounding frantic even to her own ears. "He's only after whatever he can get and if he thinks you believe him then he probably got exactly what he wanted."

"Oh, yeah. I think he got what he wanted." Mason drawled the figure he'd paid out to Evan. Helena's breath caught in her throat.

"You bought him out?"

"It was worth every cent. I've spent the past twelve hours assessing the position here and, Helena, it's not looking pretty."

"Of course it's not. I told you on Friday he was ruining the company. I asked you for your help."

"It's not that simple. I'm requesting a full audit."

Helena's shoulders relaxed in relief. Thank goodness she'd finally have some proof of Evan's scurrilous dealings. Once they found out what, exactly, he'd been doing, they could put into action a recovery plan. The sooner she could get onto that, the better. "I'll get you our accounting firm's number."

"That won't be necessary. I'll be calling in my own team of experts."

"But we've dealt with Flannigans for years. Patrick went to school with Ed Flannigan, for goodness sake."

"Which is exactly why we need a fresh eye on the books." Mason leaned a hip against the side of the desk and crossed his arms. "There's one other thing. Until the audit is completed you're suspended from your duties."

"Suspended? Why?"

"I don't want any question about your involvement, influence or otherwise, with this audit."

"So can I continue to work from home?"

Mason's brow furrowed and his eyes trapped her piercing intelligence. "Do you usually work from home?"

"Sometimes, yes. Patrick often did and I've found it necessary sometimes since he passed away. The computer at home is linked to the mainframe here. It just makes things easier, especially if something unexpected crops up after hours."

"I'll bet it does." Mason's comment was spoken so softly Helena wasn't even certain he'd said anything, but his next words rang loud and clear. "No. You won't be working from home anymore."

"That's ridiculous. Who's going to do my work? With Evan gone as well there won't be anyone here in authority."

"Except me."

"You? You have your own business to run. When will you have time?"

"You forget. This is my business now, at least half of it, anyway. I have perfectly capable managers at BKT who can reach me if they need to."

Helena kept her hands firmly at her sides—difficult to do when all she wanted was to bunch her fists and let loose some of the frustration bubbling up inside of her. "And will I still be on full pay during this suspension?"

Mason let out a laugh that had nothing to do with humour. "Money. It's always about the money with you, isn't it? Surely you have enough to manage on, or have you burned through all of Patrick's funds already?"

"Of course not! Patrick's estate is frozen, awaiting the grant of probate from the High Court. In the meantime I rely on my salary to meet day-to-day expenses. Brody's boarding fees are due this month, too."

"Well, they may not be your worry for much longer." Mason paused before continuing. "If the money's that important to you, then yes, you will still be on full pay."

"Thank you." He'd never have any idea how much it galled her to be discussing money like this right now. All through her childhood, they'd scrimped and scraped.

She'd sworn she'd never be a victim of straitened financial circumstance again.

Mason leaned across the desk and flipped the switch that put him through to reception. "Mandy? Would you send up the security detail I brought with me this morning?"

"Security?" Helena could only manage an incredulous whisper. "Is that really necessary?"

Mason ignored her question, his expression stony.

"The guards will take you to your office where you can get your bag. When you're done, I'll escort you home."

"Why are you doing this? It isn't what I asked of you at all." What lies had Evan poisoned him with? Now that her stepson had what money he wanted by selling out his shareholding to Mason, did he have to try to destroy her, too? The answer was painfully simple. Of course he did. It's what Evan did best. But even *he* probably couldn't have imagined that Mason would treat her this way. Like a criminal.

"You need to learn, Helena. I do things on my terms, no one else's."

A knock sounded at the door and two burly uniformed guards came in at Mason's request. Helena caught the Black Knight Transport logo on their sleeves, leaving her in no doubt that Mason meant every word he'd said. Already he was infiltrating Davies Freight with his staff. How long before her son's inheritance disappeared into the ether?

"You can't do this, it's…it's underhanded. You're raiding Brody's inheritance—robbing him. Stealing your own son's birthright!"

"Birthright? Isn't that exactly what's under examination? Right now, Helena, I'd advise you to be careful about who you hurl your insults at. Until Brody's parentage is confirmed keep your opinions to yourself, or you will find out exactly how underhanded I can be."

Helena stiffened at his threat but it wasn't enough to dampen the blaze of red-hot fury that flashed across her eyes. The old Helena would not have thought twice about lashing out to score her nails across that stony visage. The new Helena had to satisfy herself with imagining it. As if he could read her mind, Mason stepped forward, a tiny smile curling up one corner of his mouth.

"I wouldn't do it if I were you."

Helena shook with suppressed anger and clenched her hands into tight fists at her sides. She thrust her chin up and demanded, "Do what?"

"Whatever it was that made your eyes flash green fire just then. You know, Helena, if we're going to sort this out, you'll have to learn to control your temper better. Your expression is a dead giveaway to exactly what you're feeling. Don't ever take up poker." He nodded over to the guards. "Please escort Mrs. Davies to her office and see that she only removes what she arrived with this morning. Everything else is the property of Davies Freight."

"You're no different than him, no different at all," Helena spat before turning for the door.

"Than whom?"

"Evan. He always wanted what was Brody's, now you're doing exactly the same thing. I should never have asked for your help. Never!"

"Perhaps you should have come to that conclusion earlier, or maybe you should have approached one of your other lovers for help instead of me."

Other lovers? Nausea rose in her throat and she swallowed against the lump that lodged there. She dragged in one deep breath, then another.

"I beg your pardon. I don't think I understand you." She was relieved to hear her voice sounded measured and level, especially when she felt anything but. Was he accusing her of infidelity during her marriage to Patrick?

"Come on, Helena. What happened? Did they all say no? Was I your last resort?"

Helena stiffened her spine. She wouldn't dignify his accusations with an answer. Last resort? He'd been her only resort and that fact alone was enough to now make her truly fear, not only for her son's future, but also for her own.

Six

Lost for words, Helena spun on her heel and stalked to her office, followed closely by the guards. The gall of the man to even suggest that she'd take anything that wasn't hers, let alone suspend her from her job. A pain in the region of her heart made her reach for the portrait photo. This would never have happened if Patrick had listened to her and slowed down a bit more. If, for once, he'd done as the doctor had urged. Helpless tears filled her eyes but she willed them back and pressed her lips together to hide their telling tremble.

"I'm sorry, Ma'am, you can't take that."

"What?" Helena paused as the guard removed the framed photo from her hands and set it back down on the desk. "You must be kidding me."

"Orders from Mr. Knight. Nothing but what you came in with this morning."

"That's just ridiculous. Let me sort this out right this minute." She moved past the desk and made for her door, only to have her passage blocked by the unyielding form of one of the guards. "Move out of my way—now."

"If you're ready to leave, we'll escort you to the lobby."

"I am not ready to leave. I demand to speak to Mr. Knight. Get out of my way."

The door behind the guard opened and Mason's imposing figure filled the frame.

"Sorry, sir. But she wants to take the picture." The older of the two guards gestured at the portrait on her desk.

"Causing trouble, Helena? Why am I not surprised? Thank you, gentlemen, I'll see her out from here."

Helena stood in absolute silence as the two men left the room, her seething gaze locked on Mason's impassive face and her mind tumbling the words that clamoured for pole position out of her mouth. Without breaking eye contact she reached across the desk to where the guard had replaced the frame, and picked the photo up. She clutched the picture to her chest with one hand while grabbing at the strap of her shoulder bag and hooking up her suit jacket with the other.

"*Now* I'm ready to go."

Mason put out his hand. "Give it to me, Helena."

Oh, this was crazy. There was no way on this earth she was leaving here without the portrait. She pressed it more firmly against her breasts.

With an exasperated sigh, Mason's hand reached forward, his fingers brushing against hers as they curled around the frame. The proximity of his fingers to her skin, masked only by the silky blouse she wore, didn't go unnoticed either. Her breasts swelled in the lacy cups that held them, her nipples tightening almost immediately into hardened nubs. Her mouth dried as a visual image of his dark head bent over her breast burned across her retina. The moment's inattention was her undoing as he gave the frame a tiny tug, causing her to lose hold of it. She gave a small exclamation of dismay as the picture dropped from their collective grips and struck the corner of the desk with a sharp *crack* before hitting the carpeted floor.

"Oh, look what you've done." Helena bent swiftly to retrieve the picture before it could be cut by the shards of glass.

"Stop. Don't touch it." Mason grasped her hand just before she could lift the photo from the debris.

"It's all right, Mason. I think I can lift the photo up without cutting myself."

"That's not what I mean." He bent down and flicked over the backing of the frame, exposing a folded sheet of paper which had been tucked behind the photo.

Carefully he unfolded the sheet, the set of his mouth growing grim as he read the rows of numbers on the sheet.

"Let me see that." Helena reached for the paper.

"I don't think so. Was this what you were trying to smuggle out of here, Helena? Is this where all the money's been going?"

"What on earth are you talking about? What money?"

"Don't play the innocent with me. If there's one thing I'm sure you know all about, it's money."

A sick feeling settled deep in the pit of her stomach. "You're talking in riddles. I just want our photo. It's the last one I have of Patrick with Brody and me."

"I'll have it reframed for you and delivered to the house. Now come on. I want you out of here."

"Surely you're not suggesting I deliberately hid

something in that frame?" A mirthless laugh escaped her tightened throat. The sound flitted across the room before falling flat when she realised by his gaze that that was exactly what he was suggesting. "You're wrong. You have it all wrong."

"We'll see about that."

"Then you'll see you're wrong. About this, about me. About everything. I was faithful to Patrick. Always. Mind, heart and body. You can think what you like but I know the truth."

"I don't think you even know what the truth is anymore, Helena. In fact, I don't think you ever did."

"How dare you!"

"Oh, I dare." He flicked the sheet of paper with his fingers. "And I will get to the bottom of this. I hope you're prepared for what comes out because if I find so much as a hint that you've been stealing from Patrick all these years, you will be sorry you ever met him, or me."

"Sorry? I'm already sorry I met you."

"Good, then we both know exactly where we stand."

As they drove in frozen silence toward the waterfront suburb where Patrick had built Helena their home, Mason itched to get to the root of what those numbers were hiding, and if they matched up with his suspicions about Helena. Patrick had been a generous man. More than generous. Mason could only be grateful that his mentor had never suspected his beautiful trophy wife of such duplicitous behaviour. The truth would have devastated him.

He took his eyes off the road long enough to flick a glance her way. Helena sat, locked in her thoughts, beside him. Her skin was pale, almost translucent, and dark shadows scored rings under her eyes. This morning had come as quite a shock to her, that much was obvious. Something she'd said earlier tickled at the back of his mind.

"You mentioned the paternity testing before. What did you find out?"

He felt her start as his words broke the frigid air between them.

"The testing lab is right here in Auckland. It's quite straightforward. You pay your money, you get your test."

"How much?"

Helena told him the figure she'd been given over the phone.

"So when are we going?" he pressed.

"I haven't booked it yet." Helena sounded surprised.

"Don't you want to know now, or is it that you're frightened I'm going to find you out for a liar?" His fingers tightened on the wheel as they turned into her gates and swung up the cobbled drive to the front of her house.

"I'm not afraid of anything, Mason Knight, particularly not the truth. Maybe that's something you should try sometime before jumping to asinine conclusions."

"I call it as I see it until I know differently. How soon can we get the results?"

"They said their general time frame is three weeks but apparently in most cases the results are available within a few days."

Mason drummed his fingers on the steering wheel. A few days. In only a few days he could find out whether he had a son. A son he knew only from a few boastful photographs shared by Patrick after a business meeting. A son he'd deserved to know from birth. The hollowness that had taken residence deep inside his chest since he'd learned he might be Brody's father ached anew. All those wasted years. If it was true, it wasn't only Helena who'd cheated him out of fatherhood, it had been his mentor, too. The betrayal didn't bear considering. Patrick had known him even better, perhaps, than his own father— he alone would have known what this news would do to him, the toll it would take. He shut the door firmly on that part of his mind and focussed on the present.

"What's involved?"

"All we need is recent photo identification of the parties involved and we can either have the samples taken at the laboratory itself or at any local diagnostic collection room."

"That simple, huh?"

Helena sighed. "Yeah. I thought it would be more complex. But all they need is the consent forms completed and either a blood sample or a swab of your mouth."

"Book it."

"I can't just do it like that."

His ire rose at her protest. "Why the hell not?" He ground the words past his teeth. She'd taken it this far. The only reason she wouldn't go all the way now was if she was having second thoughts. As far as he was concerned it was way too late for them now.

"I have Brody to consider."

"Yeah, so?"

"Well, I don't want to upset him. He doesn't need to know yet that Patrick wasn't his father. He's just coming to terms with his grief. I can't do that to him. I need to tread carefully here."

"Helena, if you don't organise this within the next few days, I can promise you that I will take whatever steps are necessary to have Brody tested."

"You can't!"

"Don't push me."

He watched as she lifted a hand to her hair, and absently twirled a hank until it wound like a corkscrew. A shudder ran through him as he remembered the texture of that hair—like warm, russet coloured silk—through his fingers, across his body. A sharp jolt of desire burned a trail below his belt. He hated that she could incite such a reaction in him.

Mason let go the breath he'd drawn in a frustrated rush of air. "I'm not negotiable on this, Helena. You came to me for help. I want proof."

"I might be able to get him tested at school, but I'm not telling him why. Not yet."

"Frankly, at this stage I don't care what you tell him. Just get it done."

"Fine. Is that everything then, *master?*"

The sarcasm in her voice was just enough to tip him over the edge. Ever since he'd dropped her home on Saturday she'd plagued his mind and body. The sooner he got this wretched physical yearning for her out of his system, the better. Denying himself the satisfaction of release on Friday night had been a bad move. It only served to make him want her more.

"Everything? Not by a long shot."

Mason hooked one arm around her shoulders and pulled her to him, his other hand reaching behind her head, grabbing the fullness of her hair and tilting her face to meet his onslaught. From the split-second it took to identify the fear in her emerald gaze to the moment his lips touched hers, he was driven by anger—by the need to dominate and force her to submit to him. But as her soft lips parted in surprise beneath his and his mouth filled with the heady intoxicating taste of her, the fury left his body, leaving it replaced instead by something far more dangerous. Something that threatened his equilibrium in a way nothing and no one else ever had.

She tasted of some sweet feminine blend he couldn't get enough of—a taste that was intrinsically her own. His tongue swept past her lips to stroke against hers, to entice her to take him deeper. She moaned from deep down in her throat and the sound drove him crazy. She was his for the taking. He should be disgusted that it was so easy—that she was so easy for him—but all he wanted was more. More of her mouth, more of her body, more of her heat.

He lifted his head and watched as she opened her eyes—the green depths hazy with desire, her pupils dilated to enormous black pools.

"Let's take this inside," he growled.

The change in her expression was as immediate and as chilling as a hail storm.

"Let's not."

Before he could stop her, she'd gathered her things and was out of the car.

Mason climbed from the vehicle and leaned over the roof, watching as she all but ran for the sanctuary of her front door. "You can run from me, Helena, but it's not over between us until I say so," he called after her retreating form.

She hesitated for a moment in the portico, her key already slotting into the front door. For a second he thought she'd turn and say something, anything, but with a flick of her wrist the door was open and she stepped inside. The resounding bang as it closed behind her retreating form echoed across the drive.

Helena watched from behind the sheer curtains in the front room as, for a full thirty seconds, Mason didn't move. Then, to her relief, he got back into the car and roared away—gravel spitting out from under his tyres.

One touch, that's all it took, and she'd melted for him again. Her body still clamoured for his. She had to shore her reserves against him somehow. She turned from the window and raced up the stairs to her bedroom and discarded her clothing in an untidy heap. As cold as the swimming pool would be, anything would be preferable to the flaming heat that seared her veins. She grabbed a black one-piece swimsuit from the drawer and pulled it on over her body, groaning slightly as the fabric caressed her breasts. Had she done as Mason had suggested, it would be his hands, his mouth, his tongue, caressing her now. And maybe, just maybe, the ever tightening knot of need that had plagued her since Friday night would begin to be assuaged.

But she'd said no, and she'd run, because she knew deep down inside that if he'd touched her once more she'd have conceded to his power over her, and done so willingly.

Her inner muscles clenched tight against the tingle of desire deep inside. Even now she wanted him, even when he so clearly despised her and had believed whatever web of lies Evan had spun. Without pausing for another thought Helena barrelled down the stairs and through the house to the indoor pool. She hadn't bothered to keep it heated since Patrick's death and the sluicing coolness would be just what her body needed right now. About twenty laps should do it, she thought haphazardly, or maybe a hundred. Whatever it took, she wasn't getting out of that pool until she felt as weak as jelly and as incapable of submitting to Mason Knight as possible.

* * *

Rain-laden skies threatened overhead, turning the late afternoon into premature night. She hoped the weather would hold off. They had the last appointment at the clinic and would miss it if the weather, and subsequently the Auckland city traffic, turned foul. Helena stood nervously in the brightly-lit portico at her front door waiting for the roar of Mason's Porsche to come up her drive. She hadn't spoken to him since a week ago on Monday when he'd driven her home. A computer forensics company had turned up at her door, just as she'd finished her gruelling marathon in the pool, to take the computer from the library and since then she'd had no contact with work at all.

The first day home had stretched out interminably and finally boredom had driven her to start going through Patrick's personal items—packing up his clothes and things that neither Brody nor Evan would want into boxes for local charities, and setting aside other items Patrick had listed in his will as bequests for Evan and some of his old friends. It had been a job she'd been putting off—the finality of it almost too much to bear. The boxes now stood, stacked like sentinels, just inside her front entrance. A physical reminder of Patrick's absence from her life.

She didn't want to think about that right now. Today would be trial enough without dealing anew with her grief. When she'd booked the appointment at the laboratory, in defiance and knowing Mason could be contacted at Davies Freight, she had deliberately left a message with his secretary at Black Knight Transport about where they had to be and when.

Caller ID had saved her from having to speak with

him when he'd called back to confirm he'd be picking her up to take her for their tests. The tone of his voice on the answering machine left her in no doubt that he suspected she was standing there, listening, and refusing to pick up the phone to speak with him personally. She'd almost hoped she could get away with taking a taxi and meeting him there, but acceded that it would only be prolonging the inevitable. She had to face him some time, somewhere.

In the distance she heard the downshift of gears as a car approached from the road and a sweep of headlights lit the foliage that lined the long driveway—it may as well be now.

As he swung the gleaming low-slung vehicle around her turning bay, she stepped out toward the car. Nerves bundled into ever-tightening knots as she reached out to open the door and settled herself inside. With nothing but a curt nod from Mason, they were on their way. Fortunately, the threatening rain held off, but despite the fact that the laboratory was a mere twenty minutes from her home, every kilometre passed in painful thickening silence. Finally, she could stand it no longer.

"So? Have you found out everything you need to prove I'm a liar yet?" she challenged.

"Not yet."

"That's because there's nothing there."

"We'll see." Mason pulled the car up in the parking lot outside the laboratory. "What have you arranged for Brody?"

"I told Brody our family doctor was concerned with how lethargic he's been lately." That in itself was no lie, although their doctor had also hastened to add that at Brody's stage of adolescent development it wasn't unusual, especially combined with his grief over losing the only father he'd ever known. The doctor had advised Helena to ask the school nurse to keep an eye on him and they could take further action later if necessary.

"And?" Mason prompted.

"And I told him that the doctor wanted to be sure he hadn't contracted glandular fever and had requested blood work be done. I don't appreciate having to lie to my son."

"Why start worrying about that now? You've lied to him his entire life." The acrid bitterness in Mason's voice flayed her like a whip and she physically recoiled from him.

"I didn't know Patrick wasn't his father until his lawyer gave me his medical records. Why won't you believe me?"

"Because I really have no cause to believe you, Helena."

"Well, you'll have to believe me when we get the results of these tests."

"All they will prove is that either you're lying now or that you've cheated me out of my son's life for the past eleven years. Frankly, I don't find anything admirable in either of them. Do you?"

"I didn't know!"

Mason ignored her as he alighted from the car and came around to open her door. "Come on. At least this will get us one step closer to the truth."

Helena walked by his side, his hand at her elbow as they entered the building. Fleetingly she wondered how many couples the staff here saw arriving like this—couples filled with anxiety at the outcome of the test. In her heart, she knew the result couldn't be anything but proof that Mason was Brody's father. She hadn't been with anyone in almost a year prior to her marriage to Patrick—no one except Mason.

The memory of that night, of the raw passion that had driven her, drove a spike of pure longing from her core and through her entire body. It had been an instinctive reaction to the trauma she'd been through, she understood that now. She'd read every book on the topic in a vain attempt to identify what had driven her uncharacteristic behaviour that night. The fact that it could be pigeonholed by psychobabble was little comfort in the face of Mason's behaviour, however.

He barely spoke to her as they went through the process of confirming their identification and completing the forms and consents. The test itself was almost disappointingly simple. Helena felt that for something so momentous it should have been more complex, more time-consuming. More important, somehow. Once the samples were taken they were free to go. Free to wait for what would arguably be the three longest days of her life.

Now, as they walked out to the car in a silence that was anything but companionable, she felt the tension begin anew. As she buckled her car seat belt, she sighed.

"Too late for second thoughts," Mason stated, turning to face her with a flare of challenge in his eyes.

"I'm not having second thoughts."

The expression on Mason's face told her clearly he thought she was lying, and since that was basically what he thought about everything that came out of her mouth, she had retrained herself not to care—much.

"I'm not scared of the truth," she insisted. *At least not in the way you think,* she added silently. When she'd initially approached Mason it had been with the sole intention of securing Brody's inheritance and seeing that Patrick's wishes were carried out. But, in the face of his animosity toward her, she'd been rattled by an even more disturbing consideration.

What if Mason wanted to take fatherhood a step further? What if he wanted to take Brody away from her?

While a part of her mind argued that surely no family court in New Zealand would allow such a thing, she knew it wouldn't take too much digging to expose the piece of her past that would sit like a big black mark against her. Digging, ha! If Evan knew, the whole world could know in only a matter of moments. She swallowed against the obstruction lodged between her throat and her chest like a malignant knot of fear. She couldn't afford to even think about that happening.

Patrick had had his reasons, whatever they were, for not telling Mason about his son any earlier. He would never have shared that information if he'd dreamed it could see her lose the human being most dear to her. Since their marriage her relationship with her parents had become strained, and her contact with them had become less frequent. It was something that brought her plenty of sleepless nights, dogged with guilt, but they'd seemed happy enough in their own world. A world Patrick had paid for, not that they knew that. The older her parents had become, the more insular they'd grown and their relief that she was financially off their hands had been huge.

Besides, she knew Patrick couldn't have lied to her about his infertility. He had neither cause nor advantage to have done so. In his letter to her he'd told her how he'd figured it out after seeing the logs of the radio conversation Mason had had with the controllers at the depot that night. How he'd saved a young woman's life and returned to her safety. Given that Patrick knew she'd lost her car on the journey north, it hadn't taken him long to figure out what might have happened when she'd told him she was pregnant. In Helena's opinion, it said a lot for Patrick's strength as a man that he'd accepted Brody as his own.

Mason was Brody's father no matter how much he distrusted her. That distrust, however, still kept her from her duties at Davies Freight. Every day she'd worried and wondered how things were going, whether Mason was any closer to discovering the soak hole that was draining the company's financial stability.

"How are things at work?" Helena switched subjects.

"I already told you. Nothing conclusive yet."

"I don't mean the investigation. What about the staff, how are they handling the changes?" Patrick had taken a personal interest in all his staff, each one handpicked for their position. In their own way they were an extension of his family, and he respected everyone who worked for him accordingly.

"Pretty well. There's been a bit of confusion but they're all keen to save their jobs. I had a meeting this week with the core team to discuss options."

"Without me?"

"Obviously."

"I should have been there." She bit her lip, forcing back the words that begged to be spoken. When Patrick had died so suddenly, the staff had turned to her for guidance within the company. With both of them gone it would be like sailing a ship without a skipper. Or, at the very least, with a man at the helm they probably had genuine reason to fear. If it became Mason's intention to merge the two companies at least half of her staff's positions would go. Worse, if he found the company was unsustainable, everyone would lose their job. "Are you talking redundancies yet?"

"Hopefully not at all. Once the audit is complete we'll know better where we stand. Suffice to say, whatever put Davies Freight in the position it's in appears to have stagnated." He threw her a telling glance.

"I suppose you think that's because I'm not there."

"Looks that way."

"Evan's not there either," Helena hastened to point out, trying to ignore the chill that swept her skin. She'd battled over the past few weeks to find the source of the problem, but it appeared too deeply entrenched in the system. Evan's flashy lifestyle had pointed the finger firmly in his direction and she was certain he was the culprit. That, combined with his sudden desire to sell after Patrick died, supported her theory. Somehow he'd gotten in too deep and need a large cash influx fast. And now he had it, from Mason.

"Worried I'm catching up to your schemes, Helena?"

"No! When will you understand? It's not me that's under question here. It's Evan."

"Funny, that's what he implied about you before accepting my cheque."

"How can you still believe him over me?"

Mason turned into her driveway and pulled the car up to a halt at her front door.

He sighed and turned off the motor, then rested his fisted hands on the steering wheel. "I don't know what to believe anymore, Helena."

Finally. A chink in his armour. Helena would've rejoiced in his indecision if for one second she thought it would do her any good. Instead, that one small indication of frailty, of uncertainty, made her wonder if she shouldn't be even more worried than before. Always, Mason had been steadfast. Focussed. Determined. She reached out a hand and rested it on his. The warmth of his skin was instantly absorbed into hers and sent a spreading heat through her arm.

"Believe the facts. Believe the truth." She squeezed his tightly fisted fingers gently. "Please, believe me."

Seven

The air between them crackled with tension as her words hovered before fading away to nothing. She'd had absolutely no impact on him if his expression was anything to go by.

Mason listened to the earnest tone in her voice. Any other man would capitulate at this point, he was certain. Any other man but him. He'd been victim to the honeyed suggestions of another lying female before and the fallout had been devastating. It had set him apart from his family and put him on his solitary road to success. His elder brother, Declan, had branched out on his own—away from the umbrella of their father's company—but even he still had more in common with the old man than he realised. Of course Connor had stayed within the family fold once he'd attained his law degree. He'd been too young, and Declan too knowing, to fall for the attention teasingly scattered Mason's way by Melanie, his father's much younger mistress.

No, it was only him. The black sheep of the family. The loner. That was probably what had made him a prime target for Melanie's manipulation of a teenage boy's wild crush. For the devastation it had wrought on his relationship with his dad. No, he wouldn't believe Helena Davies. Not until he had quantifiable proof that she was as innocent as she claimed.

"Mason?" She broke into his thoughts.

"What?"

"Would you like to come in for coffee before you head back?"

"Sure." He clamped down his surprise at her sudden offer. She'd avoided all contact with him this past week, now she was inviting him inside the house. In itself, that made him suspicious. So he'd play her game. As the saying went, "Keep Your Friends Close. Keep Your Enemies Closer."

Mason's shoulders stiffened as they entered through the ornately carved front door and into the tiled entranceway. He almost expected Patrick to come through from the formal sitting room area, booming his welcome. God, he missed him.

"It's almost like he's still here, isn't it?" Helena spoke softly, a thread of tears in her voice. "I feel the same way every time I come through that door."

"Yeah. He's kind of hard to forget."

They walked into the kitchen in silence.

"How did you meet Patrick?" Helena asked.

"He never told you?"

"At the wedding, when I saw you standing there...well, suffice to say I never asked." Helena bent her head as she filled the jug at the kitchen sink, her hair obscuring her expression.

Mason would have liked to have seen her face right at this minute. He'd lay odds it was a darn sight more expressive than it had been that afternoon when she'd come floating down the aisle of the cathedral, an ethereal vision of beauty. A beauty that belied the bedraggled creature he'd pulled from certain death only hours before. The calm serenity on her face at complete odds with the driving passion of her body as she'd ridden him in the darkest hours of the night.

The memory of that passion stirred him anew, making his skin heat with need and his body tighten with a coiling hunger that whorled deep inside.

"Milk?"

"What? Oh, yeah. Just a bit, thanks. We met when I came out of the army. I responded to a call for owner drivers at the time. I was young, full of balls and bursting to make my own mark on the world." He laughed, a short harsh sound that had nothing to do with humour. "I didn't even have my own truck. I rolled up to the depot with nothing but a dream and a plan. Anyone else would have sent me on my way, or laughed so hard their gut would've burst, but not Patrick. No, he listened. Then he outlined a plan where I could do exactly what I wanted to do. What I needed to do."

To his horror, his voice broke on the last words. For a moment he was that defensive young man once more, searching for a means by which he could purge his anger and disappointment. He cleared his throat before continuing.

"Anyway, he made things happen for me."

"Mason, I'm so sorry."

"Sorry?"

"He meant so much to you and I took him from you, didn't I? If I hadn't slept with you that night, you would have seen more of him, spent more time with him. Heaven knows, maybe he'd even have listened to you instead of ignoring me when I asked him to cut back on his workload—to start to hand over the reins."

"And who would he have handed them over to, Helena? Evan? You? It's no wonder he worked himself to death." Mason flung an arm out, gesturing toward her home and possessions. "He worked for you, for this. For what you wanted."

"No. No, it wasn't like that." Tears glistened in her eyes.

"Wasn't it? Until he married you he was happy with less."

"Mason, you know what he was like. Don't let your bitterness toward me cloud your memory of Patrick. He was the most generous of men. Look at yourself. Look at what he did for you. Can you honestly say you'd be where you are now if he hadn't believed in you and what you believed you could achieve? Okay, so maybe you'd have gotten there eventually, but I'd lay odds that it wouldn't have been that fast." She rubbed at her eyes with a haphazard swipe. Even as she denuded her face of the evidence of her emotion he heard the change of tone in her voice—from soft and cajoling to hard and concise. "Be angry at me, for sure, but don't take what he gave you away. You both deserve more than that."

Her words chipped at him like a hammer and chisel, eventually fracturing the shell he worked so hard to build over his wounded heart. The pain of loss swamped him anew, mingled with the anger he'd been harbouring, not only against Patrick for marrying Helena, but also against his father for believing Melanie over him when he'd finally confronted them both. The ensuing argument had seen him become a pariah in his own home, while Melanie had sat like the cat who'd gotten the cream. Smug that her sexual prowess had allowed her to manipulate not only an older man, but his son as well.

That his relationship with Patrick had ended up destroyed as history repeated itself had come as an unbelievable blow. But this time, the responsibility had been his and his alone. He hadn't been the love-struck teenager of his youth. He'd been a young man on the fast road to success. He could've spoken up to stop Patrick from marrying Helena. He'd chosen not to, and then he'd chosen to allow himself to be closed away. His contact with his mentor diminishing each year until they barely saw or spoke to one another anymore in the months leading up to Patrick's death.

"You're right." His voice sounded foreign, strained, even to his own ears.

"Right?"

"Yeah. You took him from me." He watched as she flinched, her eyes filled with shock at his bluntness. "But worse than that, I let you."

"I never wanted to come between you. Until I married Patrick I had no idea who you were, or how close you were to him." He watched as she automatically went through the process of making their coffee, not even aware of what she was doing until a drop of hot water backwashed from the mug she was pouring into and splashed painfully against her hand. She jumped, dropping the mug onto the counter top. As the liquid began to spill across the dark granite surface she reached for a cloth.

"You need to get cold water on that."

"I'll be fine."

Mason rounded the kitchen bench and grabbed her hand, pulling her gently toward the sink and running the cold tap water over her reddening skin. She tried to pull her fingers from his grasp but he held her firmly as the cooling water did its work to pull the heat from the burn.

Helena closed her eyes, compliant at his touch. One minute they were arguing and the next she was the recipient of his care. The paradoxical situation was enough to make her want to weep. But there'd been enough tears. For Patrick, for Brody—and yes, even for Mason. No more. She was wrung out.

"How does that feel now?" His head was so close to hers his breath brushed against her hair, the sensation sending a trickle of awareness like a warning signal down her neck with a shiver.

"Okay. It's fine. You can let go of me now."

Their proximity was at once intimate, yet impersonal. His body covered hers from behind, his hips cradling her buttocks. Helena could barely breathe. Every nerve in her body almost painfully attuned to the heat radiating off his body, to the hard-muscled plane of his stomach pressed against her back.

"I—I think that's enough now," she murmured. Surely now he'd back off. Stop this mental and physical torment. He was so much bigger than her, so much stronger, although she didn't feel intimidated as much by his size as she was by her own craving for him. A craving that went soul deep. She prayed he'd back away.

Mason flicked off the tap with his free hand and, still

holding her injured one gently in his, reached across for a towel. Helena held her breath, waiting for the sting as he carefully dried the moisture off her hand. But the sting never came.

Instead, she only felt the soft pressure of Mason's lips. Her fingers curled involuntarily around his, the words she desperately needed to utter—to beg him to stop—stuttered to a halt in her throat. All pain fled as his tongue snaked out and trailed a path along the back of her hand. Her knees turned to water as he turned her wrist and laved his tongue across her pulse point before covering the wetness with his lips.

"Mason?" His name sighed from her, like a plea.

"Yes?"

"Don't, please don't. We're not ready for this. Not now. Not yet."

"Ready, Helena?" He tilted her chin with one finger so she looked directly up into his eyes, eyes that glowed with a molten heat that seared right through to her core. "When it comes to you, I'm so ready it hurts."

Her heart fluttered in her chest. This was too much, especially when she was still raw from the painful aftermath of the night when they'd begun to make love, only to have it end with such wrenching desolation. She wasn't ready. Not for this.

"I can't. *We* can't."

"Scared?" He bent his head and pressed a kiss against the corner of her mouth before fleetingly darting his tongue across her lower lip.

Terrified was the word that immediately sprang to mind. But for the life of her she couldn't pull away.

He was like a drug. Once sampled, instantly addicted. Oh sure, she thought she'd conquered this addiction, but twelve years of marriage to a man she'd loved and revered had merely dulled the hunger.

A warning flashed in the back of her mind. Would Mason just use her weakness against her and fling her clawing desire for him back into her face? She had to take the risk, had to give in to the overpowering craving to be with him every way she could.

Mason kissed her again, this time coaxing her lips apart with a pressure that hinted at the power behind his restraint.

"Don't worry, I'll hold you."

She was in his arms and they were ascending the stairs before she realised she'd even so much as whispered the word *yes*. As he neared her bedroom door she stiffened in his arms.

"No, not in there. Please. One of the guest rooms."

At her request, Mason strode the short distance down the carpeted hallway, the sound of his footsteps swallowed by the thick pile of the carpet. At the door to the furthermost guest room he slowly lowered her, allowing her to drag against his body as her feet found the floor, making sure she was left with no doubt about his desire for her. His hardness was an insistent pressure against her belly. Knowing she had such an effect on him both empowered and awed her.

This strong, vital man wanted her. He'd wanted her before, that first time, although she had to admit that she had taken advantage of him. Taken his chance to make a choice away from him, almost as she'd taken Patrick away from him. Hearing Mason talk back there in the kitchen finally brought it home to her what a devastating effect she'd had on him. Worse, she'd unwittingly taken from him his chance to be a father to their son.

She owed him—everything—and she had to make it up to him, as much as she could. That making up started now.

Instinctively, Helena reached for the doorknob behind her, turned it, and pushed open the door. She took each of Mason's hands in her own and, walking slowly backward, she drew him into the room. Mason kicked the door shut behind them. Helena reached for the light switch.

"Don't."

"But I want to see you," she protested softly.

"Leave it off. I want...I want it to be like the first time."

"Our first time?"

"Shh." He grazed her lips with one finger. "No more talking."

Helena's eyes hadn't even adjusted to the dark when his mouth closed on hers, his hand sliding up her back to the nape of her neck and holding her against him as if his life depended on her. She opened her mouth to his assault, and in that moment, opened her heart to him as she'd never allowed herself to ever before. The emotion that turbulently cascaded within her was nothing like the strong secure love she'd shared with Patrick. Love? Was this crazy roller coaster of feeling she went through every time she thought about Mason, love?

If it was, she wanted more. More than this moment of lovemaking, this slaking of their lust for one another that even after twelve years burned as hot and vivid as it had that one fateful night. The truth tore through her, sweeping away reason, opening the floodgates of her desire once again.

She lifted her hands to his face, and drove her fingers through his hair, the blunt cut strands grazing against her palms. Every thought, every sensation was heightened. Every particle of her focussed solely on Mason Knight.

Impatient hands pushed at her clothing with scant regard for fasteners or zips. On the periphery of her passion she heard and felt the buttons pop from her knitted top but she didn't care. She had an agenda of her own—to feel his skin against hers again, as quickly as possible. In moments they were both naked, their bodies aligned against one another. The hard, hot skin of his erection pulsed against her bare belly and a new wave of need radiated through her body from her centre to her very fingertips.

Mason's hands cupped her buttocks, lifting her hard against him, positioning her so the throbbing tip of him nudged against the slick hot entrance to her body.

A groan tore from his throat, feral in its ferocity. "Protection."

One word that could halt them in their tracks. One word that should have hammered home its message to her that night in his truck, in the warmth of his comforting embrace. One word she knew she could deliver on this time.

"It's okay, I'm on the pill."

For a moment Mason allowed a single stray thought into his head. Patrick had let on one night over drinks that the physical side of his marriage had all but ended. Was it consideration for her husband's erratic libido, in the belief that he was still fertile, that had her on the pill, or was it so she could keep her lovers without a care for any consequences? He didn't want to think of that now, now when his body wound ever tighter, demanding release. Demanding surcease from the ever-present tension he knew would only ease if he satisfied his hunger for her. For now it didn't matter if she had other lovers, so long as he had her.

Then, his senses went on full alert. The air in front of him moved with a shimmering heat. A question rose in his throat, only to stall, unsaid, as small warm hands cupped his balls, stroking and kneading with a firm, gentle rhythm. Anticipation almost made him jump out of his skin as the hot, wet stroke of her tongue started at the base of his arousal, the merest touch enough to make his body jerk and thrust forward.

He'd been a fool to keep the lights off. Right now he'd give anything to watch her, to see her expression as she stroked her tongue in tiny flicks from base to just below the tip of his penis. Then her lips closed over the head. She stilled and for a moment he simply relished the heat of her mouth, the texture of her tongue as she swirled it about his shaft. He was about to explode. He had to hold back—he hadn't waited for her for twelve years merely to lose it in twelve seconds.

With a raw growl he pushed his hands in her hair—fighting the urge to plunge against her—instead withdrawing from her heat and reaching for her, to pull her upright.

"I want to be inside you, to feel you."

"Like the last time?"

Her voice was unsure and he briefly felt a twinge of unease, a hint of regret for how he'd treated her the last time they were so intimate.

"No. Like the first."

He swept her into his arms again and carefully made his way in the dark to the bed. Laying her down on the covers he knelt down on the bed next to her. Helena's voice whispered through the darkness.

"If it's going to be like the first time, then you have to pretend to be asleep."

"Pretend? I wasn't pretending."

"So pretend now." Her breath stroked across his cheek.

"Is that an order?"

"If it needs to be."

His skin raised with goose bumps as her breath travelled down his chest, over his nipples, past his navel. Small deft fingers sheathed him, then, mercifully, the mattress shifted as she positioned herself over his body. Without hesitation she slid down the full length of him until they were joined, almost seamlessly. Sensation poured through him, pushing at the edges of his control. He had to last the distance.

A deep sense of rightness rocked through Helena as she settled her body over Mason's, as she drew him deep inside to her inner core. He completed her physically. Their joining felt so right. Gently she undulated against him, feeling the restraint within him that held him still as she increased the depth of her movements. Swells of pleasure grew in intensity, rising and falling through her body until she no longer felt in control. Only felt the instinctive need to ride the current of longing that craved release.

Mason's hands gripped her hips, his fingers digging into her skin, holding her firmly, not allowing her to withdraw from the journey they took together. Suddenly, she could bear it no longer. All control fled as sensation built to a peak and then poured, molten through her veins. Her body slicked with perspiration as she rocked harder, every movement silently imploring for release.

As slowly as the tension had risen, pleasure began to radiate through her body, her climax growing in strength, building like a giant wall of colour, heat and light until it crashed with terminal velocity through every nerve in her body. Mason thrust upward then shuddered against her as she collapsed against him, her body vibrating with the eruption of release.

Mason wrapped his arms around her, holding her so close she felt as though she were moulded to him. Against her ear, his heart thudded in rapid beats in his chest. His lungs drew in great gulps of air. Helena sighed in satisfaction, her eyelids drooping in sheer physical exhaustion. As she drifted off to sleep hope began to grow within that maybe, finally, she could start to make things right with him.

More than that, she *wanted* to make things right with him. It went beyond the sex. She wanted much more than that. She wanted the chance to make up to him all she'd inadvertently denied him—from his lost years with Brody, to the lost chance she'd had to love him as he deserved to be loved.

Eight

Mason woke to rumpled sheets and an empty bed. Despite the fact they'd slept little during the night, somehow he felt more rested—more satisfied—than he had in years. He got up and made his way into the guest bathroom, taking a quick hot shower before dragging on the clothes that lay strewn about the room.

Downstairs, he found Helena in the family room— her fingers wrapped tight about a large coffee mug and a stack of books in front of her on the coffee table. A flush of colour painted her cheeks as he came in, brightening the green glitter of her eyes. His gut clenched. She was an incredibly beautiful woman. Her looks deceptively fragile. Although she'd lost weight since Patrick's death, and looked as though it would take little more than a strong sou'-westerly to knock her off her feet, he recognised that her backbone was made of pure steel.

She was strong, she was tough, she was smart. If they'd met under the right circumstances who knew where they'd be now?

"Good morning." He leaned down and kissed her, hard. Desire flamed instantly. Even after their lovemaking last night he still hadn't slaked his hunger for her. He wanted her now even more.

"Let me get you some coffee." She started to get up but he gently pushed her back down in her seat.

"No problem. I can help myself. You look like you've been busy." He gestured toward the stack of books on the coffee table in front of her.

"I gathered some albums I thought you might like to go through."

"Albums?"

"Of Brody. You didn't come over much after Patrick and I married. You missed so much."

A searing shaft of anger stabbed through him, quenching his desire as effectively as an extinguisher on a fire. Did she seriously think a few photographs would make up for the lost years if Brody proved to be his son? Mason swallowed back the retort he knew would flay her to shreds.

"Take a seat. The albums are in chronological order."

"Look, Helena, now's probably not a good time. Why don't we wait until we know for sure?"

Helena rose from her seat and tipped the remnants of her coffee in the sink. He saw a shiver go through her body. She kept her back to him as she spoke, her hands gripping the bench, her face staring out the kitchen window.

"Are you afraid of the truth, Mason? Is that why you won't look at the albums?" She turned abruptly and locked her temptress's green gaze with his. "He's more like you than you could imagine, you know. Now that I know the truth, I can see it in him. *He is your son.*"

As far as he could tell there was no guile, no deception in her clear-eyed stare. No, there was nothing there but challenge. Damn her. She knew he wouldn't ignore the gauntlet once thrown down. Even their lovemaking last night had been like that. Challenge, counter challenge. Driving one another to new heights of pleasure.

He was having a hard enough time adjusting to the fact that taking her body hadn't eased the driving hunger in his—was even beginning to wonder just how much it would take before he'd had enough of Helena Davies. And now she wanted to throw this into the equation.

Fine then. He'd pick up the challenge. He threw himself into the comfortable sofa in front of the coffee table. Late morning winter sun beamed watery rays across the table, illuminating the collection of albums there, each painstakingly labelled in Helena's copperplate-style handwriting with Brody's name and the dates. Mason slid the album nearest him off the stack and flipped open the pages. A photo of her—almost naked and proudly displaying her swollen bare belly—sucked every last vestige of breath from his lungs.

The picture was deeply intimate, yet sensual at the same time. The joy in her eyes and the possessive touch of her hand on the lush curve of her stomach were both offset by a forest green strip of satin that was swathed lovingly across the fullness of her breasts and around her body, trailing under the mound that protected the new life inside. The shimmer of light and dark on the fabric drew his eye across her figure in a way that celebrated the joining of two bodies to result in new life and motherhood.

Desire flowed with thick heat through his veins as his eyes devoured the flush of warmth on her creamy skin, the hidden promise of her beauty beneath the satin, of the ripe enticing shape of her. If Brody was his, she'd cheated him of this—of watching her grow full with his baby, his son. No matter what came now, he'd never have that time back.

He could finally identify his anger toward Helena for what it really was. She'd taken a vital piece of him with her the morning after he'd saved her life. She'd taken his hope, then she'd encased it in ice as cold and brilliant as the diamonds of the wedding band placed on her finger by another man. A man she should never have married.

Mason slowly worked through each album, turning the pages one by one, his vision blurring as the pictures of a newborn baby with indistinct features firmed and shaped as Brody matured, until Mason knew without a doubt that he was staring at his own image in a younger form. He blinked away the moisture from his eyes, refusing to give in to such weakness in her presence, determined instead to feed on the energy that welled in frustrated fury from deep inside him.

He closed the final page on the album and looked up. Words failed him. Across the table from him, Helena sat, silver tear tracks shining on her cheeks.

"I wish I'd known then," she said, brokenly. "You deserve more than this. More than a photographic summary of Brody's life."

"That still remains to be seen." Even though he knew the words for a lie, he had to give them voice. In his heart, to the depths of his soul, he understood this child was his, and understood why he'd fought so hard to deny it. Feeling cheated didn't even begin to describe how raw he felt inside right now.

"Why are you so stubborn? Why can't you just accept it?"

"Accept it? Accept that the man I admired more than my own father betrayed me? Accept that you slept with me, allowed me to impregnate you, and then married someone else and let him raise my son as his own?" Mason pushed back his chair, the legs skidding across the terracotta-tiled floor with the force with which he stood. "You ask too much."

He covered the distance between the kitchen and the front door in a haze of anger, oblivious to the soft pad of Helena's bare feet on the floor as she followed him.

"Mason, wait!"

He ignored her and pulled open the front door with a wrench that did little to assuage the tension that controlled him. He had to get out of here. Away from the memories of Patrick Davies, away from Helena and as far away as possible from the truth he couldn't deny.

It no longer mattered how long the paternity test results took. He would put matters in motion today to ensure that he attained sole custody of the boy. By the time he was through with Helena she would wish she'd never been born.

Several days later, Mason stood in his office at Black Knight Transport and turned an envelope over and over in his hands. The discreet logo of the diagnostic laboratory taunted him. Now that the moment of truth had come, for some crazy reason he was reluctant to know the outcome of the paternity test. Not that it mattered anymore, anyway. In his heart he knew he was Brody's father. The albums he'd leafed through last week had convinced him beyond a shadow of a doubt and had made the family gathering he'd endured at his father's place this past weekend, together with his brothers and their expanding families, all the more stilted and painful.

At Connor's suggestion, he'd spoken with one of Auckland's foremost solicitors in family law. He had an outside chance, at best, of removing Brody from Helena's care, but as far as he was concerned a chance was all he needed. It was all he'd ever needed to succeed and this was one matter he was determined would go his way, no matter what.

His finger slid under the flap of the envelope, tearing the adhesive strip away and pulling out the folded sheets of paper. His eyes skimmed the report—assimilating the data quickly before shoving the papers back into the envelope and grabbing his keys off the surface of his desk.

It was time to face Helena with the truth.

As he pulled up outside her house he noticed another car off to the side of the parking bay. The bright red European sports car shrieked money. Had Helena bought the car for herself? If so, what with?

The auditors had presented him with an interim report this morning. Money had been siphoned off systematically for years—starting at about the time Helena had taken up her position there, when Brody had started school. Everything pointed to her, but still he had no actual proof as to who the culprit was.

Something kept niggling at him, though, and begged the question—why had she come to him for help? If she had something to hide he was the last person she should have come to. He knew that it had been Patrick's instructions that had sent her to him. Patrick had to have seen the money trickling away. Maybe he'd even suspected her already but lacked the wherewithal to confront his beautiful young wife. He certainly wouldn't be the first older man to be hoodwinked by a pretty face and a lithe body.

Or the first *younger* one either, Mason reflected bitterly.

One thing was patently clear. Patrick's indulgence of Helena had cost the company dearly.

He wandered over to the car, taking a look inside. A sale and purchase agreement lay on the passenger seat. He picked out the name on the agreement. Evan Davies.

Evan? What the hell was he doing here? Heavy morning dew lay in big round droplets on the showy red paintwork. From the looks of it he'd been here a while. All night?

The money Mason had paid out to Evan would make him a fine candidate for Helena's apparent insatiable financial hunger.

An ugly black rage rose within Mason's chest. Was she still sleeping with him? An even more unpalatable thought crossed his mind—had she ever stopped?

Mason ground gravel beneath his foot as he pivoted and made for the front entrance, ignoring the doorbell and hammering his fist against the heavy wooden door. He forced himself to calm down. What did it matter to him if she was still in bed with Evan anyway? It would only serve to make his case stronger—to give him the additional leverage he'd need to petition the family court.

The sound of someone pounding down the stairs from inside filtered through the door. He heard locks tumbling open, then the door swung wide.

Evan Davies stood before him—hair dishevelled, dressed only in a loosely-fastened robe, with a stain of lipstick on his unshaven cheek. Bile rose in Mason's throat at the thought of Helena's body meshed with this man's. Of her hands entangled in his hair. Of her lips against his skin.

His hands clenched into fists and Mason was hard-pressed not to drive one of them into the smug, sleepy features of the man standing before him.

"I thought I told you to stay away from her."

Evan's smirk widened into a smile. "Can I help it if the woman's insatiable?"

"Where is she?"

"Showering. I was just about to join her. We're both kind of…dirty."

Mason clenched his teeth so hard he thought his jaw might snap. It didn't matter, he kept telling himself. None of it mattered. He'd gotten rid of Evan Davies before, he'd do it again.

"You might like to reread that contract you signed," Mason growled warningly.

"What contract?"

"The one where you waived independent legal advice and sold me your shares to Davies Freight." Mason hesitated a moment before continuing, his voice low and dark with fury. "The one where you agreed to forfeit the money if you went near Helena again."

"That'll never stand up in court." Evan paled markedly.

"Won't it?" Mason narrowed his eyes.

"That clause was absurd and you know it. The lady's fair game."

"Let's just see about that then." Mason reached into his pocket and withdrew his cell phone but before he could flip it open Evan began to speak again.

"Don't bother. I concede. To be honest, she's not worth it. After all, if she was, you'd still be tucked up in her bed instead of hammering at her front door, now wouldn't you? So what happened? You weren't man enough for her that she had to call me back?"

Mason saw red. He took a step toward the other man, his shoulders bunched with suppressed rage. Evan scooted back on bare feet and reached out to the hall table where he swiped up a set of keys.

"Don't waste your energy, mate. Look, I'll get out of here and you can sort it all out together."

Dressed only in a robe, Evan jogged to his car and took off down the driveway, leaving a few feet of twin strips of rubber in his wake.

Mason stepped in through the front door and closed it with a resounding thud. Every instinct screamed at him to take the stairs, two steps at a time, to burst into Helena's room and wipe the remnants of her night with Evan from her body with his own. He thrust his hands into his jacket pockets and rocked on his heels, his fingers brushing the envelope he'd pushed in there on his way out the office. The crunch of the paper reminded him what he was here for.

Brody. *His son.*

"Who's there?"

Helena's voice echoed from the top of the stairs. Mason looked up. Her hair was swathed in a towel and she was encased in a neck-to-ankle thick towelling robe.

"Your lover's gone," Mason said as he started up the stairs toward her.

"What are you talking about?" Confusion marred her forehead with a frown.

"Evan. He just left."

"He's not my lover!"

"No? That's not what he said. And," Mason leaned

forward to flip the lapel of her robe, "given the evidence, I believe him."

"What is it with you? I've already told you, he's not my lover."

"You want to know what it is? I'll tell you. Quite frankly, you disgust me. We all know he's going to burn through that money I paid him for his share in Davies Freight. Is that your plan? Are you going to help him through it? Is your thirst for money so great that you'll sleep with anyone, anytime?"

Smack!

His head reeled back with the slap, his skin stinging from where her fingers had whipped across his cheek. He ran his tongue around the inside of his mouth, the tang of blood where his cheek had been cut against his teeth fuelling his anger.

He reached into his pocket and pulled out the envelope from the diagnostic lab, shoving it toward her. Her hands reached out instinctively to take it from him.

"What's this?"

"The proof you thought you wanted."

"What do you mean 'thought I wanted'?"

"Brody is my son."

Even though she had known the truth, her knees buckled and she reached for the balustrade for support. "I knew it."

"Then you might have considered that before you jumped between the sheets with Evan Davies."

"But I didn't!"

"Let's leave that for the lawyers to decide."

Her face drained of colour. "Lawyers?"

"I'm suing for full custody of my boy. You're unfit to be his mother."

"You're going to try to take him from me?"

Mason leaned so close he could smell the lingering scent of vanilla and cinnamon soap on her skin. "Make no mistake, Helena. *Try* doesn't even enter into it. I will win, and I'm sure Evan will make a convincing witness."

"I did not sleep with Evan!"

"Having had firsthand experience of your appetite, I suppose 'sleep' is a relative term under the circumstances. Oh, and by the way, my auditors have almost completed their investigation. You have some explaining to do. Get dressed."

Helena heard the words but they didn't make any sense. Mason was going to take Brody from her. He couldn't have hurt her more if he'd taken a knife to her body. She remained frozen where she stood as the reality of his claim started to sink in.

Evan had turned up at her house late last night, boastful about his new car and definitely the worse for wear after a meal that had obviously been more liquid than solid. As much as he had revolted her with his behaviour, her conscience wouldn't let him drive home. He would be dangerous behind the wheel of any car let alone the over-powered European import he'd indulged in. She'd suggested a taxi, but instead he'd staggered upstairs and he'd fallen asleep in the first bedroom he'd come across. Unfortunately, that bedroom had been hers. She had left him where he'd lain and locked herself in the guest room at the end of the hall. The one she'd shared with Mason.

She'd barely slept, always keeping a wary ear out for his unwelcome attention and plagued by memories of the night she'd last spent in the room. Eventually, though, she must have fallen asleep, waking groggy when she'd heard Evan up and about.

"Come on, I haven't got all day, Helena."

Mason took her by the arm and led her back up the stairs and to her bedroom. At the door he hesitated and suddenly she knew why. Strewn all over the floor were Evan's clothes. The bedcovers and sheets were tangled over the mattress, one pillow on the floor. A cold uncomfortable chill crept down her back as she felt him stiffen at her side.

"I'll wait for you downstairs."

His voice was arctic. A sense of impending disaster wrapped around her heart and squeezed tight.

"I need to dry my hair so I'll be a few minutes."

"Don't fuss on my account. Your charms are wasted on me."

With that he turned and she heard his footfalls as he thundered down the stairs and the front door opened and closed again. Helena flexed her hand, her fingers still smarting from the slap she'd dealt him. She couldn't believe she'd lost control like that, that she'd actually struck him. With the way things were going, no doubt he'd be charging her with assault as well. She looked again at the paper Mason had pushed at her. The proof she'd wanted so desperately so he would help to get Davies Freight back up on its feet again.

It all came down to the old saying, "be careful what you wish for" in the end. Now she had what she needed—what she'd hoped for to ensure that Brody would never want the way she had, would never have to settle for second best or waylay his dreams for lack of money—she ran the very real risk of losing her son. Fear was an ugly, insidious sensation, she decided as she unwound the damp towel from her hair and reached for the blow-dryer. A very ugly sensation indeed.

Despite Mason's insistence that she not take any bother over her appearance, Helena needed the armour that a formal business suit and full makeup gave her. By the time she made it down the stairs and to the front door she could almost fool herself into believing it would be just another day at the office. Almost.

Mason sat in his Porsche—she could see his fingers drumming on the steering wheel. As she locked the front door behind her and approached the car he leaned across and pushed open the passenger door.

"I was on the verge of coming to get you. Dressed or not."

"It's a good thing I'm ready then, isn't it." She took her time settling herself in the seat and putting on her seat belt. "So what is it the auditors have found?"

"I'm not discussing that with you without witnesses to record the meeting. You'll have to wait."

Helena's brow furrowed.

Mason flung her a dark look. "Worried? You should be. I told you I'd get to the bottom of this. You should have learned to hide your tracks a little better."

It was pointless arguing with him. She'd learned that now. No matter how hard she pleaded her innocence, no matter what she said, he wouldn't believe her. She stared blindly forward, oblivious to the familiar scenery as it whipped by on the journey to Davies Freight.

Why had it come to this, she wondered. Why had it come to the point where she would lose everything she'd worked so hard for? A gaping hollow hole opened in her chest, the ache going straight through her heart.

Brody. How on earth would she be able to fight Mason in court? He had the means, the influence and the support to do whatever it took to win. To take her son from her.

The prospect of saving Davies Freight came a very poor second to the thought that she'd lose Brody.

"We're here." Mason's clipped words penetrated the fog of worry that clouded her mind.

"Fine. I'll be as glad to get to the bottom of this as you are."

"Don't be so sure about that."

His words hung like an ominous knell in the air as they walked across the car park and into the building. At reception Mandy looked startled as Helena came through the door.

"Mrs. Davies. Good to have you back. Are you feeling better now?"

"Fine, thank you." Helena shot a questioning look at Mason as they made their way up the stairs to the next floor. "What was that about?"

"I thought it better under the circumstances if they didn't know you were being investigated. You never know where misplaced loyalties might lie that could jeopardise the investigation."

"My staff are loyal to me because I'm a good employer. Not for any other reason."

Mason didn't respond, instead leading the way to her office. He held the door open for her, gesturing that she should precede him into the room.

A comforting sense of familiarity swept over her as she entered. The pictures on the wall, the bookcase, her desk. All of it reflected her personality. Her framed degree hung on the wall opposite her desk so she could see it and remind herself daily of how far she'd come. Of what she'd achieved. All her life, all she'd wanted was to be able to say she'd made it. Now, it looked like she was going to lose it, too.

She put her bag down and sat in the chair behind her desk, silently staking her claim. She clasped her hands together in front of her, squeezing her fingers tight to hide the trembling that threatened to give away her anxiety. If Mason saw even one sign of weakness she had no doubt he'd be in for the kill and she'd be out of here before she could so much as say the words *balance sheet*.

A knock sounded at the door and a tall willowy blonde walked in, a bunch of reports in her arms, and a smile on her face as wide as the Auckland Harbour Bridge when she saw Mason standing there.

"Mason." She acknowledged his presence with a warmth in her voice that went way beyond professional acquaintance.

Helena fought to quell the swell of envy that rose from deep inside her when Mason turned and smiled welcomingly at the newcomer.

"Ah, Sherie, all ready?"

"Yes, I think you'll be surprised at the results." The blonde flung a look in Helena's direction. "Mrs. Davies, I'm Sherie Watson. Mason contracted my firm to conduct the audit on Davies Freight. I can see why you were all concerned, I just don't know if we're going to be able to act soon enough to bolster things back up."

A young man arrived at the door with another stack of files. Sherie cleared a space on the desk for his armload of information.

"This is Alex, my assistant."

Mason took a step forward and put his hand on Sherie's sleeve. To Helena's annoyance the cool blonde blushed at the contact.

"Is there anything else you need before we commence?" He phrased his question with the type of smile Helena would have walked over hot coals to receive from him.

"No, thanks. We're all ready." Sherie smiled back.

Over the next two hours, Sherie and Alex systematically went through their report and Helena had to brokenly admit to herself that the facts were damning. Within a very short period of time after she'd started working at Davies Freight, sums of money had been filtered through an account—false invoices were being paid. The sums had been small at first, probably so as not to raise any flags with the accountant at Flannigans, who finalised their year-end accounting after the data was initially collated at Davies Freight. But over the past three years the sums had incrementally increased until the company had virtually been haemorrhaging money into one account.

"So it's simple then, track down whose account the money is going to and we have our culprit." Helena pushed her chair back from the desk and rotated her shoulders to work out the kinks she'd gained while poring over the reports.

"We, umm..." Sherie shot a wary glance in Mason's direction. At his nod, she continued. "We believe we know what account the funds have been filtered into."

"So, you know who it is. What are you waiting for? Why haven't you called the police?"

"It's a bit more difficult than that." Mason spoke up from where he'd been leaning against the wall, arms crossed and watching Helena. His scrutiny had made her uncomfortable at first, but once she'd started looking through the reports and listening to Sherie and Alex, he'd faded into the background.

"I don't see what the problem is."

"Would you like us to leave the room?" Alex offered.

"No. I want two impartial witnesses to what I have to say."

"Impartial?" Helena snorted. "They're hardly impartial when they're in your employment."

"Actually, they're not in my employment. They're independent of Black Knight Transport."

Helena settled back in her chair. Whether they were independent of BKT or not, Sherie was certainly not impartial when it came to Mason Knight. Well, she was welcome to him.

"So?" Helena lifted her chin and looked Mason square in the eye. "Who's the thief? Whose account has the money been going into?"

Mason stood up and removed a sheet of paper from his breast pocket. He carefully unfolded it before putting it down on the desk in front of Helena.

"Do you remember this?"

Helena picked up the sheet and examined it. All she could see were rows of figures, none of which seemed to make a great deal of sense. "It's a piece of paper. Why should I remember this one in particular?"

"Perhaps because you'd hidden it behind the photo you were so keen to remove from the office when you were suspended from your duties."

"Hidden it? Don't be ridiculous. The first time I saw that was when you picked it up out of the broken glass."

"I could almost believe you, if not for one thing. Helena, the account the money has been going into is yours."

Nine

Mason watched through narrowed eyes as every last vestige of colour drained from Helena's face. Her green eyes grew huge, the pupils dilated. A fine bead of perspiration raised on her upper lip. From his point of view she couldn't look more guilty if she tried.

"Nothing to say?" he prompted.

"I didn't do it. I don't know where the money's gone but I certainly didn't put it in any bank account in my name." Her hand fluttered up to her throat as her words choked in a voice thick with tears. "Please, Mason. You have to believe me. I didn't do it."

"I'd hoped you'd be reasonable about this, Helena. That you'd have the guts to come out and admit it when faced with the truth. It seems I was wrong."

He picked up the sheet of paper and folded it carefully before putting it back in his pocket. He turned to

Sherie and Alex, both of whom looked uncomfortable at the scene that had unfolded before them.

"Thank you. I think we have everything we need."

"Sure. We'll send through the finalised report once the computer forensics people get back to us in writing—I've been told their information will confirm everything here. Should be sometime tomorrow." Sherie put out her hand to shake his.

When they'd gone, Mason dropped into the chair opposite Helena's desk. She hadn't said a word since her tearful plea, but had remained frozen in her chair.

"I don't want to have to take this to the police, Helena. If you return the money to Davies Freight and formally resign from your position, I'm prepared to leave it there." He lifted a hand to the back of his neck and rubbed wearily at the tension there.

"No."

"I don't think I heard you right." Mason leaned forward. Surely she didn't mean to still deny it. She'd been shown the proof.

"I am not going to take responsibility for something I didn't do."

"You have to admit the evidence is fairly damning."

"Yes, it is, but even evidence can be fabricated. Which computers have you had analysed aside from mine?"

"We did your home computer and the one from the office here."

"You didn't have Evan's computer examined?"

"No need. It wasn't him."

"What makes you so sure? Why are you so prepared to believe that he's not responsible for this?"

"Because, while Evan is money-hungry, he has neither the finesse nor the patience to carry something like this off for so long. If it had been him, he would have simply skimmed off several large sums and gone shopping." There had been some misdealings by Evan—overspending on expense accounts, exorbitant lunches and hotel bills purportedly for company business, but that's as far as it went. Mason could stomach those losses, sure in the knowledge that Evan had no chance to do any further damage to Davies Freight. Helena's activities, however, were another thing entirely.

"Then it was someone else. Someone who had access to my password."

Mason expected to feel anger at her repeated protestations of innocence, but instead, he was devoid of anything but relief it was nearly over. "I'm only glad Patrick didn't live long enough to discover what you were up to. It would have broken his heart to know what you're really like."

"What I'm really like? He knew exactly what I'm really like, which is more than I can say for you and your crazy accusations."

Helena's mind spun in dizzy circles. Faced with the same evidence, she knew she would have come to the same conclusion. It was devastating to realise she had so little to go on—so little with which to prove her innocence. Bit by bit, everything she had worked so hard for during her married life was sliding through her fingers. Her security, her identity—even her very own son. And for what?

What was security anyway? She knew now, for sure, it wasn't tied up in her marriage or her job. Everything she'd ever believed in, had ever put faith in, was systematically shattering about her.

Mason remained silent after her last outburst,

choosing to cross his arms and observe her from across the desk. His very reticence gave her hope. He wasn't immune to her; she knew that with the intimacy of a lover. But would he listen—would he give her the benefit of the doubt? The answer was a resounding no. It was time to change tactics.

"It might surprise you, Mason, but I actually agree with you about Patrick."

He uncrossed his arms and shoved his hands deep in the pockets of his charcoal-grey suit. His body language implied he was open to discussion but the frigid expression on his face told her differently. "Really? You're right, I am surprised. Why start now, Helena? Running scared?"

"Scared? Not me." She shook her head gently. "No. I agree with you in being glad that Patrick didn't live long enough to see this—to see you behaving like this. He loved you like a son, Mason. Like his very own son. And now you're undermining everything he stood for."

"You're being melodramatic."

"Do you think so? I don't. You forget. You may have known Patrick for, what, fifteen years, max? I lived with, and loved, the man for twelve years, twenty-four-seven."

"And were paid handsomely for the job from what I can tell." The curl of his lip was enough to make her want to strike out at him, but she would never succumb to such emotional weakness in his presence again.

"If you think repaying Patrick's devotion to me by loving him unreservedly is something to be ashamed of then I'm sorry, but you have another thing coming. You have no right to denigrate our love for one another, or our marriage." She pushed herself upright, trying to meet him eye-to-eye. "You can do your damned best to try and discover what has gone wrong here at Davies

Freight. You can crunch numbers, you can interview staff, you can lay your unfounded accusations. But you can never take from me the life and the love I shared with Patrick." She paused for a moment, locking eyes with him before continuing, "And maybe that's the problem."

Helena pushed past him and rushed out the office. She'd braved it out long enough, but now she could barely see for the tears that blinded her vision. Tears for Patrick and for Brody, but most of all, tears for herself that she'd managed to fall in love with the one man on the face of the earth who'd never believe in her.

As she tore down the stairs and out the front door she realised that all the things she'd thought came first in her life came a distant second to knowing she loved and was loved in return. And if she couldn't have that love, she would darn well have to learn to live without it. She could rebuild her life and her son's life—brick by brick if she had to.

Suddenly it was clear that all her adult life she'd been barking up the wrong tree. Sure, it was okay to want things. But under everything remained the security of a strong and happy relationship. An equal sharing of life and love and personal philosophies.

She'd had that to an extent with Patrick but, even so, she knew in retrospect that major aspects of their relationship were missing—unbalanced. She and Mason could have those things together, had he been willing. Yet he wasn't. He was so bent on his vendetta against her—against the wrongs he perceived she'd wreaked on him. They didn't stand a chance. Not when he didn't trust her. Not when he didn't believe in her as a person, let alone as the mother of his son.

She only hoped now that she could still retain

custody of Brody. Mason would enter the fray with all legal guns blazing. He'd made his stance perfectly clear. And now, with the financial evidence he'd amassed against her, she doubted she'd stand a chance in any family court. His suspicions now, intertwined with her past, would give him all the ammunition he needed.

A dry, harsh sob shook her from deep within. She could cope with starting over if she had Brody. Surely he couldn't take Brody?

In the crisp, wet winter air she dragged one breath after another into her aching lungs. Eventually the constriction that bound her chest began to ease off, and her breathing came easier. What to do now?

She had to talk to Brody. Maybe, if he was in agreement, she could sell his share of Davies Freight to Mason on condition that he drop the custody proceedings.

But it wasn't Davies Freight Mason was after, a little voice reminded her. It was their son.

Mason raked a weary hand through his short, cropped hair. What a day. Helena had barely uttered a word as he'd taken her home after the confrontation at the office. It drove him crazy that she continued to deny any wrongdoing. He'd have been open to discussion if she'd just been honest with him, but the evidence was damning and yet she still wouldn't budge an inch.

He'd spent the rest of the day at Davies Freight, going over the figures again and again, searching for some clue that might show if she was telling the truth. The truth? Why would he even begin to think that she was capable of such a thing? Sure, she'd argued back, convincingly, that she was innocent. But his deep-seated mistrust of her told him a different story.

One way or another he'd been frustrated at every turn today and eventually he'd given up and headed for the oasis of his own company's offices. He took the elevator to the top floor of the BKT building and his shoulders started to relax. Thank goodness he had staff he could rely upon to do the right thing by him and to keep things running smoothly while he split his days between here and Davies Freight.

The situation at the latter really worried him. If the business was to stay up-and-running it needed a cash infusion and it needed it right now. The thing was, who would be fool enough to get involved when the success or failure of the company was so precarious? His instincts told him it would be best to cut his losses. Wind up the company and absorb only those operations that would benefit Black Knight Transport. But there was more than that at stake.

The company was Patrick's legacy to Brody. Patrick had often said that the boy had an old head on young shoulders and had genuinely looked forward to showing him the ropes. Could he, Mason, honour the wish of a dead man or would he simply be courting financial suicide?

As the elevator doors slid open he was no closer to finding a solution. The lights were still on in his front office and as he entered the reception room of his inner sanctum he could hear the familiar rat-a-tat-tat of his personal assistant's fingers as they flew over the keyboard. Margaret Daniels had been with him since he'd first started the business and she'd mothered him from day one. Now widowed, and with her children grown, she frequently stayed to work late.

"Margaret, what are you still doing here? It's past time you went home."

"Oh, you know it's no bother, Mr. Knight. Besides, you have an unexpected appointment waiting for you in your office." She arched one greyed eyebrow in his direction. "When you're finished, you have some explaining to do."

A sinking feeling settled in his stomach. Had Helena decided to come clean? Was she waiting for him in his office to finally admit to her theft? A piece of him hoped like crazy that he was right and that he could start to put this whole episode behind him, but as he pushed open the door and saw who waited in his office his heart stuttered in his chest.

Brody.

The slender-built boy turned from Mason's desk to face him and it was as if he was looking into a mirror—a mirror from over twenty years ago. The boy's face, above his neatly knotted school tie, was pale but stoic, his chin held high and his black-brown eyes met Mason's full on.

"You're my father."

There was no question in Brody's voice and the shock of those three simple words stopped Mason in his tracks. Behind him he heard Margaret discreetly close the office door. Something which no doubt cost her dearly given the bald statement she couldn't help but have overheard. He'd worry about that later. For now, there was one pressing issue to take care of, yet for some weird reason words failed him.

"I've known for ages, so don't bother denying it. Dad told me just before I turned ten. He said I was lucky to have two fathers, that it was more than some boys ever got." The boy's shoulders squared and he stood as rigid as a post, challenging Mason to respond.

"Yes, it's true. I am your father. I didn't know for certain myself until today." Mason stepped forward and put out his hand. Brody shook it like a man, but the handshake felt all wrong. Mason's arms ached to take his son in his arms, as he'd been cheated of doing for far too many years, and acknowledge the boy as his own. He dropped Brody's hand and gestured to the long settee against one wall.

"Take a seat. We have a lot to talk about. Not the least of which is, does your mother know you're here?"

The boy had the grace to look shamefaced. "No, I— I kind of ran away from school. It's just that I knew something was up. I knew Mum was stonewalling me, trying to protect me from something. The blood tests— they weren't for glandular fever, were they? It was to prove you're my father."

"Yes." Mason sat down next to his son. "We didn't want you to know just yet. Looks like your dad had other ideas, huh?"

"He was like that. Always wanting to be one step ahead, y'know?" Brody's eyes shone with unshed tears as he determinedly blinked them back. "I miss him."

"Me, too. He was a great man."

"He helped start you up, didn't he?"

"Yeah, he did. And he gave me some stiff competition until I diversified, too."

Brody nodded. "He told me that. He said if anyone could beat him at his own game it was you. Are you going to close down Davies Freight now?"

The boy's question shocked him. "Why would I do that?"

"It's your only real road-transport competition. Dad reckoned you would have already done it if he hadn't helped you get started."

It was galling to realise, but Brody's words were true. And he *was* thinking about shutting down Davies Freight, even if for an entirely different reason.

"You won't close it down, will you? I mean, when I grow up, I'm going to run it. It'll be my turn to give you stiff competition."

The thought of mentoring his son bloomed in his chest, but the question of whether it would be at Davies Freight or not had a severe dampening effect. Given the same circumstances he wondered what Patrick would do. Would he fight to retain a flailing business, or would he read the writing on the wall and invest his energy in another direction? The answer eluded him.

Mason looked at his watch. It was late and it suddenly occurred to him that Brody's school would be frantic by now. "I need to call your school. Let them know you're okay."

Brody sat back against the cushions on the couch. "Don't worry. I asked your secretary to ring school for me."

Mason's eyebrows raised in surprise. "And what about your mother? Did you ask Margaret to call her, too?"

Brody squirmed a little in his seat. "No. Mum would only have yelled at me and made me go back before I got to meet you. She's always got to do things right. It was her idea not to tell me the truth about the tests, wasn't it?"

"She thought the news would upset you. She didn't want you to have to deal with it so close to losing your dad." The last word stuck in Mason's throat.

"I'm not a baby! She should have told me!" The boy quietened a little after his outburst, sneaking a sideline look at Mason. "Are you mad at me?"

"To tell you the truth, Brody, I really don't know." And it was the truth. By the time his heart had resumed a normal rhythm he'd simply been blown away by the fact Brody was even in his office.

"Mum'll be mad. I don't suppose we can get away with not telling her?" Brody looked at Mason's face. "Nah, I didn't think so. So, do you want to ring her or should I?"

"Let's just take you home and deal with it then. What do you reckon?"

The boy's face brightened. "Yeah, that's brilliant. She wouldn't dream of yelling at me in front of you."

Mason wondered if that were true. He still vividly remembered the day, not long after his mother had become so ill she could barely move from her bed, he'd taken off from school and raced home. He could still see the joy in her eyes that he'd come to look out for her, but he still felt the sting of her quiet disappointment that he'd left school to do it. She'd ordered him back to class in no uncertain terms. She'd been firm with all three of her boys that way, but they'd never doubted her love for them. Even when she grew so ill that she could no longer leave her bed.

Connor barely remembered that time. Declan had simply gotten on with the basics of looking after the family and their dad had just about worked himself to the point of exhaustion. Through it all, Mason had spent every possible minute at his mother's side. Strange that he should think of that now. Those memories had been supplanted by other more painful ones as time had gone by.

He stood up. "C'mon, let's go. She's got enough on her plate right now without worrying about you."

The lights in the house were blazing as they drove up the drive to the front door. Before the car's engine had even stopped Helena was flying out the door toward the passenger door. She yanked the door open and pulled Brody from the car and into her arms. She hugged him so tight Mason thought the boy would suffocate, before pushing him away from her and holding him at arms length.

"I rang your school to talk to you and they said you'd gone. Oh my God, I was so worried about you. What were you thinking? You know you can't just up and leave like that whenever you want to." There was no mistaking the fear in her voice. The fact that Brody was perfectly safe didn't begin to touch the terror she'd obviously gone through.

"I'm sorry, Mum." Brody hung his head.

Helena stared at her son hard, then shook her head before turning her eyes on Mason.

"And you. Why did you have to get involved? Couldn't you wait before starting your campaign to take him from me?"

"It's not his fault. I went to him," Brody protested. "If you're going to be mad, be mad at me."

"Oh, don't get me wrong, young man. I am thoroughly mad at you. But I'll deal with you later. Go inside, now." Her tone brooked no argument.

Suddenly Mason was seeing a side of Helena Davies he'd never seen before. The lioness with her cub. It was an aspect of her he'd never considered. The front door slammed with a hollow thud as Brody shut himself inside. If anything, his action made Helena's spine stiffen even further.

"Explain yourself," she demanded.

Mason felt the familiar anger that always simmered beneath the surface when he was around her begin to bubble to the surface.

"Explain myself? I had nothing to do with it."

"Don't be ridiculous. You told me this morning you were going for custody of Brody. You had to have talked to him. Why else would he have run away from school like that? Couldn't you have waited? Couldn't you have damn well let me handle my son my way?"

He wanted to argue back, to point out that Brody was his son too. Yet there was an edge to her fury that hovered on a distress so deep it forced him to hold back the words he wanted to shout in defence.

Instead, he spoke quietly. "Brody was waiting for me at my office. I had no idea he'd be there."

"You expect me to believe that? You never just accept what happens around you, Mason Knight—you make things happen."

"I'm flattered by your observation, but in this case you're wrong." Mason looked toward the house just in time to catch the movement of a net curtain in one of the downstairs windows. The boy was obviously watching. "It seems that Patrick beat us both to the gun."

"Patrick?"

"He told Brody the truth just over a year ago."

Helena's face paled in the reflective glare of the outside lights. "He told Brody? Why?"

Mason sighed heavily. "Goodness knows what was behind Patrick's thinking. God knows how he even knew it was me and not some other random guy you might have slept with."

She took a step back as if he'd physically struck her and he instantly felt shame for what he'd said.

"I'm sorry. I shouldn't have said that. It was uncalled for."

"But it's what you think, isn't it? To you, the test

results only confirmed that you are Brody's father, but deep down you thought he was some Russian roulette baby. That he could have been anybody's. Not *just* yours or Patrick's." She crossed her arms defensively across her body, as if by doing so she could somehow shield herself—as if she couldn't bear to take another emotional blow from him. "I didn't deliberately keep the truth from you about Brody because I truly didn't know. You're not the only one that Patrick lied to by omission. We're in this together. We could have something here, Mason. Something special. We already share a child, we could share so much more. But none of that matters, does it? No matter what I say or do, you won't ever believe me, will you?"

Words choked in Mason's throat. He honestly didn't know what to say. Everything concrete told him he couldn't trust her but a tiny niggle in the region of his chest urged him to listen to her words and to seek the truth in them. He hissed an expletive under his breath.

The crunch of her footsteps on the driveway as she walked back to the house told him he'd had his chance to speak and lost it, and with that knowledge came the weight of realisation that with his silence he'd lost far, far more.

Ten

Mason paced the confines of his study in his home nestled on the side of Mount Hobson in Auckland's prestigious suburb of Remuera. The ice in his shot of whiskey melted, unheeded, and the lights reflected in the distance did little to soothe his fractured thoughts.

Just when had Helena managed to creep under his skin so far that he'd begun to think she might be telling the truth? He threw himself into the deep button-back chair positioned by the lit fire and stared, mesmerised by the flames licking and dancing over the wood.

He didn't want to believe she might be right, but again and again her words echoed in his mind.

We already share a child, we could share so much more.

What would it be like, he wondered, to share a life with her? He looked around the study, his hideaway when he was at home. On the mantel he had framed shots of his family and the walls displayed the work of his favourite New Zealand artists. The furniture in here was nothing but the best, like everything he surrounded himself with. But even so, his picture-perfect residence was lacking in the warmth that would make it a home. It was little more than another testament to his success.

He'd worked hard to be where he was today. He'd accumulated so much and now stood poised on the brink of diversifying across the Tasman into Australia as well. After that, who knew? He'd achieved so much in a very short period of time—success many men and women spent a lifetime working for. And for what? To enjoy it on his own?

Mason thought of his brothers. Both workaholics who'd been corralled in the past couple of years by a couple of gorgeous women. Connor had married his secretary, but not without a whole lot of stress on the journey. Declan had married his dead fiancée's best friend. Neither of them had done it the easy way, but both had loved the women involved enough to work past their problems. And that's where he differed from his brothers—he didn't love Helena.

Even as the thought took shape in his mind, his heart thudded painfully in his chest.

Was that the problem? Despite everything, was he in love with Helena? He pushed the thought stubbornly from his mind. He would not go down that road. His father had loved Melanie, or so he'd said when he'd blamed Mason wholeheartedly for the breakdown in that relationship.

But a small voice continued to niggle at him. If he didn't love Helena, why had he agreed to help her? He hadn't wanted to believe her about Brody, and under any other circumstances he'd never have bought into Davies Freight. He'd have done what he'd done with the other smaller companies he'd absorbed over the years and bided his time to make an offer. Then, when they finally stood in a position where they couldn't say no, he would have swooped in for the acquisition. So why was he working so hard to plug the holes and make Davies Freight work?

It was no longer out of any loyalty to Patrick. His mentor had lost that when he'd deliberately hidden Brody's parentage. The words Helena had taunted him with days ago came back to haunt him. The words where she'd made it clear she didn't believe he'd be where he was in his life right now without Patrick's influence. Okay, so that much was true. But the man had stolen eleven years of his son's life from him. At what stage had Patrick planned to tell him—to let him in on the secret of what he was missing?

It was impossible not to be bitter, not to regret the lost years. But hoarding bitterness could only lead to a slow poisoning of the system and eventually to complete shutdown. He'd already learned that the hard way with his father.

Mason studied Tony Knight's craggy brow in the photo and, in his father's face, began to see himself in another thirty years. He didn't like what he saw. A man still driven by the mighty dollar, still driven to hide from the grief of losing the one woman he'd loved.

The woman he loved? Did he love Helena Davies? He'd tried to convince himself she was no more than a sexual release, but sex with Helena had done anything but release him. It had only served to wind his desire for her tighter and tighter, until he was certain no one else could ever satisfy the hunger that grew within—no one but her.

Mason shifted uncomfortably in his seat. Damn, but she drove him crazy—even with just a thought.

The last time he'd felt like this he'd been a teenager and look at the trouble that had gotten him into. He'd been unable to refuse the advances of his father's mistress and in the end his weakness had driven a wedge between him and his dad that still remained.

So was it Brody that drove him to keep Davies Freight alive? No. His son could learn from the ground floor at BKT if he really wanted to. Mason understood how important it was to understand every aspect of the business. And if Brody didn't want to work from the bottom up, that was okay, too. He could provide his son with every opportunity to ensure he could never want for a single thing in his life.

A single thing but his mother.

When he won sole custody—and he was confident he would—how would Brody cope with the change in his lifestyle? Kids are adaptable, sure. But how would three dramatic life changes—losing a father, gaining another, then losing his mother—affect Brody in the long term? Did he want his son to be just like him?

The similarities between them went beyond the physical. Mason had been almost eleven, just a few months younger than Brody was now, when he'd lost his mother. But he knew he wouldn't do to his son what his father had done to him, nor betray him as Patrick had done. Never in a million years.

Damn, but his head hurt thinking about this.

But soon the loneliness he felt would be a thing of the past. There'd been a message on his answer machine from the family law solicitor he'd engaged to petition for custody of Brody. Once he won, he'd enrol the boy in a school here in Auckland, keep him close. Begin to make up for the lost years.

He looked up at the heavy wooden mantel that framed the fireplace, and in particular at the recent photo he had of his dad and brothers. What would they do in the same situation, he wondered. There really was no argument. No matter the circumstances, blood ran thicker than water. Well, at least part of the time.

That certainly hadn't been the case when Melanie had cried wolf, and insisted Mason had been the one to initiate things between them. The atmosphere at home had become unbearable after that night, and the situation had grown even worse after Melanie left. It hadn't taken long to get to the point where Mason couldn't stand the estrangement, or the guilt, any longer and two days after finishing his last year at high school he had walked straight into the New Zealand Army recruitment office and signed up.

His father's farewell when Mason left for training camp had been cold, stilted. They still had too many words left unsaid between them. And all because of a woman like Helena.

Mason lifted his tumbler and took a sip of the warmed whiskey. He grimaced at the watered-down flavour and set the glass on the table beside him.

We could share so much more.

The cynical side of him tried to convince himself that when she talked about "more" she was probably talking about money, but his heart told him different. He thought again of the look on her face—the horror in her eyes—when she'd been presented with Sherie's evidence. Either she'd been giving an award-winning performance, or she really was telling the truth and the account information was completely news to her. Thinking now about that look was enough to make him doubt his own opinion, a fact he wasn't comfortable with in the least, especially since he'd been so driven to find her accountable.

He wasn't the kind of man who doubted himself. But then again, he wasn't the kind of man who normally would unreasonably search for evidence to prove that Helena was the culprit without casting a wider net. He'd judged her guilty based on his feelings for her. Feelings that right now battered against his heart and his head with all the subtlety of a fully laden eighteen-wheeler travelling at a hundred kilometres an hour.

They were missing something. It galled him to admit it but he'd been totally, deliberately, blind to the possibility that someone else was the thief. For goodness sake, the paper had been found behind a photo he'd seen on Patrick's desk himself. It was entirely possible that Helena hadn't even known it was there. It was a possibility that flickered to life like a reluctant flame in his mind—a possibility he hadn't even allowed himself to consider before.

Could Patrick have hidden the evidence there? Surely not. But maybe he knew about the thefts? Perhaps he'd believed it was Helena and had chosen to do nothing about it. Or maybe he'd known it was someone else and was biding his time, waiting for the right moment to expose the thief.

With a sigh of self-disgust, he pushed himself up out of his seat and took his glass through to the kitchen, rinsing it out in the sink before stacking it in the dishwasher. He looked around the room, a room which in most houses was the hub of the home. It looked perfect. It looked as though no one lived there, and in reality, with the hours he worked, no one did. It was nothing like the warm friendly room at Helena's house with potted herbs in the kitchen window and the detritus that showed frequent and comfortable use of an area.

No, this wasn't a home, this was merely what he'd allowed himself to be reduced to. An accumulation of wealth and success in an unconscious bid to prove he was the better man. He'd allowed Helena's marriage to Patrick to drive him into this solitary domain and he'd had enough. It was time to step up to the plate and admit he'd been wrong.

She'd been right on the money when she'd said the love she'd shared with Patrick had been his problem all along. He'd been so driven by jealousy, and by the what-might-have-beens he'd refused to see her for what and who she really was. Worse, he'd allowed his disillusionment over Melanie to sway him to find similarities between the women. Amplifying the flaws in Helena that he thought he'd found, and making himself miserable in the process. His feelings for Helena, no matter how hard he tried to suppress them, had kept him from forming any lasting relationship with another woman. But then he hadn't ever wanted anyone else the way he wanted her.

A single truth shattered through his mind—*he loved her.* No one else would do. No other woman had impacted on him the way she had and now that she was free, he could dare to want her for himself—provided he hadn't irrevocably ruined his chances by his truly awful treatment of her over the past few weeks.

It wouldn't be enough just to have Brody. He wanted the whole package. He wanted them both, forever.

For Helena's sake, he knew know he had to prove she was telling the truth or he would die a very lonely man. He'd treated her appallingly. It was time to make that up to her, if she'd let him.

So far, he'd done everything he could in the investigation to remain above board—the audit, the computer forensics, the lot. Now, it was time to dig deep below the surface—whatever the financial price. If he could find out what had happened to the money when it passed through the account set up in Helena's name, he'd be a giant step closer to finally winning the woman he'd loved for longer than he wanted to admit.

His brothers would help, he was sure of that, and their anonymity in the investigation might be just the leverage he needed.

Ding dong.

Mason flicked a glance at his watch. Ten o'clock. Who the hell visited at this time of night? The doorbell went again.

"All right, all right. Hold on, I'm coming," he shouted as he strode through the echoing house and opened the door.

"Hey, bro'. Nice welcome." Declan Knight turned to face his other brother, Connor. "Looks like we made the right decision to come over. He's alone."

Connor merely eyed Mason from the front step and nodded.

"Too bad if I wasn't, right? Like you guys would just leave if I had company?" Mason fought to keep a welcoming smile from his face.

"I hear you've been holding out on us," Declan

drawled. "Connor tells me congratulations are in order—*Dad.*"

From behind his back, Declan produced a twelve-year-old bottle of Scotch and pushed past Mason. Connor followed close behind.

Standing at the door, Mason spoke to the empty front porch, "Sure, c'mon in, guys." Then, with a sense of rightness he hadn't felt in a long time, he turned and followed them down the hall. His brothers were just what he needed right now. Among the three of them, they'd get to the bottom of this.

And then it would be time to reach out and get the woman he loved, just like he should have done twelve years ago.

Helena saw the real estate agent to the gate, where she hammered a For Sale sign in the grass verge at the front of the poperty. The agent had impressed her with her professionalism and enthusiasm. She'd assured Helena that she had several buyers on her books for the home already. With any luck, she wouldn't even have to endure so much as a single open-home day. The sooner she could get this over with, the better. She wanted everything cut and dried and off her hands.

Two nights ago it had finally occurred to Helena that if she sold the house, as was her right to, she could put back into Davies Freight a good deal of what had gone missing—whether she'd been responsible or not.

She still couldn't understand how so much money had been filtered into an account in her name and then been siphoned off elsewhere unknown—she might never understand it. But one thing she knew without doubt. If Mason Knight wasn't going to save Davies Freight for Brody, she'd do it herself.

The fact that the company was now half Mason's wasn't lost on her. Maybe though, with this act, she could finally get him to accept that she wasn't the money-loving whore he'd all but accused her of being. She caught a glimpse of herself in the hall mirror. Well, she wouldn't attract any punters looking like this. Her face was pale, her hair lank and dull, and her eyes red-rimmed from lack of sleep.

Since that night a week ago, when she'd stayed up for hours watching Brody sleep, she'd struggled through the dark hours. Her breath caught as she thought of her precious boy. He'd have died of embarrassment, for sure, if he'd known she'd remained in his room long after he'd drifted off. But it had been with a sense of fatalism that Helena decided this might be one of her last chances to spend time with her son before his feelings toward her were poisoned by the knowledge that she'd decided not to contest Mason's bid for custody.

When she'd bid Brody goodbye at the train station early the next morning to send him back to school, it had taken every ounce of her courage to remain strong and not break down.

She was confident she'd made the right decision. It was more than her heart could bear to drag her son through her past, and her reasons for marrying Patrick. She was certain she'd have rights to see Brody. There wasn't a judge living who'd deny her that. But she was prepared to stand aside. For now. For her son. In years to come, when he was mature enough to make his own decisions, when he could understand the sacrifice she'd made out of her love for him—out of what was right, for him—she had no doubt he'd come back to her. But if she forced Brody to decide now, or put him through the agony of a family court trial and the push-me pull-you that would come about, she could do irreparable damage.

She strolled slowly up the drive, looking at the garden with a sense of loss that she wouldn't be here to see the newly pruned roses burst into bloom again in the spring, or the tulip bulbs she'd planted last April push through the ground to give a carpet of colour on the edge of the driveway.

The bulbs reminded her of her love for Mason. How there was so much evolving beneath the surface, reaching for the light of day, reaching for the warmth of reciprocated love. But it wasn't to be. She knew they didn't stand a chance together, no matter how much she loved him. In her heart of hearts she knew if she could just set this one thing right, then knowing how he felt about her wouldn't weigh like a millstone about her neck.

Helena looked around her again. She'd come so far from the twenty-year-old bride she'd been when this house was built. She had everything, and yet she had nothing. Nothing but her single-minded purpose to set things right in her world again. No matter what the cost.

It would be worth it, she consoled herself. It had to be.

Eleven

She'd just pulled the front door closed behind her when she heard a vehicle roar up the drive, its wheels skidding slightly as it drew to a halt. At the sound of a car door being slammed shut, soon followed by rapid steps up the front stairs, filtered through the heavy front door, she froze. *Oh no,* she thought, *please not Evan. Not today.*

"Helena?"

Mason? She snuck a peek through the peephole. Maybe she'd have been better off if it had been Evan after all. Him, she could handle. No wonder she hadn't recognised the sound of the car. Behind Mason stood the big black truck she'd crashed on his private road. He'd obviously finally gotten it back from the panel and paint shop. Maybe he was here to give her the bill, she thought, on the verge of hysteria.

"Helena!" She jumped as he hammered at the door. "C'mon. I know you're in there. Open the door."

She made a decision to face him—so she could say goodbye. This time, for good. She took her time turning the key in the lock and only opened the door sufficiently wide to show her face.

"What the hell is this?" Without so much as a hello, Mason pushed the door open and held up the For Sale sign the Realtor had just finished hammering into the ground. Soil from the stakes attached to the sign dropped on the tiled entrance.

Helena crossed her arms and stood firm in the doorway. "Last time I looked I didn't answer to you. I don't have to tell you anything."

Mason's dark eyes narrowed suspiciously. He hurled the sign off to the side of the front porch. "What are you up to? Why are you selling the house?"

Helena sighed resignedly. He wouldn't leave without an answer and if she wanted him off her front porch she'd have to tell him the truth. "If you must know, it's because I won't need it soon. It's far too big for me, anyway."

"Downsizing? That doesn't sound like you." He sounded surprised.

She shook her head. "You don't know me."

You never did, and you never will. The knowledge cut her like a knife. She fought to control the tremor in her voice—she had to hold it together. About now, her lawyer would be calling his to say that she'd chosen not to contest his petition to have custody of Brody. Her insides felt as though they were being torn apart but she daren't give him so much as an inkling of how much this killed her inside, inch by slow painful inch. She lifted her hand to close the door but he was faster and inserted his large frame in the doorway.

"You're right, I don't. But what if I want to?"

"It's too late for that, Mason. Look, if you really want to know, I'm selling the house to put the money back into Davies Freight. Okay, are you satisfied? Now you know, you can leave."

She lifted her hand to the door again, but he held his stance refusing to budge.

"But I'm not nearly satisfied, Helena." His voice was low and rich, like the texture of velvet. "Are you?"

"Don't play games with me, Mason. I'm not in the mood."

"Okay. No games. But do one thing for me."

"One thing. And then you'll leave me alone?"

"One thing, and then, yeah, if that's what you really want, I'll leave you alone."

He was up to something, she was certain, but for the life of her she couldn't gauge what it was. There was a look in his eyes that she couldn't quite define. Surely he would be satisfied she was selling her home to refinance the company. Something didn't sit right with her though, and caution urged her to find out what he wanted before she would agree to anything.

"So what is it?" she demanded. "What's this one thing you want from me?"

Your forgiveness would be a start. The words echoed silently in his head and Mason had to think twice before answering. He'd set this process in place and he planned to follow every step to the letter. No shortcuts. If he got this right, everything would be worthwhile. If he didn't…well, it didn't bear thinking about. Failure was not an option. Not now, not with Helena.

"I need you to come with me." He reached out to take her hand and urged her gently out onto the front porch.

"Come with you? Where?" She pulled back, resisting his gentle coercion.

"You'll find out when we get there."

"Just because I'm paying money into Davies Freight doesn't mean I'm admitting anything. It had better not be a police station you're taking me to, Mason, or God help me, I'll—"

"Don't worry. It's not the police."

"Let me lock up then. Do I need to bring anything?"

"No. We won't be long."

To his relief she turned and locked the front door, slipping the house key in her jeans pocket. The black sweater she wore highlighted how pale she was, and how exhausted. Guilt struck him square in the chest. He'd done this to her—even driven her to try to sell her home. So much hinged on the outcome of the next hour. He hoped like crazy that his instincts had been right and that it wasn't entirely too late.

Mason handed her up into the cab of the truck, and walked around to the driver's side. When he realised how much space lay between them he instantly regretted bringing the larger vehicle. In the Porsche they'd have been closer together. He sensed her stiffen when she realised where they were headed—Davies Freight.

"What are you doing? Why are you bringing me here?"

"There's something you need to see for yourself." He clenched his jaw tight. She wouldn't like what was coming next. It had taken him and his brothers the better part of the past week to nail this. Like anything important, it all came down to the finer details. Now they had the conclusion he'd been seeking all along.

As they pulled up in the car park, Helena swiftly undid her seat belt and alighted from the truck before he could come around and open her door. He watched as she straightened her shoulders and smoothed her clothes and as her face assumed calmer lines. It was as if she was determined to put on a brave face for whatever he had lined up for her inside. Pride swelled inside him. She was so strong. Stronger than he'd ever realised or given her credit for.

"They're waiting for us upstairs," he said quietly.

"Then let's get this over with," she snapped and started to walk toward the front door.

She abruptly stopped in her tracks in the foyer, and looked at him, accusation clear in her voice when she spoke. "Who's this?" She gestured to where his PA, Margaret, was sitting on reception. "What's wrong with Mandy? Don't tell me you've started firing my people."

"Just come on in. I'll tell you everything in a minute."

They crossed through reception quickly and headed up the staircase to the next floor. At the door to Patrick's office Mason hesitated a moment, turning to face Helena and holding both her arms just above the elbow in his warm firm grip.

"Now, you're probably not going to like what you're going to hear, but I want you to know I'll be right by you."

He pushed the door open to reveal the two uniformed police officers standing on either side of what had been Patrick's desk. Mason heard Helena's breath catch as she recognised the person leaning back in a chair in the corner of the office. Mandy. Gone was the friendly and welcoming receptionist she'd grown accustomed to. Instead, a hard and mutinous glare distorted her features.

"Mandy? What…?" Helena's voice trailed away, one hand fluttered to her throat as the truth slowly sank in.

"Go on," Mason nodded at Mandy, who turned her head away from Helena, refusing to make eye contact.

"Okay, okay. It was me."

"Why?" Helena demanded, her voice low, steady and resonating with an anger he'd expected. "Why did you steal from us?"

The other woman snorted and shook her head. "We're the same age, you know that? And from the same background too. I couldn't see why, when I was right under his nose for the taking, he had to go and choose you. Why should you have it all? The clothes, the education, the beautiful house. He should have chosen me.

"I was mad when he brought you into the office, all proud as punch about his trophy bride, so I thought I'd teach him a lesson. Just a little one at first, but when no one noticed I decided to take a bit more."

"Then you started gambling, and that's what strung you up," Mason interrupted in a voice colder than a Southland winter.

"Yeah. I started to take too much and Patrick found out about it."

"That explains the paper behind the picture," Helena exclaimed. "He must have started looking into it just before he died. Why didn't he talk to me about it?"

"I'm sure he would've, given time. He wasn't the kind of man to make decisions lightly. In fact, if I know him, he would even have given Mandy a chance to pay it back—isn't that right?" He fixed his stare at the receptionist who nodded. "But when he died, you thought you could keep going and that no one else would know."

"I had to. I owed too much money." The woman's face crumpled and tears shone on her cheeks.

Mason nodded to the police officers. "Thank you for waiting. You can take her now. I think Mrs. Davies has heard enough."

He waited while they escorted Mandy from the room, then turned to face Helena.

"Are you okay?"

"Okay?" She lowered herself into a chair and dropped her head in her hands. "No, I'm not okay. I can't believe she did that to us. She's like one of the family. And I can't believe Patrick kept it from me. Didn't he think I could cope with the news? She was systematically decimating our company and he wanted to give her another chance?" She shook her head as if she couldn't believe her own words.

The phone rang shrilly on the desk and Mason reached forward and flipped on the speaker.

"Yes, Margaret?"

"Sorry to interrupt you, Mr. Knight, but I have your solicitor on the phone."

Mason looked at Helena. She was shaking from the after-effects of the episode with Mandy. She needed him right now. "Tell him I'll call him later."

His solicitor? Fear slammed into Helena with devastating force as she remembered her instructions to her lawyer this morning. She'd given up her son! And for what? She groaned in despair. What had she done?

Mason hunkered down in front of her, taking her frozen hands in his and heating them between his long, warm fingers.

"I know it's a shock, but you can't feel sorry for her. She hasn't even expressed remorse for her actions—in some weird way she still believes she was totally justified. Don't worry, the police will deal with her from here, you won't have to see her again."

Helena couldn't speak. Mandy's betrayal was the least of her worries. Her world was imploding and all Mason could say was "don't worry"?

"Let me take you home. Will you be okay to walk?"

She nodded, incapable of speech. Her mind was racing with what she had to do next. As soon as she walked in that door back home she would be straight on the phone to her lawyer to countermand her earlier instructions. She'd been a fool for the last time.

The cabin temperature in the truck was set to high and it wasn't long before she began to feel sleepy. The somnolent sound of the four-by-four's tyres as they hummed along the road made it difficult to keep her eyes open. The past weeks' events had taken their toll and she battled to stay awake, but somehow it was just easier to let her heavy lids slid closed. They'd be home in half-an-hour at the most. That's all she needed, just a short kip to refresh herself and get ready for what was going to be the biggest fight of her life.

Twelve

Mason sensed the moment Helena fell asleep and loosened his vice-like grip on the steering wheel. She looked done in. The purplish bruises under her eyes spoke volumes as to how ragged she'd been running herself. It was up to him to make sure that changed.

Her breathing was low and steady, she didn't look like she'd wake for some time. That was probably best, but he knew if he took her straight home she'd probably coolly flick him off at the front door and that would be it. His chance would be gone. *No.* There was no way he'd settle for that.

They approached the motorway interchange, but instead of going straight ahead toward the suburb where she lived, he made an instant decision and turned onto the southern motorway instead. She needed the sleep, he told himself. He'd handle her anger when she realized he was taking her to his holiday home.

He shifted slightly in his seat, patting his trouser pocket with one hand just to confirm his plans would still work. Yes, it was still there. All he had to do now was get her to agree.

During the two-and-a-half-hour journey he kept checking her to make sure she was still okay, that still she slept. It wasn't until he started up the steep grade of the private road leading to the house that she began to stir.

"Wha—? Where are we? This isn't home." She stretched her neck and rubbed a hand across her eyes. "Mason! Where have you brought me?"

"My home."

She looked around in confusion. "But… No! Take me back. Take me back right now."

"I will, I promise. Look, you needed to rest, it was simpler to just keep driving. Besides, we need to talk. This place is as good as any." Mason pulled into the garage and hit the button to close the door behind them.

"We could have talked at my place."

She sounded madder than a wet cat.

"I know. Look, we'll be back in Auckland tonight if that's what you want. Just hear me out first, okay?"

He got down from the truck and walked around to her side, giving her a hand down. She snatched her hand away from him the instant both her feet hit the concrete garage floor.

"I don't have much choice, do I?" her tone was as acerbic as the expression on her face.

"I'd say sorry, Helena, but I'm not. There are things we need to discuss. After that, well, we'll have to see."

"If you think I'm not going to fight you tooth and

nail for custody of Brody, you can think again. He's my son. Mine!"

Mason didn't answer. This was going to be hard enough without antagonising her further. She followed him inside the house, stalking past him and heading toward the large ranch sliders facing the bay. Her body was rigid with anger, an anger he needed to dissipate.

"Are you hungry?" he asked, checking the upright freezer in the kitchen. He pulled out some frozen soup and a loaf of bread and put them on the bench.

"No. I'm not hungry. Just get to the point, Mason. Why have you brought me here?"

He walked into the sitting room and came and stood behind her. She flinched as he put his hands on her shoulders and turned her to face him.

"Okay, you want to know, here it is. First things first. I want you to know I was wrong. Wrong to treat you the way I did and wrong to threaten you. I was furious when I found out about Brody—I just wanted to hurt you back. I'm not proud of my behaviour, and I hope you can find it in your heart to forgive me for the unforgivable things I did and said."

"I don't know if I can forgive you. You refused to trust me, refused to even listen to me. I meant nothing to you."

"No. You never meant nothing to me—if anything you meant too much. From the beginning I deliberately poisoned myself against you because I knew if I didn't I would end up doing everything in my power to take you from Patrick. Everything."

Her eyes dilated at his words, the forest green pools consumed by her dark pupils. Her lips parted on unspoken words of denial.

"It's true. You have no idea how difficult it was for me to see you come down the aisle that day—how hard it was for me to keep my mouth shut. I'd already decided I wanted you. I was going to do whatever I could to find you again and there you were. Right in front of me, and completely out-of-bounds.

"It was easier to tell myself that you were a gold digger, just like any other, than to admit how much it killed me to see you married to him, to see you have what I believed to be his child."

"Mason, I...I don't know what to say." Confusion clouded Helena's features.

"I know. Look, let's sit down." He led her to the couch in front of the fireplace and bent to light the paper and kindling set in there. This wasn't going as he'd planned. He'd just wanted to get his confession out of the way and move on. But she hadn't reacted as he'd hoped. She was just as closed to him, just as emotionally distant, as she'd ever been. He added a couple of logs to the kindling and then sat down next to her. Somehow he had to do this on her terms.

He noted with relief that she didn't flinch this time as he came closer. Maybe this wasn't a lost cause after all.

"Helena, I don't want to take Brody from you. But I want to be a part of his life. I'll understand if you don't want me around when you're there, but please, let me get to know my son."

"You're going to drop the custody proceedings?" Her voice came out as a breathless whisper, laced with hope.

"Yes. I couldn't do that to you or to him. I was acting out of anger when I said I'd take him from you. Anger at you, anger at Patrick—but most of all, anger at myself.

"I should have spoken up at the wedding. I should never have let you out of my grasp. But that's my cross to bear. I had some hard truths come to me this week. I finally had to admit that I was the instrument of my own failures. I'm not going to let that happen again. I've decided to make my shares in Davies Freight over to Brody, but in your care until he's old enough to look after the company himself. The money problems we can sort out with an interest-free loan from BKT—though you'll never see a cent back from Mandy, unfortunately. I'll be there to help if you want me to. If you don't, I'll understand."

He searched her face for some sign of softening. Some sign that maybe she believed him.

Helena held her breath and waited. There was more that he wasn't saying, she could see it in his eyes, feel it in the tension that held his body. But he continued to keep it in. Suddenly she realised why. Though it had taken a huge amount of courage for him to open up to her like this, he wasn't about to give her an instrument to flay him with unless she showed some sign of forgiveness.

"It's okay. We can sort out Davies Freight later," she murmured. "So where do we go from here, Mason? What next?"

"Helena, I want you to understand that whatever happens next, it's your choice."

"Thank you." She paused, choosing her next words carefully. "I was going to let you have him, you know. That call you didn't take from your solicitor, it was to tell you that I'd decided not to contest your petition. And I wouldn't have, until this morning when you brought me to hear Mandy's confession. Why did you do that?"

"I learned to listen to my heart."

"You what?"

"I learned to listen to my heart," he repeated. "I finally admitted to myself that I love you, Helena. I had to find out who was responsible for what had happened at Davies Freight, for you. Only for you. If I didn't do that I'd never be able to face you and ask you for a future together."

Helena's heart began to swell with hope. *He loved her?*

"I want to know if we stand a chance, as a couple and as a family." His eyes burned into hers as he spoke, leaving her in no doubt of the truth of his words anymore.

"You want *me,* too?"

"Always. Can you forgive me for having been a complete and utter fool?"

Tears sprang in her eyes and she lifted her hands to his face, drawing him toward her. "Of course I forgive you. How could I not? Can we really try again?" she whispered against his lips.

In response he covered her mouth with his and drew her hard against his body, where she belonged, where she finally felt at home.

His tongue teased her lips open and with a joyful moan, Helena surrendered to his caress. Her body sprang to life, every nerve ending on full alert as their tongues entwined in a ritual of belonging. She pushed her hands through his hair and cupped the back of his head, drawing him closer to her, relishing the strength of him, relishing the knowledge that he loved her.

He dragged his lips from hers and stared into her eyes, the question in them obvious.

"I love you," she said, answering his unspoken plea.

"I will never stop loving you, I never could. You know, I have done many things in my life that I've regretted afterward but I have never regretted that first night we had. Never. How could I? Without it we wouldn't have Brody. Without it, we might not have each other now. Patrick was my salvation from a bad situation in my life. I can't say he wasn't important to me, he was—but you, you were my light. You saved my life and I had no other way to thank you but with myself. In the dark, in the cab of your truck, nothing had ever been as perfect as that moment. You're still my light, Mason. Today, and always."

She slid gracefully from the couch and stood on the soft rug in front of the fireplace facing him, drinking in the masculine beauty of his face, the strong plane of his forehead and the slant of his straight nose enhanced by the glow of the fire in the winter light. His eyes simmered with unspoken desire, making her feel more beautiful, more wanted, than any woman in the world could possibly have the right to feel.

She lifted up the bottom of her sweater and pulled it over her head before letting it drop in a dark flurry to the floor. She reached behind her back and unsnapped her bra, delighting in the torment she knew she was inflicting on Mason as he watched, his lips slightly open, his breathing ragged.

Gently, she drew the straps off her shoulders, cupping the lacy pink fabric to her breasts until the last possible moment before letting the garment drop beside her sweater on the floor. She cupped her breasts with her hands—a spear of want, sharp and true, piercing her body with throbbing desire at the apex of her thighs. Her thumbs ran lightly over her nipples, hard and jutting, begging for a stronger touch. Begging for him.

Helena let her fingers trail down over her ribcage and down to the waistband of her jeans where, unable to control the quake of need that shuddered through her body, she fumbled the steel button out of its loop and rasped the fly of her jeans undone. A tiny shimmy of her hips and they, too, lay in a denim pool at her feet.

Mason emitted a harsh masculine groan, and Helena smiled enticingly as she hooked her thumbs into the waistband of her panties and slid them down her slender thighs. On legs that trembled like a newborn foal's, she stepped out of the pile of clothing and toward Mason's waiting arms.

She almost purred in delight as he pulled her down onto the couch beside him and trailed hot kisses along her cheek, her jawbone, and down her throat, laving at her collarbone and sending shudders of exquisite torture coursing through her.

Her hands fisted in the fine cotton of his shirt as she tugged it free from his trousers, then carefully undid each button, pushing the fabric aside, exposing his hard ridged abdomen and the constricted brown discs of his nipples. Unable to help herself, she lowered her lips, nipping gently at the gleaming tanned skin that stretched across his broad, muscled chest, swirling her tongue around his nipples and taking unprecedented delight in the tremor that rocked him as she closed her lips and pulled, rasping her teeth over the tightened sensitive flesh.

Finally, she pressed her own aching breasts against the heated strength of his body. Mason wrapped one arm around her back, possessively splaying his fingers across her buttocks, the action making her clench her thighs and inner muscles, and sending her desire to a fevered peak. She rubbed herself against the bulging pressure at his crotch, delighting in the uncontrolled spasm the tiny friction elicited.

But she wanted more, needed more. *She needed him.*

Helena unsnapped the fasteners on his trousers and slid her hand inside his briefs. A smile of triumph played across her lips as his impressively evident desire for her jumped against her palm. She closed one hand around him, savouring his silky-smooth texture, his heat, his hardness.

"Wait!" Mason's voice was strangled as he grasped her wrist and pulled her hand away. "If we're going to do this, we're going to do it right this time."

Helena watched, confused—her body screaming for the attention she knew only he could give—as he pulled away from her and reached deep inside his trouser pocket. He withdrew his fisted hand, slowly uncurling his fingers to reveal a solitaire diamond ring, the large square-cut stone radiant in the flickering firelight. Her heart swelled in her chest, her breathing stuttered to a momentary halt and tears threatened to fall as she saw what he held so carefully in his hand.

He reached out for her left hand and slid the ring on her finger. "You *will* marry me."

"Yes." She could barely speak through the lump of pent-up emotion in her throat.

"Now," he said with quiet urgency, lifting her hand to place a hot, moist kiss on her knuckles. "Now it's right."

He shrugged out of his shirt and removed the rest of

his clothing as she lay prone on the wide sofa. Then he lay down beside her, their legs entwining, their bodies urgent to join as one. He positioned himself at her entrance. She was so slick with desire, so hot with need; it was an intense pleasure pain as he began to fill her with excruciating slowness. Helena focussed on his face, on the love she saw reflected there, satisfied to be joined together yet craving more at the same time. And then he started to move, sending wild sensation spiralling from deep inside her as he withdrew then filled her again. Her lips parted and she dragged in a breath. She couldn't believe she could be so lucky as to have this second chance at love—a chance to build a life together with Mason. Silently she vowed never to throw this precious gift away.

Pleasure swelled within her, building stronger, harder, deeper, until she fractured apart with a cry. Mason's hips drove against her, sending another wave of pleasure as he reached his own fulfilment and spilled himself within her.

Mason raised himself slightly and twirled one finger in a thick length of her hair, drawing it to his face and inhaling the fragrance it imparted, a fragrance engraved in his memory as deeply as the feel of her body and the strength of her love.

His voice rippled with emotion as he spoke. "I love you, Helena. You are my life. I'm going to do everything in my power to make sure you know that everyday for the rest of your life."

She reached up and pressed her lips in a kiss against the base of his throat before pulling his face to hers and taking his lips, desperate to impart how privileged she felt that this strong, vital man loved her so deeply.

Against his lips she made her vow, "Thank you. I will never betray your love for me. I promise."

Finally she was where she belonged and she knew beyond a shadow of a doubt she could never willingly hurt him again. She and Mason could continue to build their lives, together, from this day.

* * * * *

Don't miss Rossellini's Revenge Affair.
Coming in December 2008 from Yvonne Lindsay and Mills & Boon® Desire™.

Danger and desire collide...

New York Times bestselling author

DIANA PALMER

Lawman

When FBI agent Garon Grier sets up home in
Texas, the strong, silent loner is certainly not
looking for love when he meets Grace Carver,
a lovely young woman unmarried and
untouched because of a dark, tragic past.

Then Garon has to tackle the most difficult case
of his career, hunting an escaped convict, whose
former child victims are all dead. All except one.

Now a desperate lawman and a proud woman
must decide if secrets will come between them
forever...or free them to love at last.

Available 15th February 2008

M&B

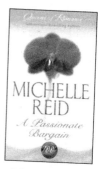

2 Books
and a surprise gift!

We would like to take this opportunity to thank you for reading this Mills & Boon® book by offering you the chance to take TWO more specially selected titles from the Desire™ series absolutely FREE! We're also making this offer to introduce you to the benefits of the Mills & Boon® Reader Service™—

> ★ **FREE home delivery**
> ★ **FREE gifts and competitions**
> ★ **FREE monthly Newsletter**
> ★ **Exclusive Reader Service offers**
> ★ **Books available before they're in the shops**

Accepting these FREE books and gift places you under no obligation to buy, you may cancel at any time, even after receiving your free shipment. Simply complete your details below and return the entire page to the address below. You don't even need a stamp!

YES! Please send me 2 free Desire books and a surprise gift. I understand that unless you hear from me, I will receive 3 superb new titles every month for just £4.99 each, postage and packing free. I am under no obligation to purchase any books and may cancel my subscription at any time. The free books and gift will be mine to keep in any case.

D8ZEF

Ms/Mrs/Miss/Mr ....Initials................................
                                                      BLOCK CAPITALS PLEASE
Surname ....
Address..

....
....Postcode ....

Send this whole page to:
UK: FREEPOST CN81, Croydon, CR9 3WZ